ERIC ROHMER

SIX MORAL TALES

Translated from the French by Sabine d'Estrée

VIKING

VIKING
Published by the Penguin Group
Penguin Group (USA) Inc., 375 Hudson Street,
New York, New York 10014, U.S.A.
Published by Penguin Group
Penguin Group (USA) Inc., 375 Hudson Street, New York, New York 10014, U.S.A. •
Penguin Group (Canada), 90 Eglinton Avenue East, Suite 700, Toronto, Ontario,
Canada M4P 2Y3 (a division of Pearson Penguin Canada Inc.) • Penguin Books Ltd.,
80 Strand, London WC2R 0RL, England • Penguin Ireland, 25 St. Stephen's Green,
Dublin 2, Ireland (a division of Penguin Books Ltd.) • Penguin Group (Australia),
250 Camberwell Road, Camberwell, Victoria 3124, Australia (a division of Pearson
Australia Group Pty. Ltd.) • Penguin Books India Pvt. Ltd., 11 Community Centre,
Panchsheel Park, New Delhi–110 017, India • Penguin Books (NZ), cnr Airborne
and Rosedale Roads, Albany, Auckland 1310, New Zealand (a division of Pearson
New Zealand Ltd.) • Penguin Books (South Africa) (Pty.) Ltd., 24 Sturdee Avenue,
Rosebank, Johannesburg 2196, South Africa

Penguin Books Ltd, Registered Offices:
80 Strand, London WC2R 0RL, England

Copyright © Editions de l'Herne, 1974
Translation copyright © Penguin Group (USA) Inc., 1980
All rights reserved

Originally published in French under the title *Six contes moraux* by
Editions de l'Herne, Paris. This translation first published in 1980 under the imprint,
A Seaver Book/Viking.

Library of Congress cataloging-in-publication data is available.

Trade ISBN 0-670-64732-2
Special Markets ISBN 0-670-03846-6

Rodrigo Corral cover design © 2006 The Criterion Collection.

Printed in the United States of America

Set in Janson Text.

CONTENTS

PREFACE

Why film a story when one can write it? Why write it when one is going to film it? Both these questions may seem trivial, but not to me. The idea for these stories came to me at a point when I did not yet know whether I was going to be a film-maker. If eventually I did turn them into films, it was because I had not succeeded in writing them. And if, in a certain way, it is true that I did write them—exactly as you are about to read them—it was solely in order to film them.

These texts, therefore, are not "adapted" from my films. Chronologically, the stories precede the films; from the outset I wanted them to be something other than "film scripts." Thus, any reference to camera angles, shots, or any other cinematic or directorial terms is notably lacking in them. From the first draft on, the stories took on a resolutely literary quality. It was as though the stories, and what they were portraying—characters, plot, dialogues—had a need to assert that they did precede the films, even though only the act of making the films gave the stories their full meaning. For one never makes a film out of nothing. To shoot a film is always to shoot *something*, be it fiction or reality, and the more shaky the reality, the more solid the fiction must be. Although I have to confess I was fascinated by the methods of cinéma vérité, I did not close my eyes to the fact that certain forms—the psychodrama and the personal diary, to name but two—were totally foreign to my purpose. These "tales," as the term implies, must stand on their own as works of fiction, even if at times they borrow, or even steal, certain of their elements from reality.

The contemporary filmmaker—and this includes me—dreams of being the sole creator of his work, which implies that he assumes, among other things, the job that traditionally devolved upon the screenwriter. Sometimes that omnipotence, instead of being an advantage and a stimulus, acts as a constraint. To be the absolute master of your subject, to be able to add to it or delete from it whatever you like, depending on the inspiration of exigencies of the moment, without having to account for what you do to anyone, is on one hand intoxicating and, on the other, paralyzing: that facility becomes a trap. What is important is that your own text be foreign to you; otherwise you flounder, and the actors with you. Or, in case you opt to improvise, be it in the plot or the dialogue, you must find a way to create a certain distance between you and what you have shot when you cut the film, so that in place of the tyranny of the written text you have that of the filmed material. And I think it safe to say that it is easier to compose images starting with a story than it is to make up a story on the basis of a series of images shot more or less at random.

Strangely, it was the latter method that tempted me at first. In these films, in which the written text was of prime importance, I was depriving myself—by the very act of writing the text first—of the pleasure of creation at the time of shooting. That the text was mine rather than someone else's made no difference: I resented that I was but the servant of that script, and decided that if that were the case, I would prefer to devote my time and effort to someone else's creation rather than my own. But little by little I realized that this confidence in the role of chance, which such a method required, did not fit in with what I had in mind, which was premeditated and very clearly defined. I realized, too, that it would have taken a miracle in which, I must confess, I did not believe, for the various elements to come together in a meaningful whole exactly as I had conceived of them. Not to mention the fact that my shoestring budget severely limited the amount of experimentation I could indulge in. And although it is true that in some cases the actors—especially in the fourth and fifth tales—participated in the writing of the dialogue, once a final text was finished, they learned it by heart, just as they would have learned a text by another author, forgetting that parts of it were their creation.

Those portions of the texts that resulted from pure improvisation are few. They affect only the cinematic form of the story, do not really emanate from the texts themselves, and therefore have no place here. For instance, in *The Bakery Girl of Monceau*, as is generally the case in any film, there were times when the actors added, because it seemed natural, such greetings as "good morning," "good-bye," "how are you?"—as distinguished from those same "good morning"s and good-bye"s that were part of the tale and not of the film. There are places, too, where descriptive phrases that on paper are expressed indirectly on the screen become direct descriptions. Finally, I might note a number of improvised expressions or exchanges, the picturesque quality of which, taken out of its cinematic context, would have jarred. I refer, for example, to the table conversation of the engineers in the film *My Night at Maud's* and Jerome's revelations in the film *Claire's Knee*.

Aside from these willful omissions, the attentive reader who has seen the films will doubtless be able to pick out certain discrepancies between the dialogues as presented in these pages and those actually spoken by the actors in the films. The fact is that, deeming I had full right to do so, I quite simply corrected occasional errors, omissions, and memory lapses on the part of the actors. My desire that we adhere as closely as possible to the written text was more a principle than an iron-clad rule. In no way did I want the quality of the acting to suffer by too rigorously adhering to the text, and I considered myself more than satisfied if my actors, who had to cope with more than their share of restrictions, could, in return for committing these venial errors, breathe a trifle more easily. There is another factor that obliged me from the start to clothe the tales in literary garb. Here, literature—and this is my principal excuse—belongs less to form than to content. My intent was to film not raw, unvarnished events but rather the account of them as given by one of the characters. The story, the selection and arrangement of the facts, as well as the way they were learned, happened to relate very clearly and specifically to the person relating them, independently of any pressures I might exert on that person. One of the reasons these tales are called "moral" is that they are effectively stripped of physical action: everything takes place in the narrator's mind. The same story, told by someone else, would be quite different, or might well not have been told at all. My heroes, somewhat like Don Quixote, think of themselves as characters in a novel, but perhaps there isn't any novel. The presence of a first-person narrator owes less to the necessity to reveal innermost thoughts—which are impossible to transpose, either visually or through dialogue—than to the necessity to situate with absolute clarity the protagonist's viewpoint, and to make this viewpoint the target at which, as both author and director, I am aiming.

In my early drafts of these tales there was very little direct dialogue, and for a time I seriously considered using a constant voice-over, from the beginning to the final shot. Little by little, however, the text initially intended for the voice-over shifted into the mouth of one character or another. In *Claire's Knee*, the voice-over disappeared completely, the gist of what it revealed being taken over by the various stories contained in the dialogue. Events, instead of being commented on at the time they take place, are only discussed afterward by Jerome, the titular narrator, in the presence of Aurora, the real narrator. In *My Night at Maud's*, the film version contains only two sentences of interior monologue, much less than was in the original shooting script. For ease of reading, however, in the present volume I have restored the balance of the stream of consciousness as it appeared in the script itself. Not that it reveals one iota more about the character than we have seen on the screen: it introduces a flexibility that the image no longer needed but that on the printed page seems once again necessary.

Here, I would like for a moment to broaden the area of discussion. The anxiety of my six characters in search of a story mirrors that of the author faced with his own creative impotence, which the quasi-mechanical process of invention utilized here—the variation on a theme—conceals but imperfectly. Perhaps it also mirrors the anxiety of the cinema, which throughout its short history has proved a terrifying devourer of subjects, plundering the repertory of the theater, the novel, and the realms of nonfiction. But when you take a close look at the vast spoils that the output of the film industry represents, you realize that what it has evolved out of its own storehouse is slight indeed, both qualitatively and quantitatively. When you scratch the surface a little, you see that there are really very few original scenarios: those that claim originality derive more or less openly from a novel or a dramatic work. There is no film literature, as there is a literature for the theater; nothing vaguely resembling a work, a "play," capable of inspiring and withstanding a thousand possible approaches, a thousand different ways of being staged. In film, the power relationship is reversed: the direction is king, the text subservient. A film script is in itself of little or no consequence, and mine is no exception to that rule. If it seems to resemble literature, the appearance is deceiving; it is rather a yearning for it. It takes as a model a form of narration already a century old and settles for it with seeming smugness, as though, when it comes to literature, it preferred the hallucinatory to the practical.

It is only on the screen that the form of these tales is fully realized, if only because a new viewpoint is added—that of the camera—that no longer coincides with that of the narrator. Here there is a perspective lacking, which, admittedly, might have been brought into being by the act of writing—by some more or less colorful or vivid description of the characters and their actions, or of the setting in which they live and move. I preferred not to attempt this embellishment; or, to be more precise, I was incapable of doing it. If I had been able to, and if it had been successful, I would have considered these tales sufficient unto themselves in this form and felt no need to turn them into films. For, as I said at the start of this preface, why be a filmmaker if you can be a novelist?

E. R.

I

THE BAKERY GIRL
OF MONCEAU

Paris, the Villiers intersection. To the east, the boulevard des Batignolles, with the outline of Sacré-Coeur looming in the background. To the north, the rue de Lévis and its open market, the café du "Dôme" at the corner of the avenue de Villiers, then, on the sidewalk across the street, the Villiers subway stop, set directly beneath a clock, among the trees of the center mall, which has been destroyed.

To the west, the boulevard de Courcelles, which led to Monceau Park, on the fringe of which the former Cité-Club, a student center, used to occupy a building dating from Napoleon III, which was torn down in 1960. It was there I ate dinner every night when I was in law school, for I lived nearby on the rue de Rome. At the same time, Sylvia, who worked in an art gallery on the rue de Monceau, used to walk through the park on her way home.

At that point, I knew her only by sight. Once in a while our paths would cross somewhere along the three-hundred-yard length of the boulevard that separated the intersection from the student center. We had exchanged a few furtive looks, but nothing more.

My friend Schmidt was responsible for urging me to action.

"Unfortunately, she's a little too tall for me. But why don't you see how you make out with her."

"What? Just go up and talk to her? Not me!"

"Why not? You never know!"

It was true: she wasn't a girl you could just go up and introduce yourself to on the street. And to confront her cold, just like that, was even less my style. Yet I assumed she would make an exception for me, as I would have made an exception for her. Despite these careful rationalizations, I was afraid of making a move too quickly. I opted for extreme caution, sometimes going so far as to avoid her gaze, leaving the task of sizing her up to Schmidt.

"Did she look over this way?"

"She did."

"For a long time?"

"Pretty long. Longer than usual, that I can safely say."

"Listen," I said, "I feel like following her. At least so I'll know where she lives."

"Go right up to her; don't follow her. If you do, you'll blow it."

"Go right up to her?"

I realized how strongly I felt about her. It was May, and the end of the school year was fast approaching. There was no question that she lived in the area. We had seen her once carrying a string basket, obviously doing her shopping. We had been sitting on the terrace of the Dôme, having an after-dinner coffee, when she walked by. It was only quarter to eight, and the stores were still open.

"Actually," I said after she had turned the corner, "she might live right around here somewhere."

"Don't go away," Schmidt said. "I'm going on a little reconnaissance mission."

A few moments later he was back.

"She went into one of the shops. I don't know which direction she'll take when she comes out. The risk is too great."

A short while later we saw her pass by again, "looking a little too straight in front of her," as Schmidt was quick to note, "not to be aware of our presence."

"The hell with it!" I said, getting to my feet. "I'm going to follow her."

I abandoned all caution and followed hard on her heels up the rue de Lévis. But I had to beat a quick retreat, for she was zigzagging from one street stall to another in such a way that at any moment she might have caught sight of me. I came back to the Dôme, and for the rest of the evening didn't see her. But even if I had managed to follow her to her door, what good would that have done me? Schmidt was right: this skirmishing could not go on indefinitely. I was on the verge of taking the matter in hand—that is, of going straight up to her and saying hello—when, at long last, fortune smiled on me.

The corner clock said seven; we were on our way to dinner. I had stopped to buy the evening paper. Schmidt, instead of waiting for me, had gone ahead and crossed to the opposite sidewalk, from which he watched me as, head lowered, I ran to catch up with him. Just as I was about to start across the street I saw him signaling frantically to me, and at first I couldn't figure out what he wanted; I thought he was trying to warn me about some imminent danger in the street. Actually, it was toward the sidewalk behind me and to my right that he pointed. I turned my head, but the sun, which was low on the horizon, blinded me. I took a step or two back, the better to see, and when I did, I ran almost full tilt into the object of Schmidt's gesticulations, which was none other than Sylvia herself, striding up the boulevard. I began to apologize.

"Oh, I beg your pardon!"

"No problem. Don't give it another thought."

"You sure?"

"There's no marked damage, so far as I can tell."

"Luckily . . . I don't know what's the matter with me today. Just a little while ago I almost killed myself on those stupid things over there," I said, pointing toward a pile of rubbish stacked along the sidewalk.

She burst out laughing. "What I wouldn't have given to see that!"

"I said I *almost* killed myself."

"What?"

The traffic noises were so loud at that time of day we could barely make out what we were saying. I raised my voice till I was almost shouting:

"I said I *almost:* I didn't really hurt myself . . . Oh, these damn cars! You can't hear yourself think!"

Any attempt at conversation was clearly futile. Sylvia began to leave, and for the life of me I couldn't think of anything to say that might keep her.

"I'm going this way," she said.

"And I'm going that way," I said. Then I added, very quickly, "I owe you an apology. What say we meet for coffee in an hour? You, my friend, and me."

I made it an hour from then because I was sure she wouldn't accept an invitation for here and now.

"I'm sorry, but I'm busy tonight. Maybe another time. We do seem to pass each other in the street fairly often. 'Bye now."

"Good-bye!"

Without even watching her disappear into the distance, I ran to catch up with Schmidt, smirking like a Cheshire cat.

During the brief minute our conversation had lasted I had kept but one thought in mind: say something, anything, that would prevent her from leaving, no matter what impression—

and it could only be poor—I might make on her. And yet there was no question that I had scored a victory. In all that rush-hour hustle, something of myself had come through. She had not seemed put off by it; on the contrary, she had seemed to relish it, to respond in kind to my remarks. That she had refused my invitation did not upset me in the least, since, the way things were left, I felt free, when next we met, to take up our conversation where it had left off. And I had little doubt we would meet again soon. What more could I ask?

Then something happened that I did not expect. The extraordinary stroke of good luck that had thrown us together was followed by a stroke of bad luck. Three days passed, a week, and not once did I so much as glimpse Sylvia in the street. Schmidt, to concentrate on his upcoming written examination, had gone home to his family to study. And no matter how madly in love I already was, the idea of diverting some of my study time to go looking for Sylvia did not even cross my mind. My only free moments were at mealtime. So I did without dinner.

I calculated that dinner took me thirty minutes. The trip to and from the student center took three. Thus, if I spent dinnertime looking for Sylvia, my chances of finding her would increase tenfold. But then arose the question of how best to use that time: stalking the boulevards had its virtues, but also its drawbacks, for since I did not know where she lived or from which direction she might come, she might well be taking other side streets, not to mention the Metro or the bus. One thing was certain: she still had to go shopping. And that was why I decided to broaden my investigations to include the rue de Lévis.

I have to confess that on these sultry late afternoons, patrolling the boulevard was dull and fatiguing. The market, on the contrary, offered variety, freshness, and the irresistible factor of food. My stomach, weary of student meals, was pestering me; in anticipation of the upcoming vacation it was clamoring for that gastronomical interlude that cherry time promised. The odors of the open market and the hurly-burly that went with it were more fun, and more relaxing for me, after so many hours of hitting the books and of memorizing the contents of the professors' lectures than were the noise of the student restaurant and the untantalizing whiffs of the student food.

And still my searches proved fruitless. Thousands of people lived in the area—probably one of the most densely populated sections of the city. Should I stay in one place? Or should I prowl? I was young, and doubtless thought, somewhat stupidly, that suddenly, in one of the windows that lined the streets, Sylvia would appear. Or perhaps she would emerge just as suddenly from one of the shops in the neighborhood and, as had happened the other day, literally run into me. So I opted to keep moving, to prowl.

It was in the course of my wanderings that I discovered, on the corner of the rue Lebouteux, a little bakery where I bought all kinds of cakes, which constituted the sum and substance of my daily fare. Two women ran the shop: the owner, or the wife of the owner, who at this time of day was almost always busy in the kitchen; and a rather pretty brunette, bright-eyed and comely, with full, sensuous lips. The first days I visited the shop, if I remember correctly, I often found her coping with the young hoods of the area, who made a point of stopping in to horse around and show off in front of her. They hung around so long that she was never able to serve me promptly.

Thus I had all the time in the world to decide what I wanted, though I almost never settled on anything but sugar cookies. The kind they made was neither better nor worse than one could find in any other bakery. In fact, it was factory made, and distributed to all the stores and bakeries in Paris. On the one hand, the empty street down which I walked, the last lap in my peripatetic search, offered me the advantage of eating my purchase in peace, without Sylvia's seeing me, in case she might suddenly materialize out of the crowd without warning; on the other, the purchase of my sugar cookie had, after a certain time, turned into a kind of ceremony between the baker's assistant and me.

To tell the truth, it was she who started it. To irritate her young boyfriend, she had at the height of one of their frequent arguments made a point of intimating—by obvious winks and smiles, to which I responded with a face of marble—some tacit understanding between us.

I had bought only one cookie, and I began to eat it as I made my way from the bakery to the open market. When I got there, I wanted another one, and retraced my steps. The smile with which the baker's assistant greeted me, as though she were welcoming a friend or acquaintance, only reinforced my coldness. At my age, if there is anything one hates to do it is run errands. I therefore made a point of avoiding the least semblance of familiarity with salespeople. I like to go into a shop as though I were there for the first time.

"I'd like a sugar cookie," I said, in my most neutral tone of voice.

Surprised, she did a kind of double take, as though not quite sure she was seeing right, and her meaningful glance made me ashamed of myself. I found it impossible to play my little game any longer and, with the same ingenuous air, asked her how much I owed her. "Forty centimes?" I queried matter-of-factly.

"Forty even," she answered quickly, apparently having guessed the game I was playing and having decided to play it, too.

And still no Sylvia anywhere on the horizon. Was she hiding from me? And, if so, why, in God's name? Could she have gone to the country? Was she sick? Or dead? Or married? I ran the full gamut of possibilities, all of which struck me as equally likely. By the end of the week my search had turned into a pure formality. I couldn't wait to return to my bakery, each day being more careful to prepare my entrances and exits, my dilatory habits and bizarre conduct.

The mask of obsequiousness and commercial indifference that my baker's assistant sported only contributed, I could clearly see, to helping her play the game, and her distortions of the rule were not so many oversights, nor did they stem from impatience, but were obviously meant to be provocative. If ever she happened to anticipate, by a movement of her hand or so much as a glance, the cake or cookie on which I had set my heart, I pretended to change my mind, even though I might eventually come back to my original choice.

"Two sugar cookies?"

"No . . . uh . . . Yes, one sugar cookie . . . Uh . . . and, well, I think maybe I'll have . . . another. Yes, that's it: two."

She went about filling my order without the least trace of impatience, happy to find some excuse to keep me there in the shop with her, for at that late hour there were few customers. And the way she fluttered her eyelashes, pressed her lips together—all sorts of little blunders she committed—betrayed feelings that

were less and less unconscious. It hadn't taken me long to figure out that the pretty baker's assistant did not find me unat-
tractive, but—call it vanity if you like—I somehow seemed to
take it for granted that any girl would be attracted to me. Besides, not only was she not exactly what I would call my type—
which is the least you can say about her—but the fact is I was
wholly preoccupied with Sylvia . . . Yes, and it was precisely
because I was thinking of Sylvia that I did not disdain the advances of the baker's assistant—and there could be no question
that they were advances. I in fact responded to them more
warmly than I would have were I not in love with another girl.

And yet the comedy, impelled as it were by its own mo-
mentum, was emerging from the reserve in which it had been
confined during the first few days, and threatened to turn into
burlesque. Sure now of the girl's feelings about me, I took
great delight in testing her malleability, making sure she
yielded to my slightest whim. I watched her do a double-take
when in contrast to my seemingly insatiable appetite of the
previous day I would surprise her the following time by order-
ing in moderation. On my greedy visits I sometimes ordered
as many as ten pastries at a time, far from sure I would be able
to consume them. And yet somehow I did, although it might
take me as long as fifteen minutes, standing there on the street
corner munching away, only a stone's throw from the bakery,
but now without the slightest fear of being seen.

So it was that each day I ventured a little farther, convinced
it was but a game that could not go very far. Besides, I told myself, it was as good a way as any of whiling away the time, and
also a method of getting even with Sylvia and being revenged
for her absence. And yet I had the feeling that this vengeance
was unworthy of me, and my way of reacting to it was to take
out my irritation on the baker's girl. What upset me the most

was not the notion that she might take a shine to me but, on the contrary, that it might enter her mind that I could end up liking her. And to justify myself in my own eyes I kept repeating, over and over again, that it was her fault and that I would have to punish her for daring to associate with her betters.

Matters had reached the point at which I decided to take the offensive. The bakery was empty. It was only a few minutes from closing time, and the baker herself was in the back checking the roast that she was preparing for supper. I remained in the shop while I munched on my pastries; I decided to offer one to the baker's assistant. She refused at first, but I knew she only wanted to be coaxed, and finally she chose a piece of pie that she swallowed as though she hadn't eaten in a week. I teased her.

"I always thought that anyone who worked in a bakery shop all day long would end up hating every kind of sweet or pastry there is."

"You know," she said, her mouth still full, "I've only been here a month, and I'm not staying on much longer. Come September I have a job in one of the big department stores."

"You work here all day long?"

"Yes."

"And what do you do with your evenings?"

She didn't reply. She was leaning back on the counter, her eyes lowered. I went on.

"How about going out with me one night?"

She took two steps forward, to the shop door, where she was framed in the waning light. Her square décolletage emphasized the line of her breast and shoulders. After a moment's silence she turned her head slightly.

"I'm only eighteen, you know."

I moved over to her and with one finger touched her bare back.

"So what? Don't your parents ever let you go out?"

The arrival of the baker enabled her to avoid a reply. Quickly she slipped back behind the counter.

My exams were almost over, and soon I would be going away on vacation. I assumed that Sylvia was lost forever. Force of habit alone made me continue my nocturnal rounds looking for her—plus, perhaps, the hope of extracting from the baker's assistant the promise to go out with me, which I admit was meager consolation for my disappointment. Two days before my departure I ran into her in the street. She was carrying a basket of bread. I stopped her.

"Would you like me to help you?"

"Do I look as though I need help?"

"Am I bothering you? Are you afraid someone might see us?"

"Not at all. Anyway, I'm leaving in a month." She gave a slight smile, which she meant to be provocative. In order to dispel her embarrassment, I suggested we start walking.

"Would it bother you if I walked with you for a while?"

"Well, actually . . ."

Luckily I caught sight of a *porte-cochère*.

"Listen, let's step inside here, just for a second. I have something I want to tell you."

Like a little lamb, she followed me into an inside courtyard. She set down her basket of bread and leaned up against the wall. Her solemn, questioning eyes looked up at me.

"Did I do something wrong? Something you took offense at?"

"No, I already told you, that's not the reason."

I looked her straight in the eye. I placed my hand on the wall just beside her, at the height of her shoulders.

"What say we go out together some night? How about to-morrow?"

"Don't . . . I should go now. I really should."

"Why?"

"I don't know. After all, I don't know you from Adam."

"That's precisely the point of going out; that way we can get to know each other. Do I look all that frightening?"

She smiled. "No, of course not."

I took her hand and began playing with her fingers.

"It's no big deal. We can go to a movie on the Champs-Elysées. Do you ever go to the movies?"

"Sure. On Saturday."

"Then let's go on Saturday . . ."

"I usually go with some friends."

"Boyfriends?"

"Boys and girls both. They're all so . . . stupid!"

"Another good reason to go with me. So are we all set for Saturday?"

"No, not Saturday."

"What about some other day? Do your parents keep you locked up?"

"Don't be silly. Of course they don't."

"All right, then, let's go out tomorrow. We'll have dinner in a good little restaurant; then we'll go over to the Champs-Elysées. I'll wait for you at eight o'clock at the café on the corner. The Dôme. You know the one, don't you?"

"Do I have to dress up?"

I slipped my hand beneath the strap of her dress and caressed her shoulder with my fingertips. She didn't stop me, but I could feel her trembling.

"Of course you don't. You're fine just the way you are. Okay?"

14

"I don't know whether my mother will—"

"But you said that—"

"Yes, in principle. But—"

"Tell her you're going out with a girlfriend."

"I suppose I could do that. I mean, maybe."

With a movement of her shoulder she forced me to withdraw my hand. Her voice was thick. Mine, I have to confess, wasn't too self-assured either. I tried to joke.

"Listen, are you romantic?"

"What?"

I enunciated each syllable carefully: "Ro-man-tic. I'll tell you what I'll do: I'll come by the shop tomorrow night at seven-thirty. In case we can't talk openly in the shop, here's what we'll do. I'll ask for a pastry. If you give me two, it'll mean you're coming, in which case we'll meet as planned at the Dôme. Okay?"

"Well . . . okay."

"Say it back to me, so we make sure you have it straight."

"If I give you two pastries, it means yes," she said with utter seriousness, without the trace of a smile or that bit of ease that would have made me feel more comfortable and eased my conscience to some degree.

What in the world had I got myself into?

The following day, a Friday, I took my oral examination and passed it. By now I had lost all desire to keep my evening engagement, but the fellow students with whom I might have celebrated my success were still bogged down in their exams, and the prospect of spending an evening alone was more than I could face.

When I got to the rue Lebouteux, it was already quarter to eight. As we had agreed the day before, I asked for a pastry, and

I watched as the baker's assistant handed me one; then, after a second's hesitation, which I must admit upped her in my esteem, a second. I exited and retraced my steps to the intersection, munching on my pastries as I walked. But I had gone no more than a dozen yards when I gave a start. Yes, it was Sylvia walking toward me, clearly crossing the street to intercept me. Her ankle was bandaged, and she was walking with the help of a cane. I had just enough time to swallow what was in my mouth and conceal the other pastry in the palm of my hand.

"Hi there!" she said, all smiles.

"Good evening! How are you? What happened? Did you have an accident?"

"Oh, nothing. I sprained my ankle. But it laid me up for three weeks."

"I was surprised not to have run into you again."

"I caught a glimpse of you yesterday, but you seemed lost in your thoughts."

"Oh, really?"

In a split second I had made my decision. Sylvia was there. Everything else vanished. All that mattered was getting away from this cursed place as soon as possible.

"Have you had dinner yet?"

"No. In fact I didn't even have an afternoon snack today." And, so saying, she stared openly at the pastry in my hand.

"The heat makes me hungry," I said lamely, as though in answer to her stare.

"You don't have to account for your eating habits," she said, laughing. But her sarcasm made no impression on me. My mind was filled with one idea and one idea only: to spirit her far away from where we were standing.

"What say we have dinner together?"

"Fine by me. But I must go back up to my place. Do you

mind waiting. I only live on the second floor; I won't be a minute."

And I saw her disappear into the door of the building cater-corner from where we had met, directly across from the bakery.

That minute she mentioned lasted fifteen, during which I had ample opportunity to reflect on my imprudence. I doubtless ought to have invited Sylvia for another night, and kept to my plans with the baker's assistant for that evening. But my choice was, above all, *moral.* Having found Sylvia again, to have carried on with the baker's girl would have been worse than a vice: it would have been pure nonsense.

To make matters more complicated, it had begun to rain. And yet it was the rain that saved me. It was already past eight o'clock, but the baker's assistant was apparently waiting for the rain to let up before leaving the shop. The last drops were falling when Sylvia reappeared, a raincoat over her shoulders. I suggested I go look for a taxi.

"With the rain you'll never find one," she said. "I don't mind walking."

"Really?"

"Really."

I moved beside her and fell into step with her. The street was deserted, and if the baker's girl emerged from the shop, she might well see us. In any case, I thought to myself, realizing how cowardly the concern, she would be too far away to cause any trouble. I didn't dare turn to look, and the walk was interminable. Had she seen us, or was she pining away, waiting, in the café? I'll never know.

. . .

As for the conquest of Sylvia, it was a mere formality. The reason for it was revealed to me later that same night.

"During the time I was laid up I managed to find a few amusements," she said, looking at me with a mocking air. "You probably don't know it, but my window looks out on the street. I saw everything." I felt myself trembling. She went on. "You're a terrible person! You came within a hairbreadth of making me jealous. Yet I obviously couldn't bring myself to let you know by some kind of signal. I loathe people who pace back and forth in front of my doorstep. Too bad for you if you want to ruin your stomach with all those silly little pastries."

"On the contrary, they're very good."

"I know. I tried them. Actually, I know all your vices!"

Six months later we were married, and for a while we lived on the rue Lebouteux. Sometimes we went to buy our bread together, but it was no longer the same baker's girl.

II

SUZANNE'S CAREER

It was at the Café le Luco, on the boulevard Saint-Michel, that we met Suzanne. I lived directly above the café, in the Hôtel de l'Observatoire. I was eighteen, and in my first year of college, majoring in pharmacy.

Guillaume, two years older than I, was majoring in political science. We were close friends, and yet in many ways poles apart. I disapproved of practically everything he did, yet I envied his free and easy manner. For him, to lay eyes on a girl meant automatically to try to make her. Any pretense would do: a word or phrase overheard, a chair borrowed, the title of a book.

At the next table, Suzanne was boning up on her Italian. Standing on no ceremony, Guillaume grabbed the book as she was putting on her glasses, and, with great pomposity and heavy accent, he began reading.

"*I promessi sposi!*"

The assault did not seem to faze her in the least. She burst out laughing.

"How many years of Italian have you had!"

"Are you at the Sorbonne?" he said, dropping his vulgar air.

"More or less. I'm taking some evening classes at the interpreters' school on the rue de la Sorbonne. I work in the daytime, right over there, across the street, at the Anti-Tuberculosis League."

"You like it there?"

"Not everything you do in life is a source of pure pleasure . . ."

21

Just then Martine, a fellow student in political science, stopped to say hello. Guillaume introduced her to Suzanne, who mumbled her name under her breath.

"I'm afraid I didn't catch your name," he said as he sat back down. "Is it Anne?"

"No, I'm sorry to say. It's Suzanne."

"Why sorry? You wouldn't by any chance be a snob?"

"No, not at all. It's just that I don't like my name."

"In any case, it's better than Suzon."

"Jerk!"

"The name is Guillaume Peuch-Drummond."

"And mine is Suzanne Hocquetot."

"With an *H?*"*

"Yes. And T-O-T at the end."

"You're from Normandy?"

"Yes. Are you, too?"

"No, but I am interested in onomastics. Do you know what that is?"

"Hmm . . . The science of names?"

"The science of *proper* names. Give me any name, and I'll tell you its geographic origin and etymology."

That was one of his favorite gimmicks, and, in all fairness, one had to admit it was less banal than telling horoscopes or palm-reading.

I was listening with one ear, while with the other I was vaguely following the plans for a party that was to be held the following Saturday.

---

*French pronunciation has often proved treacherous for generations of foreigners: one of the trickiest letters is "h"—generally silent, except in some proper names. *(Tr.)*

"Guillaume," shouted Jean-Louis, sitting nearby, "are you going to Pfeiffer's bash?"

"No," he said, turning to face the caller. "I can't. I'm having a dinner party at the house that Saturday. In fact, you're invited." Then, turning back to Suzanne, "You want to come?"

"Why not? Where is it?"

"At Bourg-la-Reine. I'll come and pick you up. You like paella?"

"I'm not sure whether I've ever had it."

"I make a neat paella. In fact, it's the only dish I know how to cook. Where do you live—with your parents?"

"No, I have a room with some people who live at the Porte de Clichy. But I'm almost never there. I don't get home from class until ten at night, and I get up at seven in the morning."

"And how about Sunday?"

"I usually spend Sundays working on my Italian. But I do prefer to do that at a café. It's so much more pleasant . . ."

With Guillaume, things rarely dragged on for very long. And yet Suzanne refused to yield to his advances, at least up to the Saturday dinner that had been discussed at the café. I was just finishing work when I saw them arrive.

"Hurry," Guillaume said when I opened the door. "The car's illegally parked."

"Listen," I began, "I'm not sure I can come. I'm way behind in chemistry."

"I like people who keep their word."

"I didn't say I'd come."

"You sure did. You heard him, didn't you?" he said, turning to Suzanne.

"Yes," she said. "You did say you'd come."

"So come on. I'll drive you home by midnight."

"That's what you always say."

"I'm serious," he said, trying to assume an air of dignity. "Besides, I have to drive Suzanne home, too."

"Okay, okay," I said. "You win." But even as I headed for the closet to get my good suit, I knew exactly how the evening was going to turn out. Suzanne had sat down on the bed, and had pulled Guillaume over to her. While I was tying my tie, they were already going at it.

"Who's going to be there?" I said, having decided that their necking had gone on long enough.

"There'll be Jean-Louis, Catherine, François, Philippe . . . and your girlfriend."

"*What* girlfriend."

"Sophie."

"You're crazy. I don't even know her." It was true: I had laid eyes on the girl twice in my life, both times in the company of Frank, a friend of Guillaume's.

"Doesn't matter. I know you have the hots for her."

"Oh . . . maybe. I mean, she's not bad."

"If Bertrand says she's not bad, that means she's a knockout. But wait a minute," he said, turning to Suzanne. "You know the girl. She was in the bar the other day: the Irish girl."

"Oh, sure," she said. "She's a real beauty, that girl. Bertrand, I commend you on your excellent taste."

Guillaume spent the better part of the year at his house in Bourg-la-Reine, since his mother traveled a great deal. That night, Suzanne was playing hostess, and taking the role very seriously. But the minute we arrived, Guillaume set off in hot pursuit of Sophie, as though he had made up his mind to win her before the evening was over. His job was made all the easier in that Frank, her presumed escort, seemed rather indifferent to her that night.

I was keeping carefully, and philosophically, out of things, but I could see that Suzanne was on the verge of tears. I kept expecting her to pick up her coat, dash out of the house, and head for the train station. Sophie, I had to admit, intimidated me to some degree, and in a sense Guillaume's relentless pursuit of her was a blessing. All I hoped was that he would go one step too far and be put back in his place. But he apparently knew just how far he could go, and as yet had gone no further. Toward eleven o'clock he took me aside in the kitchen.

"How are things progressing between you and Sophie?" he asked, patting me on the shoulder as he posed the incredible question.

"Shouldn't I be the one asking you that question?"

"Come off it, man. I don't give a damn about Sophie. I'm just doing that to make Suzanne jealous. How is she, by the way? Is she taking it badly?"

"Suzanne? I don't think she's overjoyed. And with good reason, I might add."

"Good! There's nothing worse than those girls who look like an easy lay but have to drag things on and on, to prove they're not . . . Anyway, I have a feeling now she's ripe to be plucked. What do you think?"

"Yeah, maybe," I said with no real conviction.

"Get rid of that long face, for God's sake! I told you: I couldn't care less about Sophie; for one thing, she's too pretentious. But I have a feeling it's all over between her and Frank."

"Please," I protested, "don't worry about me, as far as Sophie's concerned. I don't have any claim on her."

25

"You can if you want. She likes you. It's plain as the nose on your face. Can't hide those feelings, you know . . . What was it I wanted to say? Oh, yes. I have to ask you one favor. When the others are ready to leave, don't go with any of them if they suggest driving you home. Say I'm going to drive you. In all fairness, I can't stay behind alone with Suzanne. She's a provincial, and has to maintain a façade of propriety."

At about midnight all the guests said good night and got ready to go their various ways. Someone did indeed offer me a ride home, which I refused. It was in the same car in which Sophie was riding, and thus I lost an opportunity to make some time with her. But did I really want to? Despite what Guillaume had said, I still suspected she was very much taken with Frank, a tall, good-looking fellow, and I had no illusions that I would succeed where my friend had failed.

So there we were, the three of us, after the last of the guests had gone. Suzanne, overjoyed at having been readmitted to Guillaume's favor, had lost all notion of time. She was tenderly cuddled in his arm while he, sprawled on the couch, was blowing smoke rings in the general direction of the ceiling. Seated across from them, I had all I could do to stifle my yawns. For want of something better to do, I began beating time on the little coffee table in front of my chair.

"You know," Guillaume said, "Bertrand can make tables move."

"Really?" said Suzanne, obviously intrigued.

"It's true," I said. "That's one of my rare social talents. Actually, nothing is easier, especially with this table. Come over, both of you, and place your hands flat on the tabletop, in such a way that your fingers are touching. There's nothing magic about it. It's all a question of our nerve impulses."

They both got up and came over to where I was sitting. They sat down across from me and placed their hands as I had instructed.

"Now, concentrate, as hard as you can. But at the same time relax, let yourself go!"

At first Suzanne had trouble containing her laughter, but finally she got hold of herself and yielded to the contagion of calm. For several minutes an imposing silence reigned; then the table began to move. First it leaned to the right, then back to the left. Suzanne, clearly skeptical, did her best to resist its movement.

"Bertrand, you're pushing!"

"I swear I'm not! It's the spirit!"

She shrugged her shoulders.

"Actually," I went on, "it's our involuntary impulses. The spirit is the result of our tripled subconscious effort."

"A very scholarly explanation."

"Quiet, please," Guillaume interrupted. "No more comments. Let's resume our concentration."

"Let's summon the spirit," I said, and I began to feel the wood cracking once again. "Spirit, are you there?"

The table rose, then dropped suddenly back to the floor.

"One knock means yes . . . Spirit, are you there?"

I explained that each letter of the alphabet was indicated by a corresponding number of knocks; that is, one for *a*, two for *b*, and so forth. When I heard the first reply, four knocks—that is, the letter *d*—I already suspected what the result would be. It's true the word was already in the air; or, more precisely, on the cover of the record lying next to the record player. And it fed Guillaume's pride to the same degree that it inspired my own sense of mischief.

27

"D-O-N-J . . ." Guillaume spelled out, already delighted. "The spirit is in all likelihood none other than Don Juan himself. And what is this Don Juan saying?"

At that he took over possession of the guiding spirit to add his own two cents, although I have to say my contribution was not exactly nil; nor in fact was Suzanne's, for the next phrase offered by the oracle surely expressed her own deep-seated desire.

"T-O-B-E . . . Why, the spirit's spelling out 'To bed'!" Guillaume exclaimed. Then, "Bertrand, I never knew you were such a low-down, vulgar guy!"

In vain I protested my innocence, while Guillaume went into gales of laughter, and Suzanne, inwardly delighted, tried to assume an air of shock and displeasure.

"All right, let's go to bed," he concluded. "The fact is, I'm ready to drop. I don't even have the strength to drive you back to Paris. But the house is plenty large enough for all of us. Bertrand and I will sleep here, and you, Suzanne, can sleep in my mother's room. You know where it is?"

"Yes," she said, somewhat disappointed, "I know where it is."

Guillaume took her to the living-room door and planted a little kiss on each cheek.

"Good night. You're not angry at me, are you?"

"Why should I be angry at you? Good night, Bertrand!" And she turned and disappeared down the hallway.

"Ah, women!" Guillaume said, sighing, lighting a cigarette.

He took a few puffs, then put an end to the little game he had been playing. "I have to go and cheer the poor girl up," he said. He turned and left the room.

I went to bed, sure I had seen the last of him for the night.

. . .

The following morning I was up at dawn. I had already spent a number of Sundays at Guillaume's house, and even under the present circumstances I was sure that Guillaume would have asked me to stay, only too happy to have me around as a witness to his triumph. But my role had already gone on too long for my taste. I tiptoed out of the house and made my way to the train station.

It wasn't that Suzanne's behavior interested me in the least—what she did was her business and hers alone—but it seemed that Guillaume took a malicious pleasure in involving me in his wicked little games; he enjoyed creating a climate of lewdness around even the most innocuous of his ploys and pranks.

A week later I ran into him along the Boul' Mich'.*

"What's new with you?" I said. "You've disappeared from sight."

"Problems," he said. "A heavy scene."

"Suzanne?"

"She calls me at all hours of the day and night. I seem to have an uncanny knack for picking girls who immediately turn into clinging vines. What about you—have you seen her since that dinner party?"

"Yeah, once or twice. But I wouldn't say there was much of a conversation."

"Did she talk about me?"

"No. I just bumped into her in the street. She was on her way to make a phone call."

"Ah! You see what I mean?"

---

*Student slang for boulevard Saint-Michel, the heart of the Latin Quarter. *(Tr.)*

The following Saturday he phoned me. He confessed that out of weakness he had taken up with Suzanne again, and wanted to know if I would join the two of them—since she bored him out of his mind—for a night on the town.

I accepted, but with great reluctance and bad grace. We went out dancing, to a nightclub on the Right Bank. Suzanne, who was dressed to kill, treated me like her newfound confidant, filling my ears with the effusions of her rediscovered happiness. It was a role I did not exactly covet: her every gesture and expression, her laughter and carrying on, put me off more than I can say. And yet I really had nothing specific against her. I hated her the way I hated all the skirts that Guillaume chased. He sought out the easiest ones, without exception, and, so far as I know, never made a move toward any girl halfway worthy of him, for in those days I still had a very high opinion of Guillaume's powers of seduction.

He drove me back to my hotel; then he and Suzanne continued on to the house at Bourg-la-Reine. At two o'clock the next afternoon Guillaume called me again.

"How about coming out to the house this afternoon for tea? It'll be nice. I swear I'll drive you back to town by seven. Don't tell me you plan to stay cooped up all day Sunday in your room."

I found a beaming Suzanne and a good-natured Guillaume, the latter in a full, fur-collared robe, lolling contentedly on the couch. It wasn't long before the idyllic scene took a quick turn for the worse. As Suzanne was bending over him to take a book off the shelf behind the couch, Guillaume gave her a smart slap on the buttocks. She responded with a slap that he barely managed to avoid. He grabbed her arm, but she twisted free and took refuge by the fireplace. Guillaume, instead of following her, remained sprawled among his pillows, his only comment on the exchange a coarse laugh that was clearly intended for me. Then he glanced over at Suzanne, who was pouting in her corner.

"Suzanne!"

He called her several times, but she refused to reply, standing there with her eyes stubbornly lowered.

"Suzanne! Don't be angry. I was only joking."

"I don't like jokes in poor taste."

"If my taste were good, I wouldn't be attracted to you."

"That's all I care about."

"What?"

"That you do like me."

"I was beginning to think that didn't matter to you."

"Anyway, if you don't like me, there are plenty of others who do, you know."

"Oh, I know. All those pimply little twerps."

"That's not true! They're as good-looking as you. Some far better."

Guillaume whistled between his teeth and gave me a knowing look. "The girl's no dummy, eh? Got a mind of her own, and knows how to use it."

I was in no mood to referee their arguments. I got up out of my chair and headed for the door.

"Wait a minute," Guillaume called after me. "There's one question I want to ask you. And you," he said, turning to Suzanne, "come over here. Next to me. What are you waiting for?"

Reluctantly she complied; and I, in spite of myself, paused in midflight, to see what was next on Guillaume's evil agenda.

"You know," he went on, "Bertrand's the best friend I've ever had. Look at him blush. Suzanne, are you in love with him?"

"With Bertrand? Of course not!"

"That's not very flattering!"

"Idiot!"

"Let's make one assumption: that he's been after you."

"But the fact is he hasn't been."

"But let's suppose he had. What if he had really badgered you, begged you on bended knee?"

"That's not his style."

"What makes you so sure? He might very easily have been pursuing you? Would you have given in to his advances?"

"No, I don't think so. I like Bertrand a lot, but I have very set ideas on certain subjects."

"What about you, Bertrand? If Suzanne—"

"Let's say that I have very set ideas on certain subjects," I said, casting a withering glance in Suzanne's direction.

"I can't believe how pretentious you both are. At least Bertrand has good reason for the way he feels, but Suzanne . . . you're the most conceited girl I've ever met. Don't you agree, Bertrand?"

"No, absolutely not. In fact, if anything, I'd say the opposite is true."

"I know what you mean: she's such a scatterbrain. But one doesn't necessarily preclude the other."

Suzanne, who was growing ever more furious, tried to get up, but Guillaume held her in place.

"Let me go!"

"Stay right where you are!"

"What for? To listen to your asinine remarks?"

"I say what I think. Bertrand, tell me in all honesty: don't you find that she's a little sweet on you?"

"No, not at all."

"You told me she was. At least that's what you thought."

"You're crazy!"

Guillaume was having a harder and harder time keeping Suzanne from wresting herself free.

"You do think it," he insisted.

"I don't!"

"Why don't you?"

"Because it's obvious!"

"The evidence is inadmissible," he exclaimed with the tone of a public prosecutor. "Case closed. Let the sentence be carried out!"

Suzanne had finally succeeded in pulling away from Guillaume and was on her knees on the couch. But he still had hold of her arms, and he pulled her down on top of him. He tried to spank her; she fought to free herself, shouting, "Ouch! Help! Bertrand! Bertrand!"

But before I had a chance to get involved she finally wrestled free and ran out of the room, slamming the door behind her.

"You're a real bastard," I said. "Why do you have to involve me in these dumb situations?"

"Don't let it worry you. I've been trying to get her off my back for the past two weeks. This said, she's really well stacked. But Suzanne's my mother's first name, too, and somehow that bugs me."

Suzanne resurfaced. She had put on her coat and went over to pick up her pocketbook.

"Do you want me to take you home?" I said, slipping into my sportcoat.

"Thanks, that would be nice."

"The least you could do would be to say good-bye," Guillaume broke in.

She paused and half turned in his direction.

"Good-bye," she said, "forever!"

He laughed, and began to sing softly:

> *"Bye-bye, my child,*
> *Bye-bye forever.*
> *It's no surprise,*
> *But your sweet smile*
> *Will linger on*
> *Long after you are gone. "*

She shrugged her shoulders. Guillaume got to his feet and went over to her.

"Listen," he said, "I didn't mean all those nasty things. I was just in a foul mood. Will you forgive me? Please? Pretty please? Come on, speak up."

Suzanne's face slowly relaxed. In spite of herself she could not repress a slight smile. One could sense that he had her again in the palm of his hand. Fed up and worn out, I quickly exited into the next room.

There I waited for Suzanne for a few minutes, which was long enough to turn against her all the pent-up anger I had amassed against Guillaume during that whole scene. After all, I was damned stupid to be worrying about that girl. She deserved what she got: Guillaume was if anything too decent. Her complete lack of dignity justified the contempt that I had always felt not only for the way she acted but for the way she looked as well.

I decided to do everything in my power to avoid seeing her, under any pretense, and for a few days I was able to. But she was on the lookout for me. She would sit endlessly on the terrace of the café across the street from where I lived and keep an eye posted on the hotel door. Whenever I went in or out, she would wave at me or call over.

"Can I buy you a cup of coffee? You're not on your way to a fire, are you?"

There were times when I couldn't manage to avoid her, particularly when she resorted to wiles and stratagems.

"Someone was asking me about you."

"Who?"

"Sophie."

"Ah!"

"We had lunch together the other day. She's really a great girl."

"Is she? I hardly know her . . ."

The conversation faltered there. But Suzanne, undaunted, made another valiant effort.

"Are you going to the big dance at the Business School?"

"No, I can't. I've got too much work."

"Really? You ought to try to make it. Just this once."

"Anyway, I'm dead broke."

"Oh, if that's what's keeping you away, be my guest."

"Please!"

"I'm serious. I just received my monthly allowance, so I'm loaded."

"I said no."

"Come on. You'll be doing me a favor. And besides, Sophie will be there."

"That's no reason."

"Yes it is. I'll tell you what: I'll loan you the money. You can pay me back later. Okay?"

In the end I gave in to her pressures. Suzanne had been telling the truth. Sophie was there, without an escort, and, what was more, seemed particularly friendly toward me. It was the first time she and I had been able to exchange as much as two words without anyone else's being present. But her talk was all about Guillaume; my reaction was to take refuge in peremptory assertions that ruined any possibility of conversation.

"Do you know him very well?"

"He's my best friend."

"That's odd. You two are so different."

"Not all that much. Actually, on a lot of points we see absolutely eye to eye."

"I find that hard to believe . . ."

I was overwhelmed by shyness, and the spark of brilliance I had counted on to overwhelm her failed to appear. Meanwhile, Suzanne was having a ball with a steady succession of dance partners, each one uglier than the last. I had a feeling that my time was almost up with Sophie, that she was itching to get away from me. She began to respond to invitations to dance so readily that I was crushed.

Finally, I lost her in the crowd, and somehow I found myself, at four in the morning, alone again with Suzanne. She began to offer me a detailed account of her unhappy experiences with Guillaume, which reminded me of my own.

"Believe me," she said, "I don't give a damn about Guillaume. It's all over between us. He's a bright enough boy; but in certain ways he's unbelievably dumb. More stupid than bad, in my opinion. Fortunately, I'm an easygoing person. But someday I suppose he'll find the right person for him . . ."

The next day, Guillaume was waiting for me as I came out of school.

"There you are, you bastard. I hear you're chasing my old girl."

"What?"

"Don't deny it. My spies saw you last night at the big bash."

"Ah! Of course I was there. So what?"

"I just want to warn you, old buddy. She's a far trickier number than you think."

"I can take care of myself."

"Look how she wrangled herself an invitation."

"Not so; she's the one who paid my way."

"No kidding. *She* paid. My my my! That's absolutely great. That gives me all sorts of ideas. We'll ruin the poor girl."

Suzanne, as was her wont, had gone to her café terrace directly after work Guillaume the Debonair went over to where she was sitting.

"Hi there, Suzanne! My God, it's been a long time. How're things with you?"

"Very well, thanks," she said icily.

But when she caught sight of me, her expression softened. "Hello, Bertrand."

"It's great to see you again," Guillaume went on, and without waiting to be asked he pulled up a chair across from her. "Do you mind?"

"I'm leaving in five minutes anyway."

I joined them. For a long moment no one spoke. Suzanne sat staring at her coffee cup while Guillaume studied her face, a waggish look on his face.

"Suzanne, word's out that you're flirting outrageously. I'm shocked. Especially when the object of your advances is none other than my best friend!"

Once again I could see her giving in. When it came time to pay, Guillaume pretended to fumble for his money.

"Dammit! I haven't got a cent with me tonight. Do you mind picking up the tab for me, Bertrand?"

I took out my wallet, but Suzanne had already opened her pocketbook.

"No, keep your money. I invited you."

"Come on!"

"You heard me."

"No I didn't. And anyway, you're boring me," I said, putting some money on the table.

Suzanne picked it up and handed it back to me. "If I feel like inviting you, that's my business, right? I'm a free person."

"Okay, be a free person, if it gives you any pleasure." And I stuck the money back in my pocket.

There followed a period of two or three weeks during which we very deliberately sponged off Suzanne, allowing her to invite us to cafés, restaurants, the movies. For the sake of "appearances," she even went so far as to slip us money under the table. After a few days the little game began to pale for me. Finally, Guillaume went off to spend a few days with his mother, but Suzanne still managed to concoct various ways to keep after me.

When the hotel phone was occupied, I used to cross the street and use the phone in the basement of the café. Once, I saw Suzanne sitting inside, right next to the window, but I pretended not to see her. She got up and followed me downstairs.

"So that's how it is," she said. "Making a point of ignoring me. I was upstairs. Didn't you see me wave to you?"

"No, I didn't."

"Do you have a minute or two? I have something I want to talk to you about."

Actually, she wanted to invite me out. I made up some excuse about not being free. She didn't believe me.

"If it's money you're worried about, don't let that bother you . . ."

"But you know what, Suzanne? It does!"

"I can't believe how middle-class you are."

"Maybe I am. Go and invite someone else."

"That's not the question," she said. "If I simply wanted to go out with no one in particular, there would be no problem. I spend most of my day turning down dates. Does it bug you that I prefer to go out with you?"

Finally I agreed to go out with her, to dinner at a little place called Paul's, which just happened to be Guillaume's favorite restaurant. That evening, as I was getting ready to go out, who should show up at my hotel but Guillaume. He had just got back from the Riviera. The news was that his mother had re-married and would be living permanently in the South. But Guillaume would be keeping the place in Bourg-la-Reine.

"What are you doing tonight?" he said. "Got a date?"

"Yes."

"Why don't we go out to dinner together? On me. I'm loaded."

"No, I can't. I'm tied up."

"Suzanne?"

"No."

"Come on, you can tell me. Is it with her?"

"Yes."

"How is your love life progressing?"

"Just great."

"You'll be bored out of your skull. Why don't you bring me along?"

"Out of the question."

"I have an idea. Where are you going? Let me guess: to Paul's?"

"You're really one big pain," I said, knowing I had already lost.

"I'll just happen to bump into you. If she pulls a long face, invite me to join you. I'll pay you back later. Come on, you can do me this one favor. I feel like raising a little hell tonight. In any case, if she asked you to go to Paul's, it means she really hopes she'll run into me there."

Everything happened exactly as Guillaume had planned it. He showed up just as we were beginning our first course and carefully managed it so that it was we who ended up coaxing him to join us.

"If it's a hiding place you're looking for," he said as he came over to our table, "you have to admit your choice is pretty lousy."

"We're not hiding," I said. "Have you eaten?"

"No, but—"

"Pull up a chair and join us. I'm paying."

"No, thanks . . . Anyway, Suzanne doesn't want me to."

She shrugged with disgust. "You're so stupid."

"Be frank about it."

"I *am* being frank."

While we were having dessert, Guillaume excused himself and went to make a phone call. While he was gone, Suzanne slipped me another ten-franc note. This time I adamantly refused.

"Out of the question. Listen, it was I who invited him."

"But you're flat broke."

"No more than you are . . . Come on, put your money back in your pocketbook."

"Okay. But I'm going to invite you all to the club."

"You're going to bankrupt yourself."

"That's my business."

We went to the same nightclub we had gone to before. At about two in the morning I was dozing away in my chair when Guillaume nudged me awake with his elbow.

"Come on. Let's blow this joint."

"What about Suzanne?"

"She's gone to the ladies' room. And don't start giving me your morality bit, about how it's not proper to leave without her."

Might as well break off relations once and for all, I thought. So I got to my feet and followed Guillaume out the door.

I had a feeling that this French leave of ours would be for naught. The next day, precisely at noon, the inescapable Suzanne pounced on me.

"How's Guillaume? Has he slept off last night?"

"He was afraid to drive home alone, so he stayed over at my place. Slept in a chair."

"Anyway, the party's over. It's only the twelfth of the month and I haven't a penny to my name."

"You have enough left to eat on, don't you?"

"Not even. But don't worry—I'll manage."

"I have a couple of extra canteen tickets I can let you have."

"No, thanks. I'll have lunch with a girlfriend; you know, the girl who works with me . . . You know what? You guys did me a favor by leaving last night. After you left I met this extraordinary guy, a Scotsman. Really terrific. I have a date to see him again tonight."

"No kidding! Congratulations. Well," I said as I started to leave, "see you around, Suzanne."

I had already started to cross the street when I heard her shout, "You can tell Guillaume if you want to!"

· · ·

Then it was Easter vacation, and I went to spend it with my family, in Normandy. I had just arrived back in Paris—in fact I was still unpacking my suitcase, carefully folding and hiding within the pages of a book the four hundred francs my parents had given me to buy a new suit with—when Guillaume knocked at my door. I had barely time enough to slip the book back into its place on the mantelpiece.

"Greetings. I just stopped by to see if you were back yet."

"Just got back this minute."

"You have a good vacation?"

"Slept a lot. How about you?"

"Terrific! Absolutely fabulous! You have no idea how many pretty girls there are in the South of France . . . The Riviera is crawling with them. Anyway, just before I left I met an incredible number. A Parisian. She'll be here day after tomorrow."

"Really?"

"The sad part is, I don't have any money to take her out. Blew my whole wad on the way up here from the Riviera. You couldn't bail me out, could you? Say, one or two hundred francs?"

"I wish I could, but I haven't got them."

"I'm expecting a money order Monday. You must have some money; you just got back from vacation."

"No, I don't. My parents send me my allowance every week."

"You mean to tell me you can't cough up a lousy hundred francs?"

"Sorry. I just paid my rent."

The bell rang in the hallway. It was the desk ringing me from downstairs: there was a phone call for me. I went down to the lobby and picked up the receiver.

"Hello."

"Hello there. This is Suzanne. How was your holiday? When can we get together? You going to the big bash at Daniel's a week from this Thursday?"

"Ah, well, I guess so."

"Sophie will be there. So be sure to show up!"

"I don't know. I have a makeup exam the next day . . . Well, okay, I'll be there."

"You see—I'm thinking of you."

"I appreciate it. And what are you up to? How's your Englishman?"

"You mean the Scotsman. Oh, he's gone home. Actually, he turned out to be a bit of a bore!"

When I went back upstairs, Guillaume was rummaging in my books.

"I'll bet that was Suzanne who just called."

"No!" I said.

"Have you seen her since that night?"

"I ran into her a couple of times before we left for Easter vacation."

"With her Englishman?"

"You knew about him?"

"More or less. Anyway, it serves her right. The guy took off and never looked back. Admit it: it *was* Suzanne who just called."

"No, I told you it wasn't."

"You're lying."

"And you're a pain in the ass!"

"It was a girl! That much is plain as day."

"It was Sophie, if you must know. You happy now?"

"Sophie? Well, well . . ." Guillaume said, slightly surprised. "In that case, my fine feathered friend, don't hold back: if there's one thing girls like, it's for men to take the offensive!"

.   .   .

At Daniel's party, while we were dancing, Sophie wasted no time climbing astride her own favorite hobbyhorse: accusing Guillaume of every dirty trick in the book, casting aspersions on his character and person.

"Everything you say may be true," I admitted, "but the fact is, there are certain things I allow Guillaume that I wouldn't condone in anyone else. Somehow, he can get away with them."

"For me it's just the opposite: I condone nothing where he's concerned, and overlook everyone else's offense, big or small. I simply loathe that kind of rich man's son who plays Mr. Tough Guy. Really, he doesn't fit the role."

"He'll get over it."

"That's what makes me most angry: he does it not out of conviction but pure snobbery. I hate snobs."

"One thing he's not is a snob. What do you have against him, anyway? You don't even know him."

"I've heard enough about him."

"Oh, you mean from Suzanne."

"Yes, you hit the nail on the head: from Suzanne herself."

"She's big enough to defend herself without your help. Besides, if she dislikes him so much, why doesn't she simply stop running after him?"

"Really! You talk like such a child!"

Our conversation was going from bad to worse, and the more we talked, the less sure I was how to handle her. One thing was sure, however, and that was that the forcing tactic recommended by Guillaume was not the way. Meanwhile, Suzanne, who seemed very popular, finally fended off suitors by claiming she was too tired to dance another step; besides, she complained, her shoes didn't fit and her feet were killing her. As she was leaving the party, she drew me aside into the kitchen.

"You couldn't lend me ten francs for a taxi, could you?"

"Sure." I took out my wallet, flipped it open, and saw that it was empty. "Dammit! I forgot to take my money. Ask Sophie."

"Are you kidding? She's the last person I'd ask."

"How about what's-his-name?" I was referring to the host.

"I hate to ask him. I already owe him some money."

"You really have been living it up, haven't you?"

"Haven't you heard? I quit my job," she said with a tight little smile.

"And what are you living on?"

She shrugged evasively.

"I don't know anyone here who has a car," I went on, growing more irritated by the minute that she had seen fit to lay all her problems on me.

"Yes," she said, "Jean-Louis does"—alluding to one of her numerous suitors—"but I'd just as soon not ask him, if you know what I mean . . ." She kept staring at me imploringly, as though I were her sole means of salvation.

"I have some money back at my hotel," I said. "Come on, if your feet don't hurt you too much."

"I can walk *that* far," she said. "Your hotel's right around the corner."

She hobbled along behind me. When we reached the hotel, she paused in front of the door and said, "Listen, you're very sweet. I don't want to make you walk up six flights of stairs twice. Besides, my feet are killing me. I don't know whether I'd even be able to make it to the taxi stand . . . If it doesn't bother you, why don't I simply come upstairs with you. I won't be any trouble. I'll just curl up in a chair and read."

"Okay," I said, less persuaded by her reasoning than taken

aback by the unexpected nature of her proposition. I merely added, "Just make sure you don't make any noise."

"You worried about your reputation?"

To which I simply shrugged and muttered something unintelligent.

As soon as she was in the room, Suzanne sat down in the only easy chair. She took off her shoes, tucked her legs up under her, and, as she was trying to find a comfortable position in the chair, caught the hem of her skirt on a nail that was sticking out.

"Damn!"

"What's the matter?"

"I tore my skirt again. You wouldn't have a safety pin, would you?"

"I have something even better," I said, moving across the room and pulling open a drawer. "A needle and thread."

"Great . . . The stupid thing is, this is the only presentable skirt I own."

"What about the dress you wore to the party?"

"Someone lent it to me. Anyway, it's too fancy for everyday wear."

I handed her a spool of black thread and a needle, which she threaded.

"I don't suppose you have a thimble."

I knelt down on one knee and took the needle from her. "I don't need a thimble. You see, when I sew, I don't push, I pull."

I was inches away from her, my hands on her knee, my face close to hers. I can't say that the combination of her presence and the late hour—however "ugly" I might have considered her in the past—was unsettling. The fact that for some time now Suzanne had been solicitous of me, that she had made a point of coming up to my room, and the incident—perhaps provoked—of her torn skirt gave me full license to make further advances, it seemed to me, if I had any designs on her. What, in fact, was she looking for? There was something particularly studied, something focused, about her attitude tonight, as though she had a well-laid-out plan in mind. Or was I imagining things, and was it simply her own embarrassment that made me think so? I was still turning all these possibilities over in my mind when she took the needle away from me, pushed me slightly away from her, and put me on the defensive.

"Oh, boys! Okay. That's enough. I see the picture."

"The hell with you, then. Do it yourself," I said, getting to my feet. I was angry, and I hoped my tone conveyed it. I went over to fetch my pajamas.

"I may be a jerk," I said, passing behind the easy chair and already beginning to undress, "but the fact is, the only place I can get a decent night's sleep is in my bed. And I have a makeup exam tomorrow."

"Please," Suzanne said, all sweetness again, "don't worry about little old me. I can cope very nicely." She stretched her legs out and rubbed one foot against the other. "I'm so tired," she went on, "I think I could sleep anywhere. What infuriates me," she said, shifting subjects in midstream, "is that I was really had by that dumb bitch of a saleslady. She sold me a pair of shoes two sizes too small for me, and I was stupid enough to buy them. And they're the only pair I have."

"Why don't you take them back?"

"How can I? I've already worn them two days." She sighed. "The worst of it is, I've already eaten into my last ten-franc note."

"It's really that bad, eh?"

"I'm afraid so."

"I'd be happy to lend you some, but I have to pay my dentist. You think you can hang on until next week?"

"Please, Bertrand, I appreciate it. Don't worry. I'll work it out one way or another."

"You know, I feel very embarrassed about this whole thing. I made you throw your money away hand over fist."

"No, you didn't. I spent it myself, and if I did, it was because I enjoyed it. We spent some great evenings together, didn't we? That's all that matters. You can always find money one way or another. All you have to do is look for it. You know, what I'd really like is part-time work. Besides, I think before long I'm going to take off for Italy. All these little uptight Frenchmen give me a pain in the you know what."

"It would appear," I declaimed, "that Italy is teeming with handsome men."

She shrugged her shoulders. "You may not believe this, but the fact is that here in Paris I still haven't found a man I like. I mean, not one!"

"You're too demanding."

"And what about you? As for Guillaume, contrary to what you think, I never for one moment took him seriously. Even admitting for argument's sake that I was a little in love with him . . . In fact, if you want to know, you're the only one of the lot I find bearable. You're a no-good bastard, but at least a girl knows where she stands with you. All the others have one thing in mind: to take you to bed, and then it's good-bye."

"I know at least a dozen who are really crazy about you."

"Name one."

"I don't know. Jean-Louis . . . François . . ."

"Ugh! If that's the best you can come up with, thanks, but no thanks. Actually, you're the only one I really like. It's rare, you know, to find a boy who doesn't spend his whole life try-ing to get a girl into bed with him."

I was washing my hands as I listened to her, and at first I didn't respond. Then, "It all depends on what girl you're talk-ing about."

"Touché!"

"I didn't mean it the way it sounded."

"He didn't mean it the way it sounded!" she said mock-ingly. "It's incredible how stupid you can be sometimes."

"What do you mean by that?"

"Nothing, really. Believe me, I really wish you nothing but the best."

I walked over to the bed and started to slip under the cov-ers. "I never doubted it for a single moment," I said, laughing.

"And how's your love life?" she said suddenly.

"Terrible," I said.

"Really? Then you must be taking the wrong tack. You have to be more aggressive. That's what girls like, you know."

"You sound just like Guillaume."

"You have to admit that he practices what he preaches."

"Not always, he doesn't. Not always."

"If you're talking about someone like Sophie, absolutely. Behind that defensive façade lies an inner self just waiting to be assaulted. If she seems defensive, it's because she always has a dozen boys hovering around her like moths around a light."

"I know what I'm doing," I said, in the same arrogant tone.

"You do? I'm delighted to hear it."

"I'm delighted you're delighted. You know, I'm not nearly so nice as you think."

"I know it, because I know *you*. In fact, I know you a lot bet-ter than you suspect."

"In that case, since we have such a profound knowledge of each other, I see no point in carrying this whole thing any further. Good night!" I finished winding the alarm clock, lay down, and turned toward the wall as she was lighting a cigarette.

At eight in the morning the alarm went off. I went over and shook Suzanne, who apparently hadn't heard a sound and was still fast asleep in her chair. She barely responded to my efforts. I shaved and washed up, then went back and tried again, this time giving her a less gentle shake.

"Suzanne. Come on!"

She staggered to her feet, took two or three steps, sighed deeply, and collapsed on the bed. In the hallway, I heard the maid's voice and the sound of the vacuum cleaner. I opened the door a crack.

"Good morning, ma'am."

"Good morning. Can I make up your room now?"

"No, not now. How about eleven? . . . G'bye, ma'am."

I turned back to Suzanne, who was still on the bed, and touched her shoulder. "Suzanne? Can you hear me?"

"Mmm. Mmm."

"Will you wait for me till eleven?"

I left the room and, after a moment's hesitation, left the key hanging in the door, so that the maid would know that I was still inside and not use her pass key to go in while I was away. A useless precaution: she was in the next room, the door to which was open, and she saw me.

"I thought . . . Are you going out?"

"Just for a second. I'll be right back up. Make up the room at eleven, right?"

"All right. Meanwhile, I'll make up the rooms downstairs."

"Fine," I said, reassured.

When I returned after my exam, Suzanne was no longer there. On the table she had left a note, prominently displayed, which read, "I had to leave. Had to meet someone." Instantly my eyes moved to the mantelpiece: the order in which I had arranged my books was changed, and it seemed to me the one in which I hid my money was sticking out slightly. I took it, slipped my fingers between the pages, and probed, then shook it out over the table. One hundred-franc note came floating down. One, and only one. In vain I kept shaking the book, always with the same results: there was no question that the other three hundred-franc notes were gone.

I went downstairs and dashed to the café. Jean-Louis, Suzanne's unhappy suitor, was sitting in the back. I went over and asked him if he had seen her that morning. Yes, he said, she had dashed in and out again. When? No more than half an hour ago. I asked him if he knew her address.

"You ought to know it better than I do," he said, obviously somewhat surprised. "Or ask Guillaume."

I went downstairs to a pay phone. No answer at Guillaume's. I called Sophie, who happened to be home. She was unusually nice, and asked how I had done in my makeup exam. She, too, had no idea where Suzanne lived. "Maybe Guillaume can tell you," she said. "But," she hastened to add, "she calls me almost every day, and, if you like, I can give her a message." She gathered from my muttered response that it wasn't something I cared to discuss over the phone, so she suggested that we meet at the end of the afternoon, after her last course at the French Institute.

While I was explaining my problem to Sophie, she listened with what seemed to be compassion rather than irony. But her suspicions were directed at a totally different culprit. She asked me if I had told the manager of the hotel about the theft.

"No," I said, "I would have had to tell him the whole story."

She burst out laughing. "And you didn't want him to know that you were sneaking ladies up to your room, eh?" She had slipped for the first time into the familiar *tu* form, and I felt less uptight with her than I had in the past. "It's a good thing you didn't," she went on, "because I'm sure it wasn't Suzanne."

"And I'm sure it was."

"It *might* have been someone else. The maid, maybe . . . In a hotel, you never know."

"No. It couldn't be."

"How about one of your friends? Guillaume, maybe?"

"You sure have a one-track mind."

"But why couldn't it have been Guillaume? You think he would have the slightest hesitation, if he needed the money?"

"Yes. He could never steal money from me! . . . Besides, he was never alone in my room." As I said those words I suddenly remembered the day I had gone downstairs to answer the phone and found him rummaging in my books when I came back up. But the thought had never crossed my mind to check in the hiding place after he had left. Besides, I had been out of the room only a couple of minutes, and he had no idea where I hid my money, or even if I had any to hide. It would have required a great deal of luck, or flair, for him to have found it in so short a time.

"No"—I shook my head—"it wasn't Guillaume," hoping my inner thoughts had not shown on my face. "That's not his style."

"It didn't bother him to bankrupt Suzanne."

"That's not the same thing. He did that as a lark."

"Some lark!" She paused and looked at me. "He really has you wrapped around his little finger, doesn't he?"

Was it Guillaume? I saw him only twice that entire semester, both of us being snowed under with work. I didn't dare tell him about the theft, for fear of his sarcastic comments. Anyway, it was Suzanne I preferred to think of as the guilty party. Somehow the notion that it was she made it seem more palatable than if it had been Guillaume, whose low blows and dirty tricks had, till now, never been aimed at me.

Sophie and I continued to see each other fairly regularly. The university was only a few blocks from where she was studying, on the boulevard Raspail, which simplified matters. But if I had made any inroads to her affections, I could detect no evidence of it.

"You see," I said one afternoon as we were sitting on a café terrace together, "what makes me think it couldn't have been Guillaume is the fact that a hundred-franc note was still there . . . There's something almost touching about leaving that behind. I can see Suzanne doing such a thing. Guillaume? Never. In a way, she was a damn nice girl."

"I'm glad to hear you say that," Sophie said.

"Not that I ever admitted she wasn't an ugly duckling, but—"

"Ugly! That's all you can ever say! It shows how limited you are. Suzanne's not ugly. I admit she may not be the classic beauty, but there's something so . . . so marvelously feminine about her. She has class. She has beautiful legs . . . lovely hands . . . In fact, I find her the quintessential French girl."

I laughed derisively. "If that's true, I can't say it makes me very patriotic."

"Very funny," she said, with obvious sarcasm. "And there's another thing about her, Mr. Smart: whether you like it or not, men adore her."

"Not this man."

"That doesn't surprise me. Anyway, I said 'men,' not 'boys.' "

"Does that mean you're the type boys like?"

"That," she said, half seriously, half ironically, "is the great tragedy of my life."

Her admission, which I thought to be aimed at me, gave me the courage to reach out and take her hand. But she quickly withdrew it. "Please," she said. "Unless you want me to get angry."

I didn't force the issue. This was but the latest in a long series of rebuffs. All was lost, although at that point I was not yet ready to admit it to myself. I limited myself to sulking for a few moments, while she watched me in obvious amusement. It was she who broke the silence.

"Oh, by the way, I might as well tell you," she began, "Suzanne's getting married."

I almost fell off my chair. "What? You mean, you've seen her?"

"Yes. For the past few days she's been calling me every day."

"No kidding? And who is it she's marrying?"

"A fellow who . . . but you know him. Frank Schaller."

"Schaller? No . . . I can't place him."

"Of course you can. He was the one I brought to Guillaume's party that night. Don't you remember?"

"In other words, she stole him from you," I managed, as the world began to gape open before me.

. . .

That unexpected conclusion caused me to revise my own thinking considerably. Till then, I had always pictured Suzanne as Guillaume's victim, the long-suffering butt of his various machinations. Actually, it was not so much that she fed his ego as that she brought out certain tendencies that he generally repressed. I realized, too, that there was a strange physical resemblance—I don't know why it had taken me so long to recognize it—among all the girls that Guillaume pursued. They were not "ugly," as I had so stoutly maintained, and they were similar less in face than in figure; that is, they didn't actually look alike, but all belonged to the same physical type. Unlike Sophie and other tall girls, whom he dismissed as "beanpoles," the type that seemed to interest him were rather small and pleasantly plump.

The school year was coming to an end. As I was failing my exams and losing Sophie, there was Suzanne, happy as a clam. I would see her from time to time, strolling along the boulevard on the arm of her handsome Frank, and despite herself she couldn't keep from glancing at me. That girl, for whom I had felt nothing but pity, was paying me back—paying us all back—and reducing us pitilessly to the level of the boys that we unquestionably still were. Whether she was innocent or guilty, shrewd or naïve, what did it matter? By depriving me of the right to feel sorry for her, Suzanne had taken her real revenge.

III

MY NIGHT AT MAUD'S

In this story I'm not going to tell everything. Besides, there isn't any story, really: just a series of very ordinary events, of chance happenings and coincidences of the kind we have all experienced at one time or another in our lives. The deeper meanings of these events will be whatever I choose to endow them with.

I will keep to a certain line, a certain order of events, a certain way in which one event succeeds another. But my feelings, my own opinions and beliefs, will not intrude upon the line of the story, even though they are very much at the forefront of the events described. I present them here without any desire to share them, or to justify them.

I was living in Clermont-Ferrand, an industrial city in south-central France, where for two months I had been working as an engineer at the Michelin tire complex. Prior to that, I had worked for a subsidiary of Standard Oil in Vancouver, before moving on to Valparaíso. Not that I had ever considered myself an expatriot. An involvement that I won't go into had kept me away from France longer than I had intended. Now I was free, and beginning to think about marriage.

Clermont, a city I had never visited before, won me over as soon as I set foot there. Geographically, its orientation was the exact opposite of the two American cities where I had lived, both of which faced west. Here, on the contrary, the Limagne plains opened eastward, whereas behind us rose the mountains of the Massif Central. I have always had a strong sense of place, and of the orientation of cities and houses I have lived in. Here, the house I chose was situated on the peaks of the Ceyrat mountains, and from it I had a splendid view, interrupted, only twelve or fifteen miles away, by the evanescent line of the Forez peaks. This panoramic but finite view I found somehow reassuring: it helped me focus my thoughts.

For the time being I have no desire to make friends. Once in a while I make a point of chatting with my fellow workers, but only on the most superficial level. I make no effort to cultivate friends. The atmosphere of this place is austere, but I have a feeling I'm one up on this coldness.

This desire to be alone is not what I would call my normal bent. Abroad, I tend to become involved with others almost too quickly, without taking into consideration any possible consequence, for I know how tenuous such relations are. Here, I keep aloof, almost as though I am on my guard.

Since my return to France I have been caught up in what I can only fairly describe as a frenzy of studying. Mathematics first and foremost, partly because my new job demands it, but also because, as seems to happen with me every two or three years, I have a thirst for it. One day, in a bookstore, where I was looking for some books on the theory of probabilities, I happened to glance at a row of paperbacks, and I bought a copy of Pascal's *Thoughts*. I hadn't read the book since high school days, yet Pascal is one of the writers who have made the biggest impression on my life. I thought I knew his work by heart; as I reread it, however, though I found the text familiar, it was no longer the same one I remembered. The one I recalled had taken to task human nature as a whole. The text I was reading now, after all these years, struck me as uncompromising and extreme, passing judgment on me, on both my past and my future. Yes, a text written for and aimed specifically at me.

My intellectual restlessness went hand in hand with a return on my part to religion. And it was here that Pascal gave me the most trouble. My limits were his starting point: "Take holy water; go to mass . . ." Between the extremes of the ungodly and the saintly Pascal left no room for the man of goodwill that I earnestly wanted to be.

Every Sunday, I go to the eleven-o'clock mass at Notre-Dame, in town. I have a car, so distance is no real problem. And as yet I don't feel my faith strong enough to face the intimacies of the suburban parish where I live. There, in the nave and side aisles of the Romanesque basilica of Notre-Dame, the crowd is thick, lively, and ever-changing: it is a setting that suits my neophyte's zeal. I have a very strong sense of my own solitude, and an even stronger wish to leave it behind. Often I catch sight of a young couple whose clear tokens of affection would, not long before, have brought a smile to my lips but that now arouse in me a feeling of envy. For the past several weeks I have also seen, at this same mass, a blonde girl of about twenty. Françoise. I know nothing else about her as yet. I'm not even sure she's noticed my presence, yet somehow there is the overwhelming notion that she will be my wife.

I know, it all seems too pat, the end all too moral. And yet I haven't the slightest doubt that that is precisely how it will turn out. I even refuse to dignify that quasi-absolute confidence I have in my own destiny as superstition. I have always had, since my tenderest years, the certainty that God was with me. That explains why I have never attached any importance to whatever obstacles have stood in my way. I knew that I would have the last word and that sooner or later I would reach the goal set jointly by me and heaven above.

That is as much as I intend to say about my motives and my beliefs. What I say from here on out will more than suffice to reveal them. I confess that I will not always speak with total candor to others, but the truth is that one can lie to oneself as well. Enough theorizing: let me come to the facts.

My faith in my destiny did not make me fatalistic: I had made up my mind to put as much of myself into the undertaking as possible. For starters, by following Françoise—which proved not as simple as it sounds. She came to church on a motorbike. I therefore had to work it that I left church before she did, in order to have time to move my car into position not far from where she parked her bike. I managed that one day, but then I lost her in the narrow, winding streets of the old quarter of Clermont. Did she live in the center of town? If so, it would have made little sense for her to use her motorbike to cover such a short distance. It seemed more likely that she drove in from some close suburb, or from the outskirts of town, which would make my search all the more difficult.

It seemed unlikely I would run into her during the week. I left my hilltop house before daybreak, and I ate lunch at the company lunchroom. After work, keeping away from the crowded center of town, I drove home via the broader boulevards that skirted Clermont. But one evening—it was, I remember, the twenty-first of December—I had some shopping to do and for once was driving down one of the main streets of town. *Driving* is the wrong term, since for several minutes I had been caught in a traffic jam and had not moved an inch when all of a sudden I saw my blonde bicyclist appear and pass me on my right, weaving in and out among the stalled cars. I can remember that one thought flashed through my head: she's going to get away! Mechanically I honked my horn. She turned around, but only for a second, without slowing her pace, then vanished in the darkness. I had the impression that in that brief second I had seen her smile.

Now I was sure of my success. I had to find her as soon as possible. Why not right now? She must have come to do some shopping herself. I parked my car and began combing the department stores, the bookstores, the cafés. But without success.

I was not discouraged by such a minor setback. Christmas was around the corner. Maybe she was going away on vacation. The streets were crowded in late afternoon, as were the shops. It was the time to try my luck.

For the next two days I made the rounds of the entire district. And so it was that on December 23, at six-thirty P.M., I ran into Vidal. I was going into a café; he was coming out, on the arm of a girl who looked like a student. We recognized each other at the same instant.

"As I live and breathe! Vidal! You're living in Clermont?"

"Well, yes . . . What about you?"

"Let's get together one of these days," I said, a trifle upset at being thwarted in my quest.

He paused for a moment, as though my presence were also upsetting his plans, then said, "How about right now, if you have the time."

The girl smiled sweetly and took her leave. I could have pretended I wasn't free, but rather than continue my fruitless search, wouldn't it be better to seize this opportunity to make contact with the student community of the town? I had gathered that Vidal was a professor at the university. Back in high school, he and I had shared top honors, he in literature, I in math and science.

"Yes," he said as we climbed up to the mezzanine area of the café, "I'm teaching philosophy at the university. And what brings you here?"

"The Michelin factory. I've been here since October. Back from a job in South America."

"You've been here more than two months? Strange we haven't run into each other before."

"You know, I live up on Ceyrat, and evenings I generally go straight home. Sometimes I eat out, but I prefer cooking for myself. When I was abroad, I spent too much time with other people. Here I had the desire to be alone awhile."

"I can leave, if you like," he said, making a move to go.

"I wasn't referring to you," I said, smiling. Then, to make up for my lack of sociability, I said, "What I meant was that I haven't gone out of my way to meet new people . . ."

"Oh"—he shrugged—"people here aren't any worse or any better than anyplace else."

"But I'm delighted to have run into you, and—"

"Aren't you married?" he asked, cutting short my fumbling explanations.

"No. Are you?"

He shook his head. "I'm in no hurry. And yet I have to admit that out here in the sticks bachelor life is not exactly my idea of heaven. What are you doing tonight?"

"Nothing. Shall we have dinner together?"

"I can't. I'm going to a concert. Leonid Kogan, in fact.

Want to join me? I have an extra ticket. The person I was taking just called in sick."

"No," I said, "I'm not in the mood to listen to music tonight."

"Everyone who is anyone will be there," he said. "Including every pretty girl in town."

"Your students?" I said skeptically.

"There are lots of pretty girls in Clermont," he said almost passionately. "The trouble is, you can never find them. I'm sure you're going to knock them dead."

"I've never knocked anyone dead . . ."

Vidal was observing me, an ironic smile playing on his lips. Doubtless he had guessed, from the way I had come barging into the café, that I had been looking for someone. But then the idea crossed my mind that Françoise might well be at the concert, and suddenly I did an about-face.

"On second thought, I will join you," I said, "if only to prove you wrong."

The idea of our meeting seemed to obsess Vidal as much as it did me, for the conversation made a quick detour back to that subject, almost without transition.

"Do you come here often?" I asked him.

"Almost never. What about you?"

"It's the first time I've ever set foot here."

"And yet it's in this place we happen to meet. Strange, no?"

"Not really," I said. "In fact, quite the contrary, if you think about it. Our ordinary trajectories don't meet; therefore it is in the realm of the extraordinary that our points of intersection are found: it's logical, my dear Watson. Actually"—I went on with a slight smile, by way of excuse—"I dabble in mathematics in my spare time. I would enjoy, for instance, trying to calculate what exactly our chances were of meeting in the space of, let's say, a two-month period."

"You think it's possible to figure out?"

"It's all a matter of information and how you treat it. We have to go on the assumption that the information exists." Of course, it was Françoise I had in mind. "The probability of my running into someone whose address or place of work is unknown to me is, of course, impossible to determine. Why, are you interested in mathematics?"

"A philosopher needs math more and more all the time. In linguistics, for example, but even for the most basic things. Pascal's arithmetic triangle is involved with the whole idea of the wager. And that's what makes Pascal so incredibly modern: the mathematician and philosopher are one and the same."

"Ah, yes," I said, "good old Pascal."

"Does that surprise you?"

"It's strange. It just so happens I'm rereading Pascal right now."

"So, how does he strike you?"

"I have to say I'm disappointed."

"Tell me more. What you say interests me."

"Well . . . I'm not sure I can put it into words. First of all, I have the feeling that I know him almost by heart. Second, it doesn't bring me anything: I find it rather empty. To the degree that I'm Catholic, or at least trying to be, what he says isn't at all parallel to my own conception of Catholicism. It's precisely because I am a Christian that I revolt against that kind of austerity. Or, if that's what Christianity is all about, then count me among the atheists! . . . By the way, are you still a Marxist?"

"Yes, absolutely: for a communist, this text dealing with the notion of 'wager' is very pertinent to the situation today.

Actually, I have serious doubts that history has a meaning. And yet I wager that there *is* a meaning to history, and I find myself in a Pascalian situation. Hypothesis A: society and any political action are totally meaningless. Hypothesis B: history does have a meaning. I'm not absolutely sure that hypothesis B has any greater chance of being true than hypothesis A. I'll even go so far as to say that it has less than a fifty-fifty chance. Let's even tip the balance further and assert that hypothesis B has only a ten-percent chance and hypothesis A a ninety-percent chance. Still I have to opt for hypothesis B, for it's the only one that makes me go on living. Let's assume that I've opted for hypothesis A and that hypothesis B turns out to be true, despite its meager ten-percent possibility: it means I've given up my reason for living . . . Therefore, I must choose hypothesis B, because it and it alone justifies my life and the acts that comprise it. It goes without saying that my chances of being mistaken are ninety to ten, but that doesn't matter."

"That's what is called mathematical hope; that is, the result of what you stand to gain as compared to the probabilities. In the case of your hypothesis B, the probability is poor, but the possible gain infinite, since for you it implies meaning in life, and, for Pascal, eternal salvation."

"It was Gorky—or Lenin, or Mayakovsky, I forget which— who used to say, apropos of the Russian Revolution, that the situation was such that you *had* to choose the one chance in a thousand, because if you chose that one chance, hope became infinitely greater than if you didn't choose it . . ."

Françoise was not at the concert. Afterward I invited Vidal to dinner at a restaurant. Perhaps under other circumstances we might not have had a great deal to say to each other, but that night each of us found in the other the devil's advocate he needed to solidify his own moral presumptions of the moment. Our conversation went on into the wee hours, and when it was closing time, we still hadn't had our say. That is why we both agreed to get together again as soon as possible.

"Tomorrow, unfortunately, I'm not free," I said. "I'm going to midnight mass . . . Why don't you come with me?"

"Why not?" said Vidal, who apparently failed to see the malice in my proposal. "Actually, I was supposed to spend Christmas Eve with a girlfriend, but I'm not sure she'll be free. Family problems . . ."

"You know," I said, "I just threw it out as a possibility . . ."

"No, no. I'm all for it. Anyway, she won't be home before midnight. She has to go pick up her daughter. She's divorced. If you like, maybe we can go up to see her after mass."

Nor was Françoise at midnight mass. After we left the church, Vidal went to a café to call his friend. When he came back, he shook his head.

"I'm afraid tonight is out," he said. "Her ex-husband is passing through Clermont, and they had some financial matters to settle. The whole business apparently wore her out. She was just on her way to bed. But come with me tomorrow."

"No, I don't know her."

"I'll introduce you. Maud is a remarkable woman, as you'll see. There aren't many like her. You'll love her . . . and she you!"

"Not so fast!"

"She lives a rather secluded life since her divorce, maybe because she doesn't feel at ease in her own crowd. She's a doctor, a pediatrician. So was her husband, in fact. A professor at the university who's transferred down south to Montpellier. Maud . . . Maud's a *very* beautiful woman."

"Why don't you stop talking and marry her?"

"No . . . And if I say no so emphatically it's because the question has been raised and resolved. We don't get along on—how shall I put it—the little daily things of life. Which doesn't mean we're not the best friends in the world. If you want to know—I asked you to come along with me because I knew what she and I would do if you didn't: we'd make love."

"In which case, count me out."

"No, you misunderstood. We would make love out of . . . lack of anything better to do. Which is no solution for either of us. Besides, as you may or may not remember, I'm a dyed-in-the-wool puritan."

"No more than I."

"A lot more."

Maud lived in a modern building on the same square as the café where I had first run into Vidal. We were ushered by a Spanish maid into a spacious living room whose simple yet tasteful appointments bespoke wealth. Opposite the door, in front of bookcases crammed with books, stood an oval table, set for dinner. At the other end of the room was a couch, covered with a vast fur the ends of which trailed onto the hardwood floor. The couch, which later proved to be Maud's bed, was surrounded by a semicircle of low easy chairs. In this cameo setting of velvet comfort, decorated with only a few abstract paintings and, above the bed, two drawings of male nudes by Leonardo, a Christmas tree with its gleaming lights and tinsel seemed almost out of place.

Maud entered the room. She was a woman about thirty years old, tall, dark, and slender. And, as Vidal had described, very beautiful indeed. Vidal went over and kissed her passionately. She submitted for a moment, then moved away from his embrace.

"My lord, you're in rare form tonight!"

"We haven't seen each other for ages."

"A week, to be exact," she said, glancing in my direction. She shook my hand and asked me to sit down. Vidal and I sat on two of the easy chairs, and Maud sat on the edge of the couch.

"So," she began, "I gather you two haven't seen each other for fifteen years."

"That's right," I said. "Fourteen, to be exact."

"And you recognized each other right away?"

"On the spot," said Vidal. He turned to me. "You haven't changed a bit."

"Nor have you."

Maud sat watching us, obviously bemused. "You might say you are both carrying adolescence as far as you can."

"How shall I take that, as a compliment or a criticism?" Vidal asked.

"Neither. As a simple statement of fact."

"And yet," I said, "we've lived very different lives."

Vidal agreed, and pointing to me, said emphatically, "He's lived a life filled with adventure."

"Ah! Tell me more."

"Don't listen to him. What he means is that I've spent several years abroad."

"In the Australian bush?"

"Nothing like that. In all kinds of middle-class cities. Vancouver, Valparaíso."

"Valparaíso was middle class?"

"Yes. At least the people I knew there. They were just as middle class as people can be in any medium-sized city in Europe, whether it's Lyon or Marseille."

"Or right here in dear old Clermont-Ferrand," Vidal said with a knowing air.

Maud obviously agreed. She reached for a cigarette and said, "Wherever you go, you are condemned to the provinces . . . Well, *condemned* might not be quite the proper word: I prefer life in the provinces."

"Then why do you want to leave Clermont?" Vidal said.

"Not because of the city itself, but the people here. I'm tired of seeing the same old faces all the time."

"Even mine?"

Vidal took her hand in his. She left it there for a few moments, then withdrew it and settled back slightly on the sofa.

"You know, my mind's made up. I'm leaving. If you love me, then why don't you come with me?"

"And what if I did?" Vidal said, moving over to sit down beside her.

"I'd be very upset."

He put his arm around her and teased her, until finally she pushed him away as though thoroughly shocked.

"Come, come now," she said, "is that any way for a professor to act? A *university* professor?"

He got up and returned to his former seat. "All right, let's be serious . . . Did you have a nice Christmas?"

"Lovely. Marie was in seventh heaven . . . She's my daugher," she added, for my benefit. "She was inundated with presents. How did you spend your Christmas?"

"At midnight mass."

She burst out laughing. "I should have guessed! You'll end up a priest before you're through."

"He dragged me there."

"No," I said, "that wasn't quite the case."

"Well, I didn't want to let you go alone."

Maud glanced at me quizzically.

"You're Catholic?"

"Yes."

"A practicing Catholic?"

"Yes, you might call me that."

"Couldn't tell by looking at him, could you, Maud?" Vidal said.

"Yes you could," Maud said. Then, to me, "I can see you quite easily as a boy scout."

"I never was a boy scout."

"If it helps, I was a choirboy," Vidal chimed in.

"That figures," Maud said. "I told you you had all the makings of a priest. Well, my fine-feathered friends," Maud said, getting up and heading toward the liquor cabinet, "if you must know, I find you both exude an unhealthy odor of holy water." She paused next to the bar. "How about something to drink?"

"Nothing for me, thanks," I said.

"How about you?" She turned to Vidal.

"A light Scotch, please."

"Not only have I never been baptized," she began as she poured Vidal his drink, "but—"

"You might as well know," Vidal cut in, "that Maud belongs to one of those families renowned in the center of France for free thinking . . . but you know, Maud, you're irreligious in such a way that it's actually a form of religion."

"I know," she said, moving back toward them, "but I have the right to prefer that religion to any others. If my parents had been Catholic, perhaps I would have followed the path you did; I mean, turned my back on the Church. Whereas at least I'm faithful."

She sat on the arm of Vidal's chair.

"One can always be faithful to nothing," he said, taking his glass.

"It's not 'nothing.' It's merely a much freer way of looking at problems. With a great many principles, in fact, often very strict principles, but without any preconceived ideas, without any trace of—"

"Please, you can spare us the claptrap."

"Don't be vulgar. It doesn't become you."

"Girls like you turn me into a papist. I don't like people who have no problems."

"Because you're abnormal. You ought to go see a psychiatrist."

"Idiot!"

"Besides, I have my problems. But they're *real* problems . . . Shall we sit down to dinner?"

By the time we came to dessert—our dinner had been enlivened by several bottles of local wine; we were all speaking loudly and rather more quickly than usual, cutting in on one another indiscriminately—the conversation had come back again to Christianity.

"I can understand people becoming atheists," Vidal said. "In fact, I'm one myself. But there's something absolutely fascinating about Christianity, and there's no way around it no matter what you think, and that's its contradictory nature."

Maud pursed her lips. "You know," she said, "your dialectic leaves me absolutely cold."

"That is what is so remarkable about someone like Pascal. Now, don't tell me you haven't read Pascal."

"Oh, sure: 'Man is thinking reed' . . . 'the two infinites' . . . Awful!"

"'Cleopatra's nose.'"

"I can't say I count him among my favorite authors," I said.

"All right. So it's two against one." Vidal said.

Maud turned to me. "Why? You haven't read Pascal? You see!"

"No, no!" I insisted. "I've *read* him, yes."

"He hates Pascal," Vidal said, pointing in my direction with obvious relish, "because Pascal is his guilty conscience. Because he's the kind of person Pascal is constantly referring to: the phony Christian."

"Is that true?" Maud said.

"Jesuitism. Pure Jesuitism."

"Let the man defend himself."

I began a long, involved explanation that became more and more embarrassing as I went along.

"I was saying that I didn't like Pascal because, well, Pascal has a very—how shall I put it—a very special concept of Christianity, one that in fact was condemned by the Church."

"Pascal wasn't condemned by the Church. At least his *Thoughts* weren't."

"But Jansenism was. And besides, Pascal wasn't a saint!"

"Hear, hear!" Maud said. And as Vidal was about to respond, she cut in. "For goodness sake, let him have the floor. You've had more than your say already!" She shot a warm smile in my direction. "You were saying?"

"Nothing, really. Simply that there are other ways of looking at Christianity than the way Pascal does. As a scientist I have the highest regard for Pascal. But as a scientist I am also shocked that he roundly condemns science.

"What makes you think he does?"

"Didn't he say, near the end of his life, 'All physics is not worth an hour of suffering'?"

"I don't call that a condemnation."

"That's because I'm expressing myself poorly. Let's take a concrete example. Take us, for instance. Right here and now. We're talking, and we forget what we're eating. We forget that excellent wine we've been drinking. It's the first time I've ever had it, by the way."

"It's drunk only by the finer families of Clermont," Vidal said mockingly. "Good old Catholic families, not to mention good old Freemason families," he said, addressing himself to Maud, who motioned for him to keep still.

"That excellent local wine—Chanturgue, right?—Pascal must have drunk it, too, since he was a native of Clermont. What I hold against him is the fact that he didn't abstain from drinking it—I have to admit I'm in favor of abstinence, asceticism; that I believe in Lent and am dead against those who would eliminate it. Anyway, the point I'm trying to make is that when Pascal was drinking the Chanturgue, he wasn't even aware of it. Since he was ill, he had to follow a strict diet, eat only the finest-quality food, but he never remembered what it was he ate."

"Yes, his sister Gilberte tells us all that, doesn't she? She notes that he never commented on the food, never said, 'My, that was delicious!'"

"Well, to my way of thinking, that's a defect, not to recognize and appreciate what's good. Speaking from a Christian point of view, I say it's a sin."

"I find your reasoning a trifle thin," Vidal said.

"Not at all," I said. "In fact, it's very, very important. But while we're on the subject, there's another thing that Pascal said that has always deeply shocked me, and that's where he says that marriage is the basest condition of Christianity!"

"I must say," Maud intervened, "that marriage is a pretty base condition. But my reasons and Pascal's for drawing that conclusion are doubtless quite different."

"Pascal's right," Vidal said. "You probably want to get married someday. So do I—"

"God forbid!" cut in Maud.

"—but in the order of sacraments, marriage falls below the priesthood."

"To tell the truth, I was thinking of that the other day at mass. There was a girl a few pews in front of me—"

"Never thought of that," Vidal interrupted. "I'll have to go to mass more often. Good spot for a pickup."

"I'm sure it's a better spot than at your political meetings," Maud said. "But go on," she said, turning to me, "what about that pretty girl?"

"I didn't say she was pretty," I said. "But for argument's sake, let's assume she was. Anyway, I shouldn't have said 'girl.' I should have said 'woman.' A very young woman with her husband."

"Or her lover," Vidal said.

"Stop it!" Maud shouted.

"They were both wearing wedding rings," I insisted.

Maud smiled. "Did you get a look close up?"

I tried to ignore her remark and go on with my story. "The fact is," I stammered, "I find what I'm trying to say very difficult to put properly into words."

Both of them leaned their elbows on the table and stared at me with obvious irony.

"And besides, I can see that you both couldn't care less," I said, "so I'm not even going to try."

"You're wrong," Maud protested. "We're very interested."

"I must confess," Vidal said, "that the idea of being obsessed by marriage strikes me as excellent. It has to do with your age—our age. This Christian couple was sublime—is that what you are trying to say? Religion gives women a whole other dimension."

"I agree," I said, while Maud made a wry face. "Religion adds something to love, just as love does the same to religion."

Just then the living-room door opened and in came Maud's daughter, Marie. She asked her mother if she could look at the blinking Christmas-tree lights, and Maud, with some slight show of irritation, acquiesced. After a few moments Maud turned off the lights and led Marie to her bedroom, saying, "There! Aren't they pretty? And now that you've had a treat, off to bed with you. Say good night to my guests."

After they had left the room, Vidal got up and sauntered off to the bookcase.

"I'd be willing to bet she has some Pascal right here on these shelves. Freemason or no Freemason . . ."

He stooped down and, on the bottom shelf, discovered a textbook edition of Pascal's *Thoughts*. He began leafing through it. I got up and joined him.

"Do you recall," he said, "whether there is any precise reference to mathematics in that part of the text dealing with probability?" But before waiting for any answer, he handed me the book, and I glanced at the passage he had referred to.

"That's precisely what the 'mathematical experiment' is," I

said. "In Pascal's case, it's always infinite . . . Unless the probability of salvation is nonexistent. Since infinity times zero still equals zero. Therefore, the argument is meaningless for someone whose measure of faith is zero."

"But if your measure of faith increases by the tiniest fraction, then once again it becomes infinity."

"That's correct."

"Then you have to back the odds."

"Yes, if I believe there is any probability and if, to boot, I think the profit is infinite."

"And is that what you believe?" Vidal said. "And even assuming you do, you don't place any bets, you don't take any risks, you don't give up anything."

"Yes I do. There are things I give up."

"Not Chanturgue. Not our lovely local wine!"

The maid was clearing the table, so we moved to the far end of the room and settled into a couple of easy chairs.

"Chanturgue is the wrong analogy," I said. "Why should I give it up? In the name of what? What I dislike most in the notion of 'wager' is the implication that you have to give up something in exchange. It's like buying a lottery ticket."

"Then think of it as a choosing. One surely has to choose between the finite and the infinite."

"When I choose Chanturgue, I'm not making a choice against God. It's a question of apples and oranges."

"And what about girls?"

"Girls, perhaps, but not women in general. At least that's the way I feel."

"You're a ladies' man."

"No."

"You used to be."

"Your memory's failing."

Maud came in at the tail end of our conversation, and was clearly amused by what she had heard. Vidal turned to her, intent on convincing her.

"I assure you, Maud, when I met him he was an inveterate ladies' man. A specialist."

"You met me when I was ten!"

"Correction: in the later stages of our friendship, after you left school."

"You don't know what you're talking about."

"Don't I? And what about Marie-Hélène?"

"Your memory's better than I thought. But I haven't the slightest notion what ever became of her."

"She took the vows. A nun, my friend, a nun!"

"What" . . . Oh, for a minute I thought you were serious . . ."

Maud, who during the entire exchange had been standing between us, cut in.

"Who is this Marie-Hélène?"

"An old girlfriend."

"To be more precise, his mistress," Vidal interjected.

She looked at me, a little more carefully than before, I thought.

"Is that true?"

"I won't try to deny that I've had several 'mistresses,' if I may borrow my friend's terminology," I said.

"You mean there were several?"

"I'm not here to bore you with the story of my life. He's not my father confessor. But I am thirty-four, and I have had a number of girls in my life. Nor do I pretend that I should serve as an example to anyone. Not in the least. Besides, all this proves nothing."

Maud moved away with obvious reluctance and went into the kitchen to put on the coffee.

"I'm not trying to prove anything, my friend," Vidal responded in a conciliatory tone.

"I know, I know," I said. "The fact that I've had a lot of girls shocks you, doesn't it? But I've never had an offhand relationship with a girl. Each time, I've been serious about her. No one-night stands, not out of any moral conviction but simply because I never could see the point of it."

"Okay, but let's assume that you take a voyage somewhere and you meet a ravishing girl along the way, someone you know you're never going to see again. How do you handle that? I mean, there are some circumstances in which it's simply hard to resist."

"Fate—I'm not referring to the deity now—has always kept me from having to cope with that problem. I never had a chance to sow any wild oats. Not that I'm proud of the fact."

Vidal heard Maud reenter the room, and raised his voice, to make sure she caught his words.

"Now, take me, for instance. 'Unlucky' is my middle name. Yet when it comes to fate and me and one-night stands, I've had my share. More than my share. Once in Italy with a Swedish girl, another time in Poland with an English girl . . ."

Maud set the tray down on a coffee table and headed back toward the kitchen.

". . . Those two nights are perhaps the most beautiful memories life has deigned to give me so far. I'm all for passing love affairs, liaisons with no future. Why? Because they're clean and simple, none of this middle-class stickiness that any long affair will ultimately lead you into."

"And I'm dead against them. At least in principle, since as I said I can't speak from experience."

"But it could happen to you."

"No."

"Come on, let's be serious. In case it did, if I understand correctly, you wouldn't turn it down?"

Maud came back carrying a coffeepot. She bent and poured the coffee into the cups as I said, "No. I was referring to times past. You're crazy. You force me to think of things that are dead and gone. Perhaps I did chase my share of skirts in the old days. But the past is the past."

"But if tomorrow"—Vidal was like a bulldog, refusing to let go—"not even tomorrow—tonight—a woman as beautiful as Maud, a woman as attractive in all senses of the term, propositioned you, or at least made it clear—"

"Stop it, Vidal," Maud said. "You're not funny."

"Let me finish. Where was I? Oh, yes, if Maud—"

"He's completely drunk." I said. "The Chanturgue must have gone to his head. Don't you agree?"

She came over and sat down on the sofa, directly across from me, balancing her cup in her hand. She looked me in the eye. Her knees were almost touching mine.

"Why don't you answer him anyway," she said at last.

I hesitated, then made up my mind.

"In the past, yes. Now, no."

"Why?" Vidal said.

"I told you. I'm a convert."

"Oh!"

"Conversion does exist. See Pascal."

There was a moment's silence. We all sipped our coffee. Then Vidal set down his cup.

"At the risk of being indiscreet," he said, "but also knowing that I'm possessed of a fair degree of intuition, I must say that I find this 'conversion' most suspect." He turned to Maud. "I found something odd about his behavior, moments of absent-mindedness, daydreaming, as though he were thinking of someone. Not some*thing*, some*one*. I wouldn't be the least surprised if he were in love."

I burst out laughing. "Now, that's news!"

Maud, not taking her eyes off me, said simply, "Is she blonde or brunette?"

"I seem to remember he prefers blondes."

Maud wouldn't let go.

"Come on, tell the truth. Confession's good for the soul. It's nothing to be ashamed of."

"And I tell you you're fabricating."

"In exchange I'll regale you with the story of my life," Maud said temptingly.

Vidal laughed scornfully.

"I warn you," he said, "you'd better settle in for a long evening."

"We'll do it over several sessions."

I'd begun to have my fill of their banter, and I knew my voice betrayed my irritation as I said evenly, "I don't know anyone. I don't love anyone. Period."

But Maud was not so easily put off.

"Does she live here in Clermont?"

"No!"

Vidal pointed at me as though he were a prosecuting attorney who had just found the hole in the witness's testimony.

"He said 'no' meaning, 'No, she doesn't live in Clermont.' Which clearly implies that she lives elsewhere. Ergo, she exists."

I shrugged my shoulders.

"My 'no' meant that she doesn't exist. And besides, even if she did, I have every right not to talk to you about her."

"You have every right to be angry," Maud said, taken aback by the violence of my reaction. "We haven't been very nice."

"I don't mind," I said. "In fact, I rather enjoy it. More than either of you know."

Vidal struggled to his feet and, going over to the liquor cabinet, poured himself a generous glass of cognac. Right to the brim.

"For God's sake, stop drinking," Maud cried out. "I'm in no mood to drive you home."

"You're not going to drive me home in any case," Vidal said. "He is," he added, nodding to me.

Now Maud rose to her feet.

"Gentlemen," she said, "I'm going to make you both a proposition. Since in the past few weeks I've been in a constant state of fatigue, the doctor prescribed as much time in bed as possible."

"The doctor?" Vidal said. "But you're the doctor."

"Elementary, my dear Vidal."

I made a show of getting up myself, figuring the message was clear enough, but she gestured to me to remain seated.

"I'm not suggesting you leave," she said. "On the contrary. I want you to stay. I order you to stay. I'm not the least bit sleepy, and I love to have people around my bed."

"What about *in* your bed?" Vidal said, somewhat thickly.

She shrugged. "In any case, not you! . . . You'll see, it will be splendidly cozy, just like in the time of the *Précieuses*. That's why I sleep out here . . . I hate bedrooms."

She headed toward the door through which, a while earlier, she had disappeared with her daughter. As soon as Vidal and I were alone I got up.

"I don't know about you," I said, "but I'm leaving. I'm dead tired."

"And leave me all alone?" Vidal said.

"Then let's both leave. The lady wants to go to bed."

"Are you kidding! That's all part of her little game." He raised his glass and downed a good slug, then tried to look mysterious. "You'll see. I think she has something up her sleeve."

"I'll see what?"

"You'll see. Sit down and take a load off your feet."

"You're drunk," I said, my patience growing thinner by the second. "I hate to be impolite. But as soon as she comes back, I'm off."

The door opened, and I turned to see if the mystery had been revealed.

"For the moment," Maud said, "I confess that I would never be mistaken for the Marquise de Rambouillet." She was wearing a kind of unbleached flannel nightgown; "minigown" might have been a more apt description, for it was cut very short, revealing her thighs.

Vidal let out a wolf whistle.

"Now I get it. You wanted to show us your legs."

"How observant," she said, heading for the bed. "And the reason is it's my only means of seduction . . ."

"Your *only?* Come, come, my dear, you're being overly modest. Let us rather say 'principal.'"

"I'm a terrible exhibitionist. Not all the time, mind you. Just when I have my attacks. You can look to your hearts' content. What you see is what there is. No additives. Nothing fake."

"I'd be the first to laugh if you slipped and broke your skull," Vidal said, as Maud literally leapt into bed. "What is that anyway, a sailor's outfit?"

"Right you are! Authentic sailor's garb."

"It may not be pretty, but it's practical. Keeps you warm."

In any case, I always take it off before I go to sleep. I always sleep in the nude. I've never been able to understand how anyone could sleep in clothing that wrinkles and creeps up your body every time you toss or turn."

"You're too light a sleeper, maybe. Why don't you take a tranquilizer?"

"Because they're very bad for you. I only prescribe them in cases where I have no other choice. Move over," she said to Vidal, who had sat down on the foot of the bed. "I want to stretch my legs."

He lay back down on top of the covers and made a show of touching Maud's body through the fur blanket.

"I love feeling your toes through the blanket. It gives one a sense of security. You must be feeling better."

I resumed my former place in the easy chair. Maud turned to me and said, "What were we talking about?"

"About girls," Vidal said. "His girls."

"Oh, yes. He was going to give us a rundown of his various amorous encounters."

"No," I said, "*you* were!"

She shook her head and, looking straight at me, said, "You know, you really shock me."

"*I* do? He's the one who's responsible. He always took great pleasure in telling horror stories about me."

"Was what I said untrue?"

"No, it wasn't, but—"

"And I say that I'm shocked," Maud broke in. "I thought that abstinence prior to marriage was a necessity for a true believer."

"I told you I didn't pretend to set myself up as an example for anyone."

"And besides," said Vidal condescendingly, "between theory and practice there's many a slip . . ."

85

"I know some men who have never slept with a girl," she went on.

"Sure," Vidal said, "me, too: hunchbacks, bald-headed coots—"

"Not necessarily."

"And I repeat once again: don't take me as an example," I said with a certain impatience. "First of all, we're talking about the past. And second, I'm not particularly proud of these—"

Maud burst out laughing. "Get down off your high horse," she said. "We were stringing you along. The fact is, I like you a lot. Especially your candor."

"Very relative, I assure you, my dear Watson," Vidal said from the bed, where he was now stretched out full length, his head on Maud's shoulder.

I began to relax slightly, and even managed a smile.

"Were you being serious when you said you were shocked? It upset me when you said it. My Christianity and my amorous adventures are two very different things—contradictory, in fact. There's an obvious conflict."

"But they do coexist in the same person."

"A rather stormy coexistence," I said, "although . . . at the risk of shocking you both even further, I have a very strong feeling that running after women is no worse, as far as one's relationship with God is concerned, than . . . than, I don't know, practicing math. Pascal, to come back to him again, not only railed against the indulgence of overeating but also, near the end of his life, against mathematics, which as you recall had been one of his earlier passions."

"Yes, that's true," Vidal said, intoning from memory, "'In the final analysis, mathematics is useless.' And I agree, don't you? Now that I think if it, you're more Pascalian than I am."

"Maybe I am. Mathematics is useless. Turns you away from

religion. It's an intellectual pastime, a diversion, an entertainment like any other. Worse than any other."

"Why worse?" Vidal wanted to know.

"Because it's purely abstract, completely devoid of anything human."

Vidal, still stretched out beside Maud on the bed, cried out, "Whereas women! . . . Ah, women! I feel like writing an article on Pascal and women. Pascal reflected a great deal on the subject, even though it's true that the *Discourse on the Passions of Love* is apocryphal and that he never knew any women—'knew' in the biblical sense—"

"I wonder if you'd mind opening the window," Maud cut in in the middle of his lecture. "There's too much smoke in here."

Vidal got up and went over to the window. As he opened it a crack he exclaimed, "What do you know—it's snowing."

I went over to look, and a moment later Maud joined us. The snow was coming down in large, lazy flakes.

"It doesn't look real, does it," Vidal said. "Phony snow. I don't really care much for it. Reminds me of childhood. And I hate anything that reminds me of childhood."

"That's because you have such a twisted mind."

"Go back to bed," he said, giving her a slap on the thighs. "You'll catch cold."

"Brute!" she said. "That hurt. You're the one who ought to go to bed."

"It is late," I said. "I don't know about you, but I'm going home."

Vidal closed the window and drew the curtain. Maud went over and climbed into bed. I walked back over to that side of the room.

"Where do you live?" she asked.

"In Ceyrat. But I have my car."

"You're liable to kill yourself on these snowy roads."

"A little snow never frightened me."

"You're wrong. It's when the snow's falling that the roads are really dangerous. I have a friend who killed himself that way, and I've been traumatized ever since." She paused. "I have an idea. Why don't you sleep in the extra bedroom. You must accept; otherwise I won't sleep a wink all night."

I didn't answer. I glanced at Vidal, who seemed lost in thought. Maud looked inquisitively first at me, then at Vidal. Suddenly Vidal broke in, "I just realized I left my windows open. My room'll be full of snow if I don't get home and close them. I'm off."

He went over, leaned down, and kissed Maud.

"I'll drive you home," I said.

"No way. You can stay." And he gave me such a strong shove that it propelled me back into my familiar easy chair. "There, that's better. Good night. Bye, Maud. I'll give you a ring."

"Hey!" she called after him as he reached the door, "you haven't forgotten tomorrow have you?"

"Thanks for reminding me," Vidal said. "What time?"

"Noon."

"And what about Marie?"

"She's spending the day with her father."

"How about joining us?" she said, turning to me. Vidal slipped on his coat.

"To do what?"

"We're going on a drive with some friends. We'll have lunch in a lovely old inn. With the snow it will be even better."

Vidal finally departed—reluctantly, it seemed to me. I felt uncomfortable. Maud suddenly looked tired, pensive, uninterested in conversation.

"Actually," I said, "I'm used to the mountains, and have driven dozens of times through snow. So you needn't worry about me at all."

"But I will! This is the worst kind of snow, the kind that melts and freezes."

"I'll be fine. You need some sleep." I got up and approached the bed.

"Stay at least for a few minutes," she pleaded.

"You really want me to?"

"Okay!" she suddenly said. "Enough's enough. Have it your way. Leave. Go home. Good night!"

I shook her hand and started for the door.

"Good night," I said, "and I'm sorry. I'd been given to understand—please don't get angry at what I say—that people in this region like to be coaxed. Gently enticed."

Again she burst out laughing.

"Actually," she said, "your informants were not all that far from the mark. But for the moment you're the one who's being difficult. As for me, when I say yes, I mean yes. And no means no. If I want someone to leave, I say 'leave.'"

"You did say 'leave,'" I replied, provocatively, I hoped. And I stood my ground, watching her very carefully. Her expression was friendly, I decided, almost imploring. I smiled. She smiled back. I sat down.

"I'll stay a bit longer," I said.

"There's no getting around the fact," she said, very seriously, "that your conduct shocks me. Profoundly."

"Yes, I know."

"It's true. I've never met anyone who disturbed me as much as you have. It's not a matter of religion. I've always been indifferent on the subject. I am neither for nor against, but what would ultimately prevent me from taking it seriously are people like you. Actually, all you're worried about is your middle-class respectability. To remain alone in a room with a woman after midnight, that's just terrible. But it would never occur to you that it might be all right for you to spend an hour or two together some evening when I feel lonely, when just possibly we might break through accepted conventions and make some kind of real contact, even if we were never to see each other again. It wouldn't occur to you, would it? And that I find not only stupid but downright un-Christian."

"Religion has nothing to do with it. My only thought was that you might be tired and want to go to sleep."

"And is that what you think now?"

"No, since I'm still here."

There was a moment's silence. Again we exchanged smiles. Then she went on.

"You know what bothers me most about you? It's the fact that you're evasive—always slipping away before anyone can really reach you. You refuse to assume responsibility. On the one hand you're a shamefaced Christian, and on the other a bashful Don Juan. Which is a bit too much."

"That's not true. I was in love, which is a whole other matter. I've loved two or three women in my life—well, say three or four. I lived with each of them for a long time, several years. I loved them, not madly perhaps, but loved them nonetheless. No, that's not fair, either. I did love them madly. And it was mutual. I'm not saying that to be boastful."

"Let's have no false modesty."

"No," I said, getting up and pacing the floor, "I'm saying that because I don't think real love can ever exist unless it's reciprocated. And it's that which leads me to believe in a certain predestination. While it lasted it was good, and it was good that it didn't work out."

"Were you the one who ended these affairs?"

"No. And neither did they. Circumstances did."

"You should have overcome them."

"They were of a sort that couldn't be overcome. Oh, I know: you'll say any circumstances can be overcome if you want them to badly enough. But that would have meant yielding to the irrational; it wouldn't have made any sense at all. No, it wasn't possible. It *had* to be impossible. It's better that it was. Do I make any sense at all?"

"Absolutely. That strikes me as being quite human, but not overly Christian."

"I know what you mean, but for the moment let's put Christianity aside. I'm not talking from that standpoint. Women have given me a great deal. Morally and spiritually. And when I say 'women,' I have a feeling I'm being a trifle—"

"Vulgar?"

"Something like that. Each time I was with a girl—and in any event every one is a separate case, so it's ridiculous to talk in generalities—I inevitably found myself in some situation that compelled me to deal with a moral problem I'd never run up against, which till then I had never had to face concretely. I was obliged to assume certain attitudes that were beneficial, which forced me out of what I might term my 'moral lethargy.'"

"You could have assumed the moral responsibility and ignored the physical."

"True, but it seemed to me that the moral aspect only existed in relationship with—oh, sure, one can always do anything—but I felt that the moral and physical were part and parcel of the same thing."

"Maybe it's only a snare set by the devil."

"If so, I would have fallen into it. In a way, I did. If I hadn't, I would have been a saint."

"And I take it you don't aspire to be a saint."

"Absolutely not."

"Oh!" she exclaimed in mock or real dismay. "Can I believe my own ears? I always thought that all real Christians aspired to sainthood."

"When I say I don't aspire to become a saint, what I doubtless mean is that I can't become one."

"How pessimistic you are. What about grace?"

"All I ask of grace is that it open up to me the possibility, however slight, of being touched by it. Whether I'm right or wrong, and going on the assumption that not everyone can aspire to sainthood, I think that there have to be people—and I count myself among them—who, given their nature, their aspirations, their talents and limitations, simply cannot aim that high. Take me: with all my mediocrity, my careful middle-of-the-roadism, my lukewarmism—all of which God despises, I know—I can still attain a kind of, not plenitude, that's the wrong term, a kind of fulfillment, again in the biblical sense of the term. I'm part of the world we live in, of this century. The Church is, too. Contrary to what you might think, I'm not a Jansenist. I believe in the possibility of human freedom, of choice."

"I never thought you didn't."

"One of you did; if it wasn't you, it was Vidal."

"He says anything that comes into his head."

"Mostly to get a rise out of me. I don't know what came over him tonight. He was drunk as a lord. I've never seen him like that before."

"How well do you know him?"

I went over and offered Maud a cigarette, then lighted it for her.

"We haven't seen each other for fourteen years. But we used to be very close, even after we got out of school."

"You weren't very nice tonight."

I sat down on the edge of the bed, then lay back, cupping my head in my hands.

"Really?"

"Like you, I have a mean streak in me. Poor Vidal isn't going to sleep a wink tonight, knowing we're together."

"But he's the one who insisted on leaving."

"Yes, by pure bravado. I can't believe you're *that* dumb. Didn't Vidal tell you he was in love with me?"

"No, he told me how much he liked you and admired you. But it was on the plane of friendship."

"He's very discreet. One of his better qualities. Actually, he's a very nice guy, although I do reproach him for his lack of humor—humor in the way he lives, I mean. I know I make him suffer, but I can't help it. He's not my type. I was stupid enough to go to bed with him one night, for no particular reason, but basically, I guess, because I couldn't think of any good reason not to. I'm very choosy when it comes to men, by the way. It's not only a physical matter: he's smart enough to understand that. I have a fairly good idea why he brought you here tonight. To test me? I doubt it. My suspicion is that he's looking for an excuse to despise me, to hate me. He's one of those people who practice the politics of disaster. Anyway, I've got way off the track. Where were we?"

I shifted position on the bed so that our bodies were parallel, my head at the level of hers, our faces only a few inches apart.

"Aren't you sleepy?" I said.

"Wide awake. How about you?"

I kept staring at her.

"I'm fine. But are you sure you're not tired?"

"If I was, I would tell you. It's been a long time since I've talked with anyone this way, and I realize how much I miss it."

I didn't respond. Maud seemed to be waiting for me to say something or to make a move. But I did neither.

"You know," she said finally, to break a silence that was on the verge of becoming oppressive, "you strike me as a very complicated person."

"Complicated?"

"I thought Christians were judged according to their acts, and yet you don't seem to attach any importance to them."

"To acts? Of course I do. A great deal of importance. But for me it's not one specific act that matters, it's the totality of all one's acts that does . . ." I moved back down to the foot of the bed. "I think of life as a total entity. What I mean is, I don't think of things in terms of this or that choice. I've never said to myself, for instance, 'Should I or shouldn't I sleep with this girl?' I've simply made an overall choice, a certain way of living."

Maud asked me if I'd bring her a glass of water. As I went to fetch it, I said, "If there's one thing I dislike about the Church, it's the whole custom of accounting, which happily is disappearing. So many good marks measured against so many bad ones. Good deeds versus sins. What really matters is your attitude in general. The way you feel that dictates your actions. For instance, when you love one girl, you don't feel like sleeping with another . . ."

I brought her the glass of water and sat down, this time in the easy chair. Maud took a few swallows, then smiled.

"It's very simple. Why are you smiling?"

"No reason," she said. "So it's true."

"What?"

"That you're in love."

"In love? With whom?"

"I don't know: with the blonde, the one and only. Have you found her?"

"I already told you I hadn't."

"Don't play games. Do you want to get married?"

"Sure, why not? Doesn't everybody?"

"I think you do a bit more than everybody. Come on, admit it."

"No! And how come you're so dead set on marrying me off, come what may?"

"Maybe I have the soul of a matchmaker. Such women do exist, you know."

"I know. And I flee them like the plague."

"So how will you go about getting married, then?"

"I don't know. Maybe through a classified ad: 'Engineer, thirty-four years old, Catholic, five feet eleven inches tall . . .'"

"'. . . good-looking, with own car, seeks blonde girl, Catholic'—correct that to 'practicing Catholic . . .'"

"It's not such a bad idea after all. You just gave me an idea. Lots of people get married that way . . . Actually, I'm only joking. I'm in no hurry."

"I'd forgotten. You still need some more time to sow those wild oats."

"That's the last thing I want."

"And if you were to find the girl you were looking for today, would you get married right away and swear to be faithful to her as long as she shall live?"

"Absolutely."

"Are you so sure you'll be faithful to your wife?"

"Of course I will."

"And what if she betrays you?"

"I think that if she loves me, she won't be unfaithful."

"Love doesn't last forever."

Again I moved over onto the edge of the bed.

"If there's one thing I've never been able to understand," I said, "it's infidelity. Even if it's only a matter of self-respect. Of pride. I can't say 'white' after I've said 'black.' If I choose a woman as my wife, it would only be because I loved her, with a love that resists the ravages of time. If I ceased to love her, I would despise myself."

"I can see what you mean by 'pride' in all that."

"I said, 'Even if it's only a matter of pride.'"

"But I think it's essentially a matter of pride . . . Anyway, if I understand you, you don't acknowledge the possibility of divorce."

"That's right."

"Then you must completely condemn me."

"Not at all. You're not Catholic, and I respect all religions, including people who have none. What I'm saying applies to me and me alone. I'm sorry if I offended you."

"But you didn't, I assure you." She sat up in bed, pulling her knees up close to her chest.

"Why did you get a divorce?" I said after a brief silence.

"I don't know . . . Actually, I know exactly why. We didn't get along together. We realized that very early on. A simple question of different chemistries."

"Maybe it was something you should have tried to work on, to overcome . . ."

"My husband is a wonderful man, in every sense. The man for whom I'll always have the highest respect. But he got on my nerves. Something deep, not just a surface thing."

"He got on your nerves how? The way I do?"

"Oh, no! You don't get on my nerves. The notion of marrying you would never have entered my head, even in my youth."

"But you did live together; you had a daughter."

"So what? Do you think it's any fun for a child to have parents who don't get along anymore? Besides, there was something else . . . You really want me to tell you the whole story of my life? All right, I will. I had a lover, and my husband had a mistress. What I find so amusing is that she was your type, that girl, very upstanding, decent, a good Catholic . . . no hypocrisy about her, nothing self-seeking. Yet I loathed her to a degree I find impossible to describe. I think she was crazy about him. Actually, he's the type of man who makes girls fall madly in love. I know I was. Anyway, I did everything I could to make him break off the affair. It was my only good deed. But I don't think she would have gone so far as to marry him. That's why I found it so funny a little while ago when you talked to me about circumstances impossible to overcome. I suspect she felt the same way."

"And your lover?"

"Well—and this ought to prove to you that I am out-and-out unlucky, and that each time I have a real chance to succeed, somehow I blow it—I was sure I had met the man of my life. I liked him completely, in every possible way. He returned the feeling. He was a doctor, too, a brilliant human being, but one who also loved life fully, who knew how to enjoy himself every minute of the day. I have never met anyone whose company, whose presence, was more pleasant than his; I never had a better time with anyone. Anyway, to make a long story short, he was killed in an automobile accident. Just like that. His car skidded on the ice. That, my friend, is what we call fate . . ."

A heavy silence fell between us. I went to the window and stared out into the night.

"Is it still snowing?"

"Yes," I said.

I came slowly back toward the bed.

"And that's the story," she said. "Finis. Over and done. It happened a year ago. *And that's that.*" She paused. "A penny for your thoughts."

"I'm sorry if I spoke lightly just now. I have the unfortunate habit of seeing everything from my own viewpoint."

"Don't apologize. In fact, your viewpoint interests me very much. Otherwise I would long since have sent you on your way."

I glanced at my watch. "Okay. It's late. Where is that bedroom you mentioned?"

"There isn't any."

"What do you mean?" I replied, taken aback. "There isn't any other room?"

"Sure: there's my waiting room, my office, my daughter's bedroom, and the maid's room. But the maid, I must warn you, is very prudish."

"But . . . did Vidal know that?"

"Of course he did. That's why he left in such a state of pique. Don't act like a little boy. Stretch out here beside me, on top of the cover, if you like. Or in between the sheets, if you don't find me too revolting."

"I can sleep in the easy chair."

"You'll have aches and pains galore. Are you afraid? Of what, me? Or yourself? I swear I won't lay a finger on you. And if I understand correctly, you have marvelous self-control."

"Do you by chance have an extra blanket?"

"Yes, in the linen closet. Bottom shelf."

I opened the closet and took out the blanket while Maud slipped out of her sailor uniform between the sheets. I took off my shoes, jacket, and tie, wrapped the blanket around me, and settled into the chair, propping my feet on the coffee table. Maud's eyes were open, and staring at me with undisguised irony.

"Id-i-ot!" she whispered, so low I couldn't hear her, but in reading her lips there was no mistaking the word.

I suddenly heaved myself up and lay down beside her, still wrapped in my blanket.

"You're going to be cold."

"Maybe so," I said. "Good night."

She turned out the light.

Day was just beginning to break. Maud's head was hardly visible, hidden in the tangle of sheets. A single ray of sunlight shot through the window and lighted my face. I awoke, sat up, then slipped beneath the fur coverlet. When I did, Maud turned over and pressed her body to mine. She put her arms around me. Her hand caressed my back. The only sound was our breathing, deep and uneven ... Suddenly I pulled myself away, half sat up, and said, "No! Listen ..."

With the same brusque reaction, Maud sat up, threw back the bed covers, and, jumping out of bed, dashed toward the bathroom. Before she was able to open the door I had reached her, taken her in my arms.

"Maud!"

"No! I like people who know what they want."

She freed herself from my grasp, went into the bathroom, and slammed the door behind her. I could hear the shower running. I dressed, and a few moments later Maud reappeared dressed in a wool dressing gown. I was halfway to the door.

"You're leaving without saying good-bye?"

"I was going to get my coat," I said. "Don't see me out. You'll catch cold."

But she paid no attention and walked me to the entranceway.

"Are you coming with us this afternoon?" she said as I slipped into my coat.

I didn't answer.

"Please do. Vidal will have us all in stitches . . . I'd like you to come."

"You would, really?"

"We won't be alone. In fact, I know one girl you might go for . . . A blonde."

"I'll do my best," I said. " 'Bye."

We shook hands, and I left.

Outside, the cold and the pristine whiteness of the snow, which I might otherwise have enjoyed and found comfort in, added to my feeling of shame at having failed: I had had neither the courage to say no candidly to what she was proposing nor the conviction, once having yielded, to go all the way. But I decided on the spot that I would not waste time raking over dead coals, trying to analyze my actions, since I was far from convinced I knew why I had vacillated so. Only one thing was clear, and that was my feeling that I would never be able to face Maud again. I didn't care what she might think of me. I couldn't care less. I made up my mind not to join them for the outing, and with that I drove back to Ceyrat without incident over the snowy roads.

By the time I arrived home I had already changed my mind. The memory of the night before obsessed me more and more, and I had a feeling it was not about to let go. I said to myself that the best way to wipe the slate clean would be to see Maud again as soon as possible and treat her as though nothing had happened.

I showered, shaved, and changed into something appropriate for the afternoon outing, then drove back into town. When I arrived at Jaude Square, I found that I was a good fifteen minutes ahead of schedule. I went into a café on a street leading from the square and I sat down at a table next to the window. Clermont, blanketed in snow, looked in the late-morning light very different from anything I had ever seen. But it was no longer a city that seemed alien to me: I had joined a circle; I had moved into someone's life. No, it was I who no longer felt as I had; or rather, I felt myself available for whatever might happen, free for any eventuality. I had no preconceived ideas, no principles; I was characterless, stripped of willpower, morals, left with nothing . . .

I must have been sitting there daydreaming for several minutes, my head propped in my hands, my elbows on the table, when suddenly I felt someone tap me on the shoulder. It was one of my co-workers at the factory. I gave a start, and almost automatically began to get to my feet.

"I hope I'm not intruding," he said. "Did I wake you up?"

"Of course not. How are you?"

"I just wanted to ask you if you wanted to join me for an afternoon of skiing, over on Mont-Dore. I'm leaving in half an hour."

"What? Oh, no, I'm sorry, but I have . . . I'm meeting some—" I stammered, but before I could finish my sentence, I saw *her:* Françoise, passing the café on her motorbike, heading toward the square. I didn't stop to think.

"Sorry, I have to run," I said, and, leaving my colleague

open-mouthed, I dashed outside, without even bothering to put my coat on. I ran down the street, crossed the square, and slowed down only when I spotted Françoise parking her bike. I walked the last few steps over to her. She turned around, and I immediately launched into a speech.

"I know according to Hoyle one is supposed to find a suitable excuse, but an excuse is always idiotic. What does a person have to do to meet you?"

She gazed at me, quizzically but without any hostility, but also doing nothing to make my task any easier. Suddenly she smiled and said, "You seem to know better than I do!"

"No, otherwise I never would have followed you this way, against all my principles."

"It's very wrong to act contrary to one's principles."

"I know, but there are times I can't help it. How about you?"

"Me, too, but I always feel bad when I do."

"I never feel guilty about anything. When I violate my principles, I do so because I figure it's worth it. At least when it comes . . ."

". . . to finding some way to meet someone."

I felt that she was more surprised than shocked at the unconventional approach I had made, but I decided to obtain a full pardon on the spot.

"Yes," I said, "I feel it would be foolish to miss meeting someone over a question of principle."

"Assuming the person in question is worth it."

"That only time will tell."

I still hadn't put on my coat, and suddenly, as the sharp cold hit me, timidity overcame me. I couldn't think of a word to say. It was she who broke the silence.

"In any case, you apparently don't believe in waiting for chance to do your work for you."

"That's not true. Life is an endless succession of chance."

"That's not my impression."

To give myself time to collect my wits, I glanced at her motorbike.

"That's dangerous, you know, in this kind of weather."

"I'm used to it. Anyway, I only use it in town. I take the bus home."

"Where do you live?"

"In Sauzet, above Ceyrat."

"When can I see you?"

"When we happen to meet next time."

"We never will."

"Sure we will," she said, laughing.

"What about tomorrow? . . . I didn't see you at midnight mass."

"Because I wasn't there. I live too far out of town."

"Good. And afterward we'll have lunch together. Okay?"

"Yes," she said. "I mean, maybe. We'll see. Listen, I have to go. But you'd better get back inside before you catch cold."

She walked away, and I ran all the way back to the café.

Maud, smothered in furs, greeted me with casual friendliness, as though nothing had happened. Vidal had arrived with a rather good-looking blonde, and was busily engaged in flirting with her so outrageously that it was totally unconvincing. As for me, my recent encounter had given me such a surge of self-confidence that I arrived in high spirits, the cause of which they would never have guessed. Perhaps they didn't even notice it, so preoccupied were they with their own concerns. We had lunch in an inn at the foot of the mountains, and in the afternoon climbed up Pariou Peak. On the way back down, Maud took matters into her own hands; leaving Vidal and his girl-friend to frolic on the slopes, she made it clear she wanted me to keep her company during the return trip. It was a fairly long walk, for the newfallen snow made it difficult to make any time, yet throughout the trip Maud didn't say a word to me. Finally, she said, "Thank God you came. Can you imagine how I would have looked being the third with those two lovebirds?"

We were down in sight of the cars now.

"Did you think I would come?"

"Why wouldn't you have?"

"I almost didn't. But whatever my other failings, I always keep a promise."

"And are you sorry you came?"

"Not in the least. I never had a better time in my life."

"Are you serious?"

"Yes. And you know it."

I took her by the shoulders and pulled her against me—the cold removed all trace of sensuality from my brace. For a moment she remained passively in my arms; then she raised her head. My lips and hers touched, ever so lightly.

"You have no idea," I murmured, "how good I feel with you."

"You'd feel even better with the blonde."

"Vidal's girl? You must be kidding."

"One should always choose the lesser of two evils."

Again I placed my lips briefly on hers.

"Your lips are cold," she said.

"So are yours. I rather like it."

"It's in keeping with your feelings."

"You're right. What I mean is, that kiss was purely platonic."

"If only it were."

"Don't you believe in the possibility of platonic relationships? Don't you think you and I can be friends?" I said, still holding her tightly.

"I don't know you well enough to answer that question."

"You're right. We've only known each other for twenty-four hours, and yet I have the feeling I've known you forever. Do you have that feeling, too?"

"It's possible. It didn't take us long to get down to intimacies, did it?"

"I don't know what's come over me the past few days. I can't stop talking. I need to pour my heart out."

"You need to get married!"

"With whom?"

"Your blonde. You know the one."

"She doesn't exist."

"Cross your heart?"

I released my grip, and we began the final stage of the descent, side by side.

"And what if I were to marry you?" I said. "How does that strike you?"

She made a wry face.

"I'm afraid I don't fulfill the requirements."

"What requirements?"

"Blonde, Catholic."

"Who told you I wanted a blonde?"

"Vidal, if I remember correctly."

"He doesn't know what he's talking about."

"And how about the Catholic bit?"

"That, yes."

"So you see!"

"I could always convert you."

"Fat chance. Especially you."

Again I seized her by her shoulders, this time from behind, and pressed myself against her back.

"Say yes! Look how well we go together, you and I. We fit, like two pieces of a jigsaw puzzle."

"Why not? You're a damn sight more attractive than Vidal."

"But you would never marry him."

"God forbid! And yet, Lord knows, I've committed many a worse stupidity in my life."

"One gets the feeling he's given up the struggle, resigned himself to the inevitable."

"He'd better. I wonder what came over him last night. Actually, he pushed you into my arms to defend himself against himself, if you follow me."

"Barely," I said, kissing her neck just above the fur collar of her overcoat. "And besides, I'm not 'in' your arms."

"I think you cured him," she went on, paying no attention to what I was saying. "That way your conscience is clear."

"It is anyway."

"Oh," she said. "I should have known."

It was dusk by the time we headed home. Vidal and his girl friend took their leave, and Maud suggested I have dinner with her. I accepted, on condition that we make it an early night. I went shopping with her—it was the maid's day off—and helped her cook as well. While we were in the kitchen the phone rang.

"You know who that was?" she said when she returned. "My husband. He really is a nice guy. He just phoned to tell me he had arranged for me to set up practice in Toulouse. A very attractive offer . . . Did I tell you I was leaving Clermont?"

"Yes, I think so. When are you going?"

"Sooner than I thought. Probably within a month. Don't you find that very decent of him?"

"You mean your husband?"

"My ex-husband. He really is terrific. I only wish we'd got along better. He was just passing through Clermont on business, and to see Marie."

"Has he remarried?"

"No. Why do you ask?"

"I just wondered. So, you're going to leave me."

"I'm afraid so."

She turned her back to me and went on cutting the vegetables while I busied myself at the stove. I went over to her and stood as close as I could without touching her.

"You know what I'm thinking?" I said, lightly caressing her hair with my fingertips. "That we've been together twenty-four hours. One whole day."

"Not even a day. This morning you were unfaithful to me."

I failed to pick up on her words, but said, very quietly, "It's strange how I don't like to leave people. I'm faithful, even to you. I'm not sorry I knew the women I did. I can't forget them; I can't pretend they never existed. That's why, in the absolute, one should never be obliged to forget. Or feel obliged. It's better to have loved and never lost. In other words, it's better to have loved only one girl. No one else, even platonically."

"Above all, not platonically."

Throughout dinner I elaborated on this same point. Maud was scoring successfully with her arguments, and I, constantly on the defensive, kept parrying her thrusts as best I could, resorting when necessary to paradox.

"Thanks to you," I said at one point, "I've progressed a step along the path to sainthood. I've already said that women have always contributed to my moral betterment."

"Even in the whorehouses of Vera Cruz?"

"I've never been to any whorehouse, here, in Vera Cruz, or in Valparaíso."

"I meant Valparaíso. That's not the point. The point is, you *ought* to have gone. It would have done you a world of good. Both physically and morally."

"Do you really think so?"

"What an idiot! Don't you see, what upsets me so about you is your lack of spontaneity."

"I've laid my heart bare to you. What more do you want?"

"I guess it's just that I don't really subscribe to your 'love but under certain conditions only' business."

"All I said was that one should love only one woman. I don't see that as being overly conditional."

"That's not what I was talking about! I meant the way you calculate, plan ahead, classify. The sine qua non for you is that your future wife be Catholic. Love will follow in due course."

"That's not it at all. I simply think it's easier to love someone whose basic ideas and ideals are compatible with yours. Now take you, for instance: I could marry you. The only thing lacking would be love."

"Thanks a lot!"

"Love on your side, not on mine."

"You mean, you'd marry me?"

"Did you have a religious marriage first time around?"

"No."

"Then there's no problem: for the Church, that marriage doesn't count. We could get married with full pomp and ceremony. Personally, I must confess I'd find the whole idea slightly preposterous, but then I see no reason to be more papist than the pope."

"I find your Jesuitical thinking amusing."

"So, you admit I'm not a Jansenist?"

"I think that's a safe assumption."

"Good, the Jansenists are so damn dour!"

At nine-thirty, having earlier agreed that we should make it an early evening, I got up to leave.

"Actually," Maud said as I slipped into my coat, "you're not dour at all, although I confess when we first met I had the mistaken impression you were."

"It's you who turns me on," I said.

"You mean you're not this positive and cheerful with other people?"

"You have no idea what a drag I usually am. The only reason I'm in such good spirits with you is that I know I'll never be seeing you again."

"Now I've heard everything!"

"What I mean is, we have no future ahead of us, and it's that notion of future that usually depresses me."

"I see. Thanks for the explanation. But we'll probably see each other again."

"Maybe yes, maybe no. But in any case only fleetingly. Passing in the night, so to speak."

"What makes you say that? Profound intuition?"

"No, logical deduction. You're leaving in a month, aren't you?"

"Not right away."

"And I'm going to be very tied up during the next few weeks, by all sorts of things."

"What kind of things—business or personal?"

"Personal, of course."

We were both standing at the threshold. I took her head in my hands.

"So it's true," she said. "There is someone you care about."

"I just like to tease," I said. "And anyway, you'll be the last to know."

"Which means there's something to know."

"If you prefer it that way."

I drew her against me, and she turned her lips to mine. But I avoided them and kissed her on both cheeks.

"So," I said, "thanks for dinner. Good night. Shall we talk on the phone?"

"You call me," she said. "I won't call you."

I climbed into my car, and since the street on the near side of Jaude Square was one-way in the wrong direction, I had to circle it and take the street on the opposite side, where Françoise had parked her bike earlier that day. In the semidarkness, lighted only by a single streetlight in whose rays I could see a few snowflakes swirling, a woman was pushing a motorbike. No, that was impossible, it couldn't be Françoise . . . But I could swear it was. I stopped the car and got out. I was right! Before she knew it, we were literally nose to nose.

"What are you doing here?"

"You see! This morning we were talking about chance."

"But how did you recognize me from so far off?"

"Even if there was one chance in a thousand it was you, I would have stopped."

She laughed, but I thought she sounded a little annoyed. All she said was, "Well, as you see, it's me, all right."

I cut back in and said, "You're going home by bike?"

"I'm afraid I missed my bus."

"I'll drive you home."

"No," she said, I thought too abruptly, her voice revealing a trace of real irritation. "That won't be necessary."

110

But I paid no attention to her words or her tone. I took her motorbike and locked it back in the bike rack.

"Yes it will. The roads are slippery and dangerous with this foul weather. And anyway, it's on my way."

As we drove, Françoise told me she was a biology major and that she was working in the lab as a research assistant, which explained why she hadn't gone home for vacation. She lived in what had once been an orphanage, but the building had been transformed into a student center and dormitory.

Just before we reached Sauzet she directed me to a steep road that had not yet been plowed out. We were only about two hundred yards from her dorm, but as we started up the hill I could feel the wheels spin and the car slow down. I tried to back down, but the car skidded and ended up athwart the road. I tried to rock it back and forth, but all I did was bury the wheels deeper in the snow, and it soon became apparent that we'd have to be towed out. At that hour, our chances of getting a tow truck were nil. Françoise suggested that I could sleep in one of the dormitory rooms; one of her friends was away on vacation.

A decrepit stairway led us to the top floor. Françoise invited me into her room and asked me if I'd like a cup of tea. I offered my services.

"Making tea is one of my rare culinary talents," I said. "Why don't you let me make it for you?"

She took me at my word. Getting stranded in the snow, the moment of fear we had shared as the car skidded out of control, had dissipated any vestiges of embarrassment, and our conversation, leaving the usual banalities behind, quickly turned personal, much as mine had with Maud the night before. While waiting for the water to boil, I sat down on the windowsill and surveyed the room. It was small and irregular in size, painted white, and furnished with the bare essentials: a narrow bed, a wooden table, two wicker chairs, and several bookcases bending beneath the weight of the books. The very rustic nature of the room struck me as both peaceful and pleasant.

"I like your room," I said. "It has a homey feel about it. I'm living in a furnished apartment. I have a kitchen, but almost never use it. Any chance of renting a room here?"

"No rooms available," she said, laughing. "Anyway, they don't rent rooms here to anyone but students."

"Girls only?"

"No, boys and girls both."

In which case I'll enroll next year in the university. Will you reserve me a room?"

"Have you been in Clermont for a long time?" she said, changing the subject to something more serious.

"Three months now. I'm working at the Michelin plant. Before that in Canada, the States, then Chile. I had some reservations about coming here, but I've grown to like it. Clermont's not a depressing place."

"You mean the people, or the town?"

"The place. I don't know many people yet. How do you find them?"

"Those I know, fine. Otherwise I wouldn't have anything to do with them."

"Do you know many people?"

"Actually, not all that many. And if you're speaking of right this minute, I'm kind of lonely, but that's only because of circumstances."

"What circumstances?"

"Nothing really. External circumstances. Friends who've gone away. Of no real interest."

"For me, or for you?"

"For you. But, speaking of you," she said, picking up quickly before I could say anything else, "you must meet people through your work."

"True," I said, smiling, "but it takes me some time to make friends."

I looked at her closely. She smiled back, then blushed and lowered her eyes.

"I've never adhered to the idea," I went on, "that just because you eat at the same table with someone or work next to this or that person you therefore ought to become friends. Don't you find that stupid?"

"Yes, to a degree. But—"

"But what?"

"Nothing, really. Essentially, I think you're right."

"Do you think I was wrong to come right up to you in the street the way I did?"

"No, but I might have sent you packing."

"Lucky is my middle name. The proof? You didn't."

"Maybe I was wrong not to. That was the first time I've answered a man who tried to pick me up."

"And I could respond by saying that was the first time I tried to make conversation with a girl I didn't know. Fortunately for me, I didn't think before I acted. Otherwise, I probably never would have done it."

The water was boiling, and I made tea. We sat down at the table, across from each other.

"Does it bother you that I keep referring to my luck?" I said.

"No, why should it? Besides, I hadn't noticed."

"The fact is, I do like to take advantage of chance opportunities. But I seem to be lucky only in worthy causes. I suspect that if I were to commit a crime, my luck would desert me."

"That way"—she laughed—"you don't have any problems with your conscience."

"Little or none," I said. "How about you?"

"With me it's almost the direct opposite. Success strikes me as slightly suspect."

"That's what is called sinning against hope. Which is very serious indeed. Don't you believe in grace?"

"Yes, but grace is something quite different. It has nothing to do with material success." She paused for a moment, then said, weighing her words carefully, "If grace were given to us like that, to fortify our clear consciences, if it wasn't deserved, if it wasn't anything more than an excuse to justify everything—"

"You're a believer in predestination!"

"No, I'm not. In contrast to you, I might add. I think that we are free to choose at every moment of our lives, that God may be able to help us make the choice, but the possibility of choice remains."

"I'm not saying I don't choose," I said, "but simply that my choice is always easy. I've always noted that to be true."

She opened her mouth as if to reply, but said nothing, seemed to reflect for a moment as though deciding how to formulate what she wanted to say, took a sip of tea, then said, "Not all choices are agonizing, but they can be."

"No," I said, "that's not what I meant. I don't mean that I opt for what is more pleasing, for what I like, but it happens to be for my own good. Take one example: I had some poor luck a few years ago; I fell in love with a girl who didn't require that love and went off with another man. In the final analysis, it was a good thing she married him rather than me."

"Yes, if she loved him."

"No, I mean it was good for *me*. Actually, I didn't really love her. The other man left his wife and children to marry her. I didn't have any wife or children to leave. But she knew very well that if I had had a family, I never would have left them for her. Therefore, that seeming stroke of bad luck was actually good luck."

"Yes," Françoise said, seeming more than routinely interested by the story, "because you had principles, and those principles took precedence over love. And she knew in her heart of hearts that for you the choice was already made."

"I didn't have a chance to choose, since it was she who jilted me."

"Because she was aware of your principles . . . But," she went on rather vehemently, "if it had been the other way around, if she had had a husband and children and was ready to leave them for you, then you would have had to make a choice."

"No, since I was lucky."

She didn't deign to smile, but remained lost in her own thoughts. I decided that it was time to say good night.

My room was just a few doors down the hall from Françoise's, and was similarly small and whitewashed. Its occupant had decorated it with a bit more flair, using pebbles and bark and branches artfully arranged around the mirror or set on the mantelpiece. I took off my shoes and lay down on the bed, wrapping myself tightly in a blanket. But I couldn't fall asleep. I sat up, took a couple of books from a shelf above the bed, and leafed through them. I took my pack of cigarettes from my suitcoat and started looking for my matches; then I remembered I had left them in Françoise's room. "There must be some around here somewhere," I said out loud, still in my room, and finally I spied a box on the mantelpiece. But it turned out to be empty. Then I searched every nook and cranny of all the drawers in the desk. A photo on the desk caught my eye: a young married couple, handsome and happy and as awkward as you could ever hope to see. But no matches. I searched high and low every possible hiding place in the room, to no avail. Then I opened my door and went out into the hallway. A thin ray of light filtered beneath Françoise's door.

Here I owe the reader a word of explanation, for the following train of thought was more than a trifle crazy. But let me give it as it came. I could have refrained from smoking. The match was only an excuse. An excuse for what? I honestly can't say. I had got what I wanted and didn't want anything else. If Françoise had fallen into my arms that night I would have been embarrassed; it would have bothered me. It was not *planned*. Then what did I want? Nothing. Perhaps to learn simply how far I could go, to what point I could push matters, before the situation itself forced me to cease and desist. Which is precisely what happened.

I hesitated for a long moment, then I walked slowly toward her door and knocked.

"Come in," she said. "Who is it?"

"I'm sorry." I said, opening the door, "I forgot my matches."

She was in bed reading; the only light still on was her bed lamp. I didn't dare look over in her direction.

"They're on the mantelpiece," she said coldly.

I went over and took the box of matches, and headed back to the door with only a faint "good night," to which I'm not even sure she responded. But her tone of voice had chilled me.

It expressed not disdain but fear, a very specific fear—not of me but of herself—the reasons for which I was unable to fathom. But in my muddle-headed way I understood that there was a point between us at which her fears and my hopes met—fears, I warrant, that were anchored in doubt.

The next morning, as I was still sleeping, she knocked on my door. She was all smiles and mocking rebuke.

"It's nine-thirty," she said brightly. "Did you forget you had an appointment?"

"What appointment?"

"With a girl. At mass."

"You're right, it's Sunday. And I'll have to do something about the car . . ."

We had a quick breakfast in her room. Over coffee, we couldn't refrain from glancing at each other and laughing. Just as we were leaving, I caught her and imprisoned her against the wall with my arms. I wanted to kiss her, but she turned her head away.

"Françoise," I said, "are you aware I love you?"

"Don't say that!"

"Why?"

"Because you don't know me."

"I'm never wrong about people."

"You might be about me."

And, saying that, she pushed my arms aside and slipped away.

My story could end here. Françoise made me forget everything, including Maud, whom I did try to telephone once, more out of form than anything else. Maud had been out. And yet the memory of my night, which I had thought exorcised, was going to resurface under circumstances that compelled me to mention her twice in front of Françoise and, on both occasions, to resort to white lies.

Two weeks after I stayed in her dorm, we were walking hand in hand in town, window shopping, when we ran into Vidal. He greeted Françoise with the familiarity of someone he already knew. I was surprised; she, seemingly embarrassed.

"Clermont's a small town," he said by way of explanation, as though to say any more might lead him into muddy waters. "Anyway, some friend you are," he said to me. "Dropped completely out of sight."

"I called you yesterday, but there was no answer."

"I was down in Toulouse yesterday, and the day before. Which reminds me, I have a message for you . . ."

He glanced over at Françoise, who seemed to be lost in thought and not even listening to our conversation. "Our lady friend has pulled up stakes."

"Has she already left?"

"No, not yet. I went with her for a short trip to check out the new place. We just got back. And she's on her way south, this time without me."

"When's she going?"

"Tomorrow, I think."

"Do you know whether she'll be home tonight?"

"I think so."

"I'll call her. I'll see you soon."

"And happy New Year," he called after us, I assumed ironically.

I didn't call. Nor did I say anything more to Françoise about Maud. And she, who seemed avid to hear every last detail of my stay in America, appeared indifferent to my recent past. She didn't pursue the question of Maud at all, or wonder what her relation was to me or Vidal. Rather it was I who asked her about Vidal.

"You know him?"

"Vaguely. He teaches at the university."

"But you're not a philosophy major."

"You know, it's as he said: Clermont's a small town. Anyway I hardly know him at all. Why, is he a friend of yours?"

"We went to school together. Do you have anything against him?"

"No. We hardly know each other; that's all."

I felt I was treading on shaky ground, so I didn't pursue it. Besides, I had other, more serious problems to cope with. I couldn't figure out why Françoise remained so distant with me, either out of some sense of misplaced modesty or, perhaps, less than passionate feelings for me. And yet by a thousand little signs I knew that her feelings for me were as strong and tender as mine for her. Obviously, she was restraining herself to make sure she didn't show what she felt, for reasons that were clear to her but that she couldn't bring herself to reveal. When I told her how much I loved her, she greeted my declarations with a stony expression, and yet she was unable to conceal completely the fact that she was delighted to hear them and only wished she could bring herself to echo them. On certain points she seemed especially touchy, such as when I tried to pay her too touching a compliment or tell how unique or special she was. No superlatives accepted. And it wasn't out of simple modesty alone.

One day we were out walking in the hills above Clermont. The snow was falling steadily. I looked down at the town, its steeples, its factories, the smoke rising from the rooftops and melting into the low-lying clouds. Meeting Françoise had cut any bonds I had with the other cities in which I had lived. Now I no longer felt in exile, as I had always felt before, but in the middle of the world, in my rightful place, in my true personality, with the woman of my life . . .

"I have a feeling I've known you forever," I said to Françoise. "Do you have that feeling, too?"

"I wish we had," she said, a bit shortly.

"Had what?"

"Known each other forever," she said.

"But I have. I swear it! The moment I met you I felt I'd always known you. And that you had known me, too. Absolutely."

I went over and took her in my arms, but she was stiff as a board.

"Sometimes people have wrong impressions," she said, struggling to free herself. But I wouldn't let her go.

"So what if I do! And besides, I know I don't!"

I raised her head and tried to kiss her, but she kept eluding my lips and pushed my hand away. I held her even more tightly.

"Kiss me!"

She wrenched free and took a step or two away from me.

"Don't you want to kiss me? What's the matter?"

"Nothing."

"I don't know; I find you strange," I said, without moving from where I was standing.

"No, I'm just being reasonable."

All I could see was her stubborn profile and the nervous movement of one of her hands, endlessly twisting the scarf around her neck.

"Listen, Françoise. I'm thirty-four years old, and you're

twenty-two, and we're both acting like a couple of fifteen-year-olds. Don't you trust me? Don't you know by now who I am?"

"Yes, I know who *you* are."

"So?"

She paused for a moment, then in clear, emphatic tones, said, "I have a lover." She didn't turn around as she said it.

I was struck dumb, could only manage to stammer.

"You . . . you have . . . You mean *now*?"

"I mean, I had . . . But not so long ago."

I went over to her quietly.

"And . . . do you love him?"

"I did."

"Who is it?"

"You don't know him." Then she gave a short laugh. "Don't worry, it's not Vidal."

"Did he . . . was it he who broke up with you?"

"No, it's more complicated than that. He's married."

"Oh, I see."

My tone was harsh, and Françoise burst into tears. I let her cry for a few moments, then said, "Listen, Françoise, I think you know how much I respect you, and respect your freedom . . . If you don't love me—"

"But I do! Don't be crazy!"

"I mean, if you're not sure about your love—"

"But I am. You're the one I love."

"What about him?"

"I did love him. I was out of my mind. I could also tell you that I've forgotten him, but you can never completely forget someone you have loved. I saw him again just before we met."

"Do you see him often?"

"No, he's moved away from Clermont. It's over, dead. I'll never see him again. Believe me."

I put my arm affectionately around her shoulder.

"Listen, Françoise, if you like, we can postpone things for a bit. But I also want to tell you that if you think I love you any less because of what you've just told me, or respect you any less, you're wrong. First because I don't have any right to judge. And second because I'm actually glad. Yes, I have to confess that my past embarrassed me, the fact that I had had affairs and you hadn't. And this starts things off on a more even keel."

"True, but your girlfriends weren't married."

"What does that have to do with it?"

"And besides, they happened on the other side of the Atlantic," she said with a wan smile.

"All right, let me make you another confession. The same morning we met, I had just spent the night with a girl."

That last revelation seemed to make an impression on Françoise, and for several moments she seemed pensive. Then her face lighted up; she brushed away her tears.

"Let's never bring the subject up again," she said, and smiled. "Okay? Let's bury it and never talk about it again."

The second time Maud came up was when, five years later, I happened to run into her in Brittany. Françoise and I were walking toward the beach with our oldest child, and as we came around a corner in the path, there was Maud. Deeply tanned, her hair blown by the wind, she struck me as more beautiful, and younger, than ever. I introduced my wife to her.

"But we know each other," Maud protested. "At least we've seen each other someplace before . . . Anyway, congratulations. Why didn't you send me an invitation?"

"I didn't know your address in Toulouse."

"You should have phoned me before I left."

"I think I did."

"No use lying. I have an excellent memory: you dropped me like the proverbial hot potato. Anyway, you had your reasons," she said, smiling pleasantly at Françoise, who seemed ill at ease and took the first opportunity to make her escape.

"He wants to go play in the sand," she said, taking our son by the hand. "Will you excuse us?"

"So she was the one," Maud said, when Françoise was beyond earshot. "How strange. I should have guessed."

"She?"

"Yes, your wife, Françoise."

"But I never mentioned her to you."

"Not much, you didn't! About your fiancée, the blonde beauty who was a practicing Catholic. I told you I had a good memory."

"How could I have talked to you about her when I didn't know her?"

"What's the point of lying?"

"I met her the day after the evening I spent at your house."

"Evening? You mean 'night,' *our* night. I remember every detail. All you did was talk to me about her . . ."

"That's true."

"And did she ever talk to you about me?"

"No, why?"

"No reason . . . I see you're still as secretive as ever. Anyway, what's the point of raking over old ashes. Cold ashes. All that's part of the dim, distant past."

"And yet it's remarkable how you look exactly the same."

"So do you."

"And yet you're right: it does seem a long time ago."

"No longer than anything else, when you come right down to it . . . By the way, did you know I remarried?"

"No. Congratulations!"

"Thanks. The only thing is, it's about to crack at the seams. I don't know how I manage it, but I just don't seem to be lucky in love." She gave a wry little smile. "But I was delighted to see you again, even if only to tell you that . . . Enough. I can see I'm boring you out of your mind." She held out her hand. "It's been nice."

"Will you be staying here for a while?" I said.

"No, we're leaving tonight, in fact."

"Do you ever get back to Clermont?"

"Never. And how about you: do you ever get down to Toulouse?"

"Never. But who knows, maybe in five years."

"Right you are: see you in five years. Now run along, before your wife comes to the conclusion that I'm filling your head with all sorts of awful stories."

I found Françoise sitting on the sand, making patterns in it with her foot. When she looked at me, her eyes were filled for a moment with a look that was both quizzical and fearful. Then she lowered her head.

"She sends her regards," I said. "She and her husband are leaving by ship tonight. It's strange, but I never knew you two had met . . ."

Françoise glanced at me with more than mild astonishment. I went on.

"When she left Clermont, I hadn't yet met you. No, that's not quite true. We had barely met. She said that neither of us had changed. And she hadn't, either . . ."

Françoise, to conceal that she was troubled, had picked up

a handful of sand and was letting it trickle between her fingers. I didn't know what to say next, to end her silence.

"Strange," I said, "I haven't seen her in five years. It's amazing how little people do change! There was no way I could pretend I didn't recognize her. Besides, she's an extremely nice person. You know what: remember I told you that the day I met you I had spent the night with a girl? She was the girl. But . . ."

I was on the verge of saying "but nothing happened between us" when suddenly I understood why Françoise was so upset and that the reason did not stem from what she was learning from me but from what she suspected I had just learned about her—and in fact it was at that moment, and only then, that the whole thing became clear to me for the first time. What I said was, "That was my last escapade. Strange that I just happened to run into her, isn't it?"

"I find it rather funny," Françoise said. "Anyway, it's so far in the past. Dead and buried. We said that we'd never talk about it again."

"Yes," I said. "It's of absolutely no importance."

And, taking her by the hand, I ran with her toward the waves.

IV

LA COLLECTIONNEUSE

Haydée

Haydée's face is round, with high cheekbones, large green eyes, a turned-up nose, and clearly defined lips that have more than a touch of the sensuous about them. Her shoulders are broad for a girl's, her breasts high and firm; her belly is flat and her waist so slight one is reminded of those women who grace the frescoes of ancient Egypt. Her long thighs and finely turned ankles explain the spring in her step. She swims like a champion, and when she races she beats everyone, including the boys.

Daniel

Daniel—Daniel Pommereulle, to give his full name—is one of those contemporary painters who during the sixties tossed their paintbrushes into the garbage and turned their creative energies to the manufacture of "objects." The art critic Alain Jouffroy called them "Objectors," and in the art magazine *Quadrum* published an article under this title devoted to their work. The year is 1966, and Jouffroy is paying a visit to Daniel's studio. He is admiring one of the artist's most recent creations: a small jar of yellow paint onto which have been glued a number of razor blades. He picks up the jar and turns it slowly in his hand, speaking as he rotates it.

"Each artist has to go as far as he can, as far as he can push himself. Those who don't are like the natives of Versailles who encircle those who go as far as they can. And those who do strive to reach their outer limits are of necessity encircled, as they are of necessity aggressive. Take this piece of work, for instance. It's perfect. Within its own limits, it could not be better. It is Unique, basing its cause on nothing, and itself encircled . . . Ow! . . ."

At that point he cuts himself, and a drop of blood appears on his thumb.

". . . not only by its own self-imposed limits but by a series of razor blades. Impossible to hold. And, as proof, I offer you my blood!"

Daniel smiles. "It was made that way on purpose."

"You enjoy seeing people cut themselves on your painting?"

"Yes, but not in your case. You're cutting enough as it is."

"I don't mind cutting myself. The people I spend most of my time with are harmless. Not dangerous in any way. You remind me of the elegance of some people toward the end of the eighteenth century who were extremely worried about their image, about the effect they had on others. That was already the beginning of the Revolution: elegance creates a kind of emptiness in the person who displays it . . ."

He looks at Daniel, who is sporting a bright-yellow knitted tie in sharp contrast to his navy blue shirt.

"This emptiness, you create it, too, Daniel. You create it through your objects, but you could just as well do without it. Razor blades are words. They could also be silence . . . And it could also be elegance: a certain yellow . . ."

Adrien

To depict Adrien and his world, let us move to the country, more specifically to the lawn of a house that belongs to a certain Rodolphe, a person who has no connection with the matters at hand and about whom, in the course of this story, we shall learn nothing more than his name.

The time is early June. The trees are in full foliage, the leaves an intense green. Bird song fills the air. Adrien is conversing with two beautiful women who, like him, are dressed in what might fairly be called tasteful simplicity. Both women have long hair, which cascades down over their shoulders. One is dark, the other blonde. We shall call them, in homage to Gérard de Nerval, Jenny and Aurélia.

The subject of the conversation is Love and Beauty. The opinions of the two ladies are diametrically opposed, Aurélia maintaining that the reason one loves someone is that one finds that person handsome or beautiful, whereas Jenny feels that love renders the person beautiful. Adrien tends to side with Jenny.

"A man can be extremely ugly yet possessed of infinite grace. And if he is loved, the person who loves him will automatically transform his ugliness into beauty."

"Not in my book," says Aurélia. "If I find someone ugly, there's nothing that can change it. It's finished before it starts."

"Finished before *what* starts?" Jenny wants to know.

"Before anything starts, no matter how superficial it might be. Even to have a drink with him for five minutes. I can't make it. I excuse myself and leave . . . Tell me honestly, can you be friends with someone you find ugly?"

"When friendship's involved, beauty or ugliness plays no part. If I like someone, I can't think in those terms."

"But it takes longer than a few minutes to become friends. It takes several encounters. How do you manage to see someone you find ugly a second time? Or several times? I can't!"

"*Ugliness* is the wrong word, anyway, as far as I'm concerned. I know all sorts of people who, by normal standards, would be considered handsome or beautiful. But the only ones who interest me are those who have something else. If beauty is all I detect, I'm bored to tears."

"When I speak of beauty, I'm not speaking of classic beauty. Absolute beauty doesn't exist. No, for me beauty can be a countless number of things: the slightest detail may render someone handsome in my eyes."

"In which case," says Adrien, "almost anyone has a chance of pleasing you."

"No!"

"Not even a chance?"

"No, and there's the rub. I find very few people handsome, and that restricts my relations with others. Because once I'm turned off, there's no going back. And a great many people turn me off . . ."

"You mean to say that once you've made up your mind," says Jenny, "there's no changing it?"

"That's right. When I'm invited to dinner, for instance, and I know my host has lined up a dinner partner for me, my first question is never 'What does he do?' but always 'Is he good-looking?'"

"And those who fail the beauty test are relegated forever to oblivion."

"My oblivion, yes."

"Irremediably."

"Irremediably, and deservedly. You see, in my eyes people are responsible for the way they look, and I'm not just talking now about how they look in repose. I include the way they move, the gestures they make, their facial expressions . . . all of which reflect how they think and express themselves. Beauty—or ugliness—is kinetic, not stationary."

In the late afternoon Adrien and Jenny are walking arm in arm near the property's edge. The sun is descending toward the treetops of the nearby wood; shadows are lengthening, and the light is more mellow.

"How long do you plan to be in London?" Adrien asks.

"At least a month, maybe a bit more."

"Will your modeling job take up all your time?"

"No, I have all sorts of friends there. I love London in July."

They have stopped, and Adrien turns to face Jenny. He puts his arms around her neck, and they look for a long moment into each other's eyes before they embrace. Finally, Jenny pulls away and turns in her tracks, her head lowered, as though lost in thought.

"Can't I entice you to come with me to the Riviera?" Adrien says. "Rodolphe is lending me his villa."

"I have too many things to do."

"I thought you just told me you didn't. Can't you come for at least a few days?"

"It's not worth it. Why don't you come to London?"

"What would I do there?"

"And what will you be doing on the Riviera?"

"Seeing some people. About business."

"What kind of business? If you want to know, I've never really taken your business matters very seriously."

"I have to go down there to take part in a closing. A really big sale, by someone who's interested in becoming my silent partner in the art gallery I want to open. He's a collector of Chinese antiquities."

"Don't you think you'd find more interesting people in London? People who could really help you even more?"

"The only people I see are those who might be able to help me. If you'd come south with me, you could see for yourself."

"I'm not coming."

"Why not?"

"Because it's high time that one of us does something serious, for once in his life."

"How can you talk like that? I'm totally serious. But I'd still like you to come with me to the Riviera."

"And I'd like you to come with me to London."

"But I've told you I can't."

"Okay. In that case . . ."

Suddenly Jenny turns and starts walking toward the house. Adrien watches her leave, and if he feels any emotion, his face does not reveal it. After a few moments he follows in her footsteps; Jenny has sat down in a lawn chair next to Aurélia, and Adrien passes them without so much as a glance and goes into the house. He climbs the stairs until he reaches the upper floor, which is unoccupied, and proceeds to wander aimlessly through the empty rooms, pausing now and then to examine the different knickknacks as though he were a connoisseur. He goes into one room whose door is shut but not locked, and his attention is drawn to a chest of drawers on top of which stands a nude statuette from the mid-nineteen-twenties. He picks it up and examines it from every angle. A plane passes overhead, and the sound it makes drowns out any other noises in the house. But as he is leaving the room, he hears sighs and the creaking of a bed, and, glancing back, he sees that the bed is occupied by a couple he doesn't know. Embarrassed, he heads for the door. But his gaze has met that of the girl in the bed . . .

Adrien's Story

No sooner had I arrived than Daniel announced the bad news: there was a girl living here, at Rodolphe's invitation, and there was no way we could ignore her presence.

"What's her name?"

"Haydée."

"Don't think I know her. Besides, I can't tell one of these broads from another. Describe her for me."

"Dumb bunny. Round face, short hair . . . sweetie pie."

"She lives here?"

"In principle, yes. But she's a real man-eater, so she's out looking as often as she's here. Sometimes she brings her pick-ups back to the house."

I wanted to be by myself, and yet Daniel's presence in no way bothered me. Living as I had throughout the year without any set pattern to my days or nights, no meetings or schedule, I had made up my mind to impose an orderly system on myself while I was here.

The monastic appearance of my room, situated under the eaves and furnished with only a spartan iron bed, suited me perfectly. There was, first of all, the matter of getting up early in the morning. For me dawn had never been a beginning but an end: I had, as it were, always backed into it; that is, as others were starting their day I was ending my night. Now I was determined to get in step with the vast majority of the world's population, for whom dawn was an awakening. The idea struck me as both invigorating and oppressive.

I had figured out that all I would have to do was move my schedule back by one-third and work it so that by evening I was too tired to think of going out. And what did I plan to do with that newly discovered portion of the day when the sun was high in the heavens? Nothing. Absolutely nothing. For once in my life I wanted a real vacation, for till now my work had begun when and where that of other people ceased: cocktails and dinner parties, weekends at the seashore or in the mountains.

But this coming year the only thing that interested me was my art gallery. And since I had done all I could in the way of preparation and planning, now I had no choice but to wait. And I was determined that for the first time in ten years I would do nothing, push inactivity to its maximum, more than I had ever done in the past.

Rodolphe's villa was a seventeenth-century manor house built in the Provençal style of the time: a two-story building with a subbasement; a façade with a small round window of the kind known as "bull's-eye." The house was rather dilapidated, a condition perhaps accentuated by an archway situated close to the house that had half fallen down, standing at the edge of a wood of cork oak. A winding path led through this wood, down to a brook that rushed merrily to the beach. The place, at this early-morning hour, was deserted. No voice interrupted the quiet slapping of the waves and the murmur of the cicadas, and I forced my mind to blank out any memories that might distract me from the impressions of the moment. At long last I was alone beside the water, far from the ritual of crowded beaches and cruises, a childhood dream, postponed from year to year, finally come true. When I contemplated the sea, I wanted my gaze to be as empty as possible, stripped clean of any painterly prejudice or preconception or botanical curiosity (for, truth to tell, if I had followed my early inclinations, I might well have ended up an art collector or amateur botanist). I surrendered myself to the gentle play of light and shadow on the water, and to the fascination of watching the ocean floor with its brownish algae and purple sea urchins, and then I surrendered myself to the water itself, floating almost without movement, in total lethargy. I let the thousand little currents carry me at will. This state of passivity, of complete availability, struck me as a perfect way of prolonging the euphoria that comes when for the first time during the summer months you go for a swim in the sea. I could easily imagine letting a whole month go by in this same frame of mind.

That is why I found unbearable the notion that anyone—with the exception of Daniel—should impinge upon my life at this juncture. The only woman in the world I would have liked to have with me was away. I had made up my mind: I had—without too much difficulty, I must say—suppressed any thought of her, not only now but, I suspected, forever. Nor was I in any mood to tolerate someone else, least of all one of the wretched little creatures who seemed to be attracted to Rodolphe.

It was in vain that I tried to convert Daniel to my new schedule. He stubbornly continued to get up at an hour when I was already back from my swim and when I felt that my day was virtually over. I spent the better part of the afternoon reading in the shade of a tall oak tree planted just in front of the terrace. What book had I chosen? The first that I had chanced upon in the house, which happened to be the first volume of Jean Jacques Rousseau's complete works. The part that reading played in my day irritated Daniel, who was in his own way pursuing the search for nothing, for emptiness, but in a much more candid and brutal way than I. His was an aggressive pursuit; mine, passive.

"Really?" he said. "You're doing nothing?"

"Nothing."

"Nothing?"

"Absolutely, positively nothing. Since I arrived here I've done nothing. Zilch. And I'm actually doing less and less with each passing day: my ambition is to arrive at absolute zero."

He was lying beside me under the tree, his gaze fixed on the lofty foliage shielding us from the sun. "But it's so hard. It requires such concentration, to reach that void."

"Maybe for you it does. I find it comes rather easily."

"Yes, but following one's own bent is more exhausting than fighting it. Besides, you're not doing 'nothing'; you're reading."

"But if I didn't read, I'd think, and thinking, when you come down to it, is the most painful thing of all, and the most monopolizing. I think people think too much anyway. A book makes my mind work, but passively, since I'm forced to follow where the book takes me. What I want to avoid at all costs is having to think on my own, to follow where my mind takes me."

"I see what you mean. Actually, in the course of one's life, one never comes up with more than three or four original ideas. People who spend their whole life thinking really don't exist."

"True. I'm looking for nothing. If I find a book, I read it. If it's Rousseau, I read Rousseau, but it might just as easily have been *Don Quixote*. And if a girl were to fall into my arms, I'd take her, assuming she happened to be pretty, simply because she came along. But the fact is, I really don't want to get involved with a girl right now, even under those circumstances."

"And what if Haydée were to crawl into your bed?"

"Who? Oh, you mean the girl who's living here. Has she crawled into yours yet?"

"No. She's always taken. And, although she apparently has a new bedfellow every twenty-four hours, she seems remarkably faithful to her man of the moment."

Three or four days after my arrival I was awakened at about two in the morning by the sound of voices, and of running water, coming from the next room. When the noises persisted, I knocked on the wall loudly to let them know they were disturbing my beauty sleep. The next day, when I was coming back from my swim, about noon, I caught a glimpse of the girl at her bedroom window. With her was a young fellow about the same age. Then, a while later, they both emerged from the house and strolled by not far from where I was reading beneath my oak. From Daniel's description, I had mistakenly pictured another girl who used to hang around Rodolphe, and who was as clinging as she was repulsive. The only thing this girl had in common with her was her short hair; I couldn't get a good enough look at her face to tell whether I'd ever seen her before, but the truth is, I'm not very good at remembering faces. Anyway, it hardly mattered, since I could tell from the outset that she and I had little chance of coexisting peacefully, for she had stopped and was bombarding the gardener's chickens, which were clucking and picking in the grass, with some pebbles. Every time she scored a hit she would celebrate by laughing hysterically. One stone, thrown a trifle too hard, missed the chicken for which it was intended and rolled to within inches of my feet. I turned my head and gave her the dirtiest look I could muster, and she responded with a vague gesture that I took to be apologetic.

But she had already figured out that I was the one who had come into her room the other day.

"We've already met" was how she greeted me when I came out onto the terrace for lunch that same day and Daniel had started to introduce me. Daniel and I made up our minds on the spot, and without consultation, to take her current boyfriend, whose name turned out to be Charlie, and make mincemeat out of him. As we insulted him with supreme elegance, Haydée, far from coming to his defense, seemed to be amused by our assault—perhaps because she did not seem overly proud of that day's conquest.

When Charlie asked me what I did for a living, I replied that I was a medical doctor, an ophthalmologist, to be precise, and that while I was on the subject, I was rather distressed to see that he was wearing such terrible eyeglasses—where had he picked them up, at some discount emporium?—and that he would be well advised to buy a better pair, something like the ones Daniel was wearing, those tiny blue wire-rimmed glasses. "You know," I concluded, "it's very dangerous to buy the first piece of junk that comes your way."

"These glasses aren't junk! I paid one hundred and fifty francs for them. They're Polaroid."

"I don't care if they're made of pure gold. The glasses themselves are lousy. Besides, the whole notion of protection from the sun has been altered by recent research, which shows that only two colors—blue and magenta—really protect the eyes from the harmful rays." I handed him Daniel's glasses, which he tried on with great solemnity.

"What," he said after some hesitation, "is magenta?"

He looked so silly that all of us, Haydée included, burst out laughing. I thought he was going to leave, but he controlled himself and finished his dessert before straddling his motorcycle and, with Haydée snuggled behind him, rode off in a cloud of dust.

The following night the same racket from the next room woke me up again. I recognized Charlie's voice. "Quiet, young lady!" I shouted as loud as I could, knocking on the wall again. I made up my mind that that night would be the last of its kind. The next day, about noon, when Charlie emerged onto the terrace, Daniel went over to him.

"Listen, old buddy, we've taken a vote, and you lost. You're no longer welcome here."

Charlie turned his back. "You're not the boss around here. I don't have to take orders from you."

I came out onto the terrace at that point. "I'm afraid you've disturbed my beauty sleep two nights running. There will not be a third," I said, tossing him the sweater that he had draped over the porch railing. Charlie glanced back at Daniel, who looked as ferocious as ever. At that point, Haydée made her appearance, and Charlie moved over to her.

"Let's get out of here," he said to her. "My father won't be back for another week. You can move in with me."

"No," she said, with a slight but candid smile.

"What?"

"I said no!"

"You don't mean to tell me you want to stay here with these jerks."

"Actually, I do."

He studied her for a moment, as if to make sure she weren't joking, shrugged his shoulders, and left without looking back.

No sooner had he left than Haydée walked over to the table, poured a cup of tea, and handed it to me with a gesture of ancestral submission.

Haydée, as though cowed, brought no more boys to the house. Not that she ceased playing the same game, but now she made phone calls in the evening after dinner. Boys would come and pick her up, and she generally arrived home around dawn, just as I was getting up. More often than not, the boy who brought her home was not the one who had picked her up the night before. Then, one evening, she asked, "Could you give me a lift?"

"Why?"

"I have to meet someone."

"Who?"

"You don't know him."

"Find someone who owns a car," I said. I was seated on the terrace, my back to her, as she stood at the terrace door.

"You really can't?" she repeated.

"I can, but I won't."

She made some vague gesture and disappeared into the house. I called after her.

"Haydée!"

"What?"

"It's merely that I think it's time you put your life in order. Look at Daniel and me: we have found happiness through virtue and the simple things of life."

Daniel, seated on the settee, surrounded by a stack of comic books, looked at her as suavely as he could, which apparently had the effect of making her brighten a bit.

"You get your kicks wherever you can," she said in a tone that she did not quite manage to make a bantering one.

"How about joining me for a swim tomorrow morning at seven?" I offered.

"Why not." And to indicate that she had nothing further to say, she took a few of Daniel's comic books, sat down in a chair, and began to read.

When the following morning I knocked on her door, she was already in her bathing suit, ready to go. That she had risen to my bait had surprised me and, I must confess, not displeased me; her reaction had helped clarify the situation. She, like Daniel, would become part of my solitude. Since she was there, the best solution was to assimilate her. That was why I wasted no time in making it clear that our relations were to be platonic, although I was well aware that she wanted quite the opposite: she would have liked me to play the mating game with her, in some ill-defined, half-insolent, half-serious manner. Which is what I would doubtless have done with any other girl. In any case, several days went by that I can only describe as harmonious, as we all went about our respective schedules and performed our assigned domestic chores without dispute. Haydée turned out to be much more compatible than we had anticipated, and she adapted herself almost immediately to our mode of living, without trying to change or reform us.

Still, there was something about the whole situation that rang false, and I was well aware of it, despite the fact that Haydée played it very close to the vest, so that it was hard to fault her but also hard to figure her out. It was this reserved quality, actually, that bothered me most. So I decided to take the matter in hand—perhaps out of fear that I might otherwise allow myself to opt for the easy road out—and see what the hell was what, no matter what the consequences. One day I let her have it right between the eyes—or the thighs, to be more exact—with a lack of couth that was totally calculated.

143

We were out for a drive, and I had parked my Jeep near the edge of a wood. I took a blanket and spread it out on the slope so that Haydée, who was wearing a miniskirt, could sit down without getting scratched by the weeds and brambles. I sat down beside her, a bit farther down the slope from where she was perched, and as I launched into a long, complicated monologue, I let my hand wander idly over her calf.

"The wines of Provence," I intoned, gesturing toward the endless rows of vineyards on the opposite side of the road, "are the worst in the world. Actually, I avoid them like the plague. People are fools to drink what they don't like, as they are to accept things they don't enjoy or see people they don't approve of. In my book, that is the epitome of immorality. In short, my worst defect is to try and verify my initial impressions. For instance, I know that if I don't like the way a girl's nose turns up, I'll get no charge out of her legs, no matter how lovely they might be."

"In that case, you have the choice of keeping your hands off them," she said evenly, drawing her legs up under her skirt.

"Besides . . ." I went on.

"Besides, what?"

"Listen, Haydée, I don't want to hurt you. But I'd just as soon you didn't covet my body."

"Covet your *what?*"

"Look, I can tell when a girl has the hots for me. And I admit that under other circumstances you could have me: I'm just too weak and accommodating. But one has to learn when to be moral, and every time I think of you as a possible bed companion, all I see is your shortcomings. And yet I'm sure, in someone else's eyes, you must have *some* qualities."

"You really think so?"

"My advice to you is to mount your offensive against Daniel.

True, he's a far better human being than you, but I strongly suspect that his moral values are far less rigid than mine."

"Listening to you leads me to believe you guys think you're the only two males in the world," she said, again with utter calm. "Did it ever occur to you the streets are filled with men, there for the plucking?"

"I know how it is, Haydée," I said with a deep sigh. "We both suffer from the same problem: we're just too attractive to the opposite sex . . ."

Obviously my verbal attack had fallen on deaf ears. My worst insults, my most offensive remarks, passed her by. All I was for her was an object, and she had made up her mind—or so I thought—to have me. She had sized me up, and nothing I could do or say would have any effect on her. Which left me with but one choice: to flee. In the morning I would sneak out of my room while she was still asleep and tiptoe down to the beach. And later, when I would see her arrive, I'd move farther on down the beach, hiding behind the rocks that dotted the bathing area. But the problem with this little game of hide-and-seek was that, far from preserving the cherished void of my holiday life, it introduced an element of drama and uncertainty. In spite of myself I was forced to spend more and more time dealing with her. And in the midst of all this, Daniel, whose own attitude toward Haydée remained a mystery, thus adding to my preoccupations, turned out to be a source of bad advice.

"Listen," I said to him one day, "do me a favor."

"I'd like to toss her out of here on her ear."

"Not so fast . . . I want you to sleep with her."

"Sleep with her yourself and leave me out of it!"

"I'm asking you to do it for me, as a favor."

"No, my friend, that's the kind of favor I never do. *You* sleep with her. If I were in your shoes, I wouldn't waste a minute."

"And I'm telling you you shouldn't either!"

"Oh, no! I'm in a mood to give lethargy full play. And besides, even if I wanted to, I'm not so sure it would work."

"You're not trying to tell me that little slut wouldn't spread her legs as soon as you snapped your fingers."

"Maybe not. But rightly or wrongly I've made up my mind not to chase any more skirts. It takes too much energy. But since she's throwing herself at you, don't fight it. She really is quite attractive."

"I know she is. But I'm fed up with all those girls everyone goes mad about. And I don't like sloppy seconds, not to mention thirds and fourths. It depresses me."

"Not me. Perversity still holds its attractions for me, but not with this crazy kid."

"Listen—"

"She wouldn't have me."

"You don't believe what you're saying."

"Of course I do. And anyway, I'm suspicious of guys who run around screwing everything in sight. I get more kick out of turning them off than turning them on. Who wants to be just one more notch in her gun?"

"You won't do it, even for me?"

"Come off it!"

"Daniel, I just can't figure you out . . ."

Despite my self-willed situation as a hermit-in-residence I had not completely withdrawn from the world. One evening I accepted an invitation to dinner, although I was not unaware that, however justified it was from a business viewpoint, it sounded the death knell of my earlier resolutions. I had a much clearer idea of things, and began to see what a blunder I had already made. The quarrel, if quarrel there was, was not between the girl and me but between Daniel and me, for it was fast becoming clear that he was taking advantage of all the irony and dissimulation that marked my relations with Haydée. As I arrived home at dawn, I had the feeling that I was playing in a game that had been fixed, and that I was lacking a trump card that would soon be revealed to me, however passively I played. Haydée was not in her own bed but in Daniel's. Through the half-open door I could see their four legs tightly intertwined.

The next morning, Daniel barely spoke to Haydée, less to throw me off the track—for he strongly suspected I was aware they had spent the night together—than to surprise me. It was Haydée who bore the brunt of his sullenness, and she seemed to react to it far more strongly than she had to my own toward her, and this upset me even more.

Since she was now at odds with both of us, Haydée was obliged to revert to her former life and resume her nocturnal escapades. There ensued a period of open hostility, during which it may well have been that our respective talents had the best opportunity to manifest themselves. I liked to play the role of district attorney. Daniel weighed the pros and cons. As for Haydée, she felt no urgent need to play the part of the defense.

"I've finally figured out what you are," I said one day. "You're a collector, Haydée, and if you sleep with anyone who happens along, without any premeditated plan, you belong on the lowest rung of the human ladder, namely the abominable ingenue . . . Now, if I felt that you were collecting in any well-organized way, with a clear-cut plan in mind; if, in other words,

I was convinced it was a plot on your part, that would change everything."

"Yes," Daniel said, "but the fact is, she is a lousy collector."

"But I'm *not* a collector, as you put it."

"Don't say that. That's the only thing you have going for you."

"But it's not true. The fact is, I'm looking. I'm looking because I'm hoping to find something. I can make mistakes."

Daniel laughed derisively. "She's not a collector. She simply picks up whatever she finds wherever she finds it. Besides, she has no idea what *distance* means."

"Maybe I don't, but I'm not afraid to try things, maybe anything. The point is, I learn from my experiences."

"Haydée, your method is to use a rake, and when you've finished raking, all you have is a little pile. Only it's a pile of nothing, since it has no substance."

"I could say the same to you."

"But I, my dear, am an admitted barbarian. If I slept with you, it was with no thought in mind whatsoever."

"You're really something! You blame me for sleeping around, and you praise yourself for doing the same."

"But you're not a barbarian; therefore, you have no right to resort to barbaric solutions. I am. Whether or not I slept with you is of no consequence. The fact is, I slept with you the moment I laid eyes on you."

"When did you see her for the first time?" I asked Daniel.

"She was dancing. How about you?"

"She was making love. In bed, with some guy. The door was unlocked, so I went in, thinking the room was empty."

"Aha, you see! So you slept with her, too. In fact, there appears to be hardly a man alive who hasn't! The bitch. This said, collectors have to be ranked very low on the human totem pole. All they're interested in is numbers: how many of this, how many of that. Purity is precisely the opposite. What counts is the process of elimination, so that when finally you do choose, it has a meaning."

During the next few days, Haydée became increasingly the center of my attention, the object of my curiosity. This girl, on whom I had initially turned my back, then accepted as an inevitable part of the furnishings, as though she had come with the house, now by slow degrees relegated Daniel to a secondary plane of interest. One night when she had stayed home I invited her to go out. She accepted, then tried to rope Daniel into the invitation, but he declined. After an eventless evening, during which most of the other girls I met served only as a foil to Haydée, I decided to speed up the course of events. Since neither of us professed to be tired, I suggested we take a drive up into the mountains before going home. I knew that Haydée was if nothing else persistent, and I reasoned that if indeed she was determined to add my humble person to her impressive collection, why not make things easier for her. And if one wanted to, one could make a case for the fact that everything she had said and done since we had first met—including sleeping with Daniel—had been done to provoke me and to arouse my interest in her. The proof was, she had succeeded.

Back home, we decided to go for a swim at our favorite spot. It was there, wanting to reassure myself as to the solidity of my hypothesis, no matter what the risks might be, that I brought the conversation around to the subject of Daniel.

"You know," I offered, making my tone as casual and friendly as possible, "if you wanted Daniel again, it wouldn't be all that difficult."

"He doesn't interest me."

"He's far better than most of the guys you run around with."

"Here, maybe. Anyway, that's my business."

"True, but it bothers me that you two don't get along."

"It doesn't bother me. Unmitigated happiness bores me to tears. A little spice livens things up."

"Your loss! For once you have a chance to make it with someone really great."

"What business is it of yours?"

"Because I came here to get some peace and quiet, and you're disturbing it."

"If everyone minded his own business, there wouldn't be a problem."

"Haydée, let's make peace."

"We're not at war."

"Yes, we are."

"You're the one who's always stirring up trouble."

"I think you're mistaking a friendly attitude for a hostile one."

"I could say the same about you."

"In other words, problem resolved."

"As far as I'm concerned. If only you'd learn to let well enough alone."

"Maybe because I can't make up my mind to like you."

"That's fine with me. Now can we live together in complete indifference?" She was seated on the beach, the waves curling gently against her legs. I was slightly behind her, leaning against a rock. She turned, looked at me, and the trace of a smile graced her lips.

"Haydée, I've always wondered what that smile meant."

"Nothing."

"That's what I thought."

It was now clear that she would not run the risk of making

the slightest opening herself. She was forcing me to commit myself, to compromise my own oft-stated position.

We fell asleep on the sand, side by side, and when I opened my eyes, it was already past noon. Haydée was snuggled against me. When she awoke, she started to pull away from me, but I held her. I kissed her, but then, all of a sudden, as though she realized for the first time who I was, she tried again to pull away. I struggled to keep her in my grasp, but she threw some sand into my face, forcing me to let her go, and she ran away, up toward the house. Still wiping my eyes, I pursued her up the pebbly path, which made it hard for both of us to run with any speed. Just as she reached the winding trail that led up to the house, Daniel appeared, on his way down to the beach for a swim. She ran up to him as though seeking his protection and nestled in his arms. He folded his arms around her and, from his lofty perch, gazed at me with obvious irony.

"What say we go for a swim?" I called up to him.

But Haydée was whispering something in his ear.

"I'm sleepy," she appeared to murmur, "Shall we go up and take a nap?"

And without a further word she led him up toward the house.

Haydée had won the first round. I had humiliated her, and she had taken her revenge. Fair enough. Maybe she really did like Daniel, but I was far from convinced. I didn't trust them singly, and certainly not as a couple. After their earlier show of mutual dislike, now they were all love and kisses. Were they doing it for themselves, or for me? And, if the latter, why did a girl who clearly would bed down at the drop of a hat take such a tortuous route to win my affections, especially since I had opened the door to a more direct route? I was probably wrong to try to apply logic where only instinct and intuition were at work. She liked to take, and be taken, when she least expected it, and she resented my constantly snatching away the opportunity and trying to pick the moment myself. But her true revenge—if she was aware of it—was to have taken possession of a corner of my mind. I who maintained that I was master of my mind had allowed it to be invaded. In all fairness, she had captured only a tiny piece of it.

At this point in the affair business matters intervened and turned my thoughts to something besides Haydée. The antique collector, the American whom I hoped would back me in my art gallery, and with whom I had been talking about a very rare vase I had with great difficulty managed to lay my hands on, announced that he would pay us a visit within the next day or two.

Meanwhile, the situation between Daniel and Haydée, after a momentary lull, again took a turn for the worse. Each sought to break off with the other, but both Daniel and Haydée seemed less intent on the break itself than on making the other look bad. It was Daniel who, in his inimitable way, pulled it off.

It was after dinner, and all three of us were in the living room. I was seated in an easy chair, Haydée was stretched out on the couch, reading some popular novel, and Daniel was leaning against the mantelpiece, looking at himself in the mirror and beating time with his foot to some inner music. The beat got louder and louder, until the walls were almost shaking. I had put down my book and was glancing at Haydée, interested to see how long she would take it.

"Shut up!" she finally shouted.

He kept on beating out the rhythm. The bric-a-brac in the room began to shake.

"I said stop it! That's enough! I can't remember when I've met a bigger jerk. What in the world am I doing here?"

Daniel turned to her suddenly and, in an icy tone, said, "Shut up, you little bitch! Who gave you the right to talk in the first place? You had the extraordinary good fortune to find yourself with guys like us. Adrien's right: you're made for the type of guy you fall in with. I made the unforgivable mistake of thinking there was more to you than met the eye, that your abject insignificance was only superficial . . . Well, I have to confess, Haydée, that it was your insignificance that fascinated me. There are those who say you're ugly, and I disagree. You aren't, but even if you were, your features, the way you look at someone, have a freshness about them that transcends the ugly. But when you are pretty, when you are ravishing, that, my love, is when I find you at your worst, your lowest, your most despicable. So I don't feel I wasted my time with you. But then, I never waste my time with anyone. End of speech. I bid you good night." As he was crossing the threshold he turned back. "Did I forget to mention that I'm leaving this place tomorrow? I've been invited for a cruise in the Seychelles."

"You're leaving?" I said. "That's really too bad. My friend Sam, the American antique dealer, is due here tomorrow at noon."

He shrugged his shoulders and left the room. Haydée, who had not responded to this diatribe, now vented her own feelings.

"Off the wall, the dumb fool! To think of all the time I've wasted on him! Me, too—I've had my fill of this place. I'm not going to waste another minute here."

She picked up the phone and dialed, then asked for "Felix,"

who apparently was a friend of Rodolphe's. But Felix had already gone out for the evening.

"If you want to go out somewhere," I said, "I'd be happy to drive you."

She did not respond, but dialed another number. No answer. She hung up, obviously put out, remained for a moment as though undecided what to do next, then looked at me pointedly and said, "Anyway, I'm *not* leaving. This house is mine as much as it is yours. I'm going to write Rodolphe and ask him to kick *you* out. Both of you!"

"And do you believe for a moment that Rodolphe will pay any attention to what you ask him?"

"Shut up!"

There was a long silence. Haydée kept her eyes glued to her book, but clearly she was not reading a line. She felt that I was staring at her, and she couldn't keep herself from raising her eyes to mine. I smiled at her. She smiled back, though without conviction, then reassumed her stolid countenance as though aware that smiling was forbidden.

"You can be sure that Daniel has spent half the afternoon rehearsing his departure speech," I offered. "Did you take him seriously?"

"I couldn't care less. I detest that kind of scene. Anyway, it's over. I've made up my mind to stay, but so long as I do I have no intention of speaking to either of you."

"Fine with me."

There was another heavy silence. She had forgotten her book and was playing with her cigarette lighter. I kept on staring at her.

"Haydée," I said, after a long moment.

She did not respond.

"Haydée!"

"What?" she said dryly.

"We've been real bastards, both of us."

"I told you: I won't say another word."

I smiled.

"Listen, Haydée, what went on between you and Daniel is your business, and I couldn't care less. But why do you lump me with him? What have I done?"

"You know very well what you've done. You filled his head with all kinds of crazy notions."

"What notions? I don't have any. All I did from the first day on was say nice things about you."

"I don't need your help, thank you very much!"

"Listen, Haydée, the only thing I hold against you, I guess, is that I assumed you had more of a sense of humor than you have. I only criticize people I like. If I really didn't like you, I wouldn't bother to say a thing, to you or anyone else."

She didn't respond. I got to my feet, went over to the bar, and poured out two glasses of whiskey. I sat down on the sofa beside her.

"Let's drink to our reconciliation," I said. "Please excuse me, Haydée. I was a real bastard."

"Don't exaggerate."

"No, I really was. You bring out the worst in me, and I confess I don't know how to refuse the bait. What bothers me about you isn't at all what you think."

"I don't think anything."

"I know. And what bugs me the most is that you don't know what it is you do want. It took me a long time to figure that out."

"It may well be that I don't *have* what I want, which doesn't mean I don't *know* what I want."

"And what do you want?"

"To have simple, normal relations with other people. I

don't know how I manage it, but I always seem to end up making things very difficult for myself. In that area, I very seldom have what I want . . . Actually, I never have."

"What about Daniel? Did you want him?"

"In a sense, yes, but not in the way I was referring to. What I really wanted from Daniel was to be friends, pure and simple. And maybe with you, too."

"With me, certainly."

"The gentleman is miffed."

"You know, I really do like you, in my own way. In fact, I like you a lot."

"You never stop picking on me, and then Daniel takes his cue from you."

"He doesn't need me to give him cues. And besides, you committed a cardinal sin when we first got here: the guys you brought home were really impossible."

"I never brought anyone home!"

"What about the guy you were in bed with when I walked into the room?"

"Oh, him! I'd already forgotten."

"And all those other creeps who used to come and pick you up?"

"If they were dumb enough to come all the way over here to pick me up, that's their problem."

"And you'll note for the past two weeks I haven't said a word of reproach. Even tonight."

"But you didn't stand up for me."

"Chalk it up to my passive nature."

"Would you really be happy if I packed up and left?"

"Not at all! I find you a charming young lady."

"You said I was ugly."

"I never said that. All I said was you weren't my type. But of your type, you're perfect."

"You mean the inferior type?"

"No, somewhere in between. Anyway, who says that my taste is necessarily good?"

"Hypocrite!"

I took her hand, and she put up no resistance.

"No hypocrisy. Charm." I paused. "You mustn't think I look down on you, Haydée. On the contrary, I find you far superior to all your lovers."

"They aren't my 'lovers.' I don't have any lovers. And if I did, it wouldn't be those jerks. Besides, it's a free country. I can see whoever I want."

"No, you're not free, any more than I am to pick on an ugly wench . . ."

"Namely me?"

She had withdrawn her hand, leaving mine on her knee. Gently I let my fingers wander idly over the black velvet of her trouser leg.

"Your case is entirely different. Generally speaking, I always wasted my time with girls like you. But you're the exception that proves the rule. I sense that with you I won't be wasting my time. In other words, you're dangerous . . . You won't believe me, and yet I fail completely to understand how you could think for one moment I didn't like you."

But she was no longer listening. "I'm afraid I've lost the thread," she said. "I'm sleepy." And she got to her feet.

"Me, too," I said.

Haydée's contained anger, the result of her hurt pride, made her infinitely desirable that night. If she had wanted to take me by the hand and lead me straight to her bedroom, I would have followed without a second's hesitation. But she didn't. She couldn't, before she had somehow managed to wash away all the humiliations and insults that Daniel and I had heaped upon her. (How she intended to go about this cleansing process I had no idea; and, I suspected, she had even less an idea than I.) At least I had the presence of mind not to try and make her stay any longer.

She sighed deeply, then said, as she left the room, "I'm finished with both of you!"

"How could you be with me, when it didn't even start?"

As she reached the door, she turned back.

"Oh yes it did," she said.

Sam came by the following afternoon at four to see the vase, which he found superb. While he was studying it, Daniel came into the living room and telephoned for a taxi. I offered to drive him, but he refused. I realized that he and Sam had never met, so I introduced them. But Daniel refused to shake hands with the American, and instead responded with a contemptuous laugh.

"So this is your 'collector'? Sir, I hope you'll be insulted if I tell you I find all collectors totally uninteresting. In fact, I believe you're the first of your species I've ever met, so I hope you won't mind my taking the opportunity to tell you how ridiculous you are."

"Daniel," I said, "for God's sake, shut up!" And, turning to Sam, I said, "Please forgive him. He's not himself."

"Ah, but I am," Daniel went on. "The truth is, all people who collect, be it art or antiques or baubles, make me sick. And anyway, Adrian, keep me out of your petty intrigues. I don't have to flatter people just because you introduce me to them. Especially people like him!" And he turned and picked up his suitcase. Haydée, who had witnessed the scene, seemed more than mildly interested in Daniel's impending departure.

"Haydée," Daniel said, nodding at her, "I want a word with you."

She got up and followed him out onto the terrace.

Sam, more surprised than upset, maintained his cool, simply remarking after they had left, "Your friends are as crazy as you are, I see."

"I'm terribly sorry, Sam. That little scene wasn't even meant for you. He's angry at the girl."

"I must say, I find her ravishing. Is she his girlfriend?"

"No."

"Yours?"

"No, not mine, either. She lives here, sleeps around with all sorts of guys. I call her the 'collector,' since she has so many notches in her gun."

"The collector? Then I see she and I have something in common. Has she notched you yet?"

"No."

"You ought to let her."

"Would you like to join the club?"

"Me?"

"Why not? She's the easiest lay in town."

"I'm only interested in girls who put up some resistance."

"Sam, I can tell you like her."

"That's beside the point. The real question is, does she like me?"

"Don't give it another thought. I have her completely under my thumb; she'll do whatever I say."

"Same old Machiavelli, I see."

The taxi arrived. We heard the door slam shut. Sam went

out onto the terrace and watched the taxi head off down the road. Then, with a twinkle in his eye, he looked straight at me and said, "Are you telling me that because you know she ran off with your friend?"

"Ran off? What are you talking about? I'm sure she didn't go with Daniel."

"How sure?"

Although I knew there was no way Haydée could have simply jumped into the taxi without packing, wearing only her light summer dress, virtually penniless, I still had a moment of panic. With Daniel, anything was possible. No, it was Sam playing a little joke at my expense. I heard her footsteps on the terrace, and there she was, bathed in sunlight, walking proud and tall, the victim arriving to offer herself in sacrifice.

I wasted no time in apprising her of the situation, and of what I hoped would be our plans for the next few days. Sam had invited us both to have dinner with him at his villa and, given the distance, suggested we sleep over.

"Listen," I said to Haydée, in the privacy of her room, where I had followed her, "Sam insists we spend the night, but I really can't. I have an early morning appointment tomorrow. But you can. I'll come by and pick you up there tomorrow afternoon."

"What precisely do you have in mind for me?"

"In what sense?"

"With your friend Sam."

"Whatever you want. But Daniel was such a boor with Sam, I'd like to make amends. With your help."

"In other words, I'm collateral for the vase."

"Forget the vase; that's only a tiny fraction of the equation. Sam may well put up the money for the gallery I want to open. In business, the important thing is to create a certain climate . . . a favorable climate."

"I adore this kind of favor. Especially for you . . . Actually, I feel safer with Sam than I would with you, now that I think about it."

"I suspect that can be taken two ways," I said, kissing her chastely.

"No," she said, with an evil laugh, "only one."

This little plot, it goes without saying, was no more than a game we were all playing, with our own ends in mind. But I had to confess I was delighted that Haydée agreed to go along with it, for it made the bond between us even stronger, a thousand times more so than the trumped-up secrets we had shared the night before. The evening unfolded uneventfully, all of us playing our roles to the hilt. At three in the morning, I finally got up and said, "I've lost track of the time. I have to be in Nice in a few hours."

"It's too late to leave," Sam said. "Your bed is all made up."

"Thank you, but I hate sleeping only a couple of hours. And the trip is quite long, especially since I have to make a detour to drop Haydée off."

"But Haydée is staying here, whatever you decide!"

I looked at her. "Do you mind?"

"Not in the least." And she cast her most seductive glance at Sam, who was ecstatic. Everything was proceeding according to plan. Almost too perfectly, I thought . . . Anyway, I said good night, and Sam invited me back to dinner, not the next night, for he assumed I'd be too tired, but the one after.

I spent the morning in Nice taking a quick look at a forthcoming auction, but I saw little that interested me. Still, it kept me from thinking. I arrived back at the villa in late afternoon, went straight to bed, and slept through until late the following morning. Once awake, I found myself upset and nervous. I drove down to town, pretending I had some errands to run, but spent the afternoon café hopping. For the first time since I had arrived here, I found time dragging unbearably, and somehow I preferred to be bored in town than back at the house. I found myself counting the minutes before it was time to head for Sam's. Yet my desire to see them both was tempered by the knowledge that once I got there, there would be nothing to discover. For either something would have happened between them, in which case they would hide it from me, or nothing would have. What irritated me most was their readiness to play the game. For even if I had made it up, they were now the center of events, and I was on the periphery. I was jealous, and however I tried to minimize it, I realized how ridiculous I was. I was not ready to admit that I actually missed Haydée. And yet whenever I visualized her among the mass of girls whom, had the occasion arisen, I would have rejected without a second thought, she stood out with disconcerting clarity.

By the time I was ready to leave for Sam's, I was in a state of rage—against him, myself, and the rest of the world. Along the way a tourist flagged me down and asked directions in halting French, and my answer was so unforgivably rude that I immediately felt sorry, which made my mood even more foul. But what should have pushed me finally over the edge actually made me feel better: Sam and Haydée greeted me with broad smiles. They stood there holding hands, like perfect lovers. But I smelled a rat; that is, I suspected that, despite appearances, Sam had not gone to bed with Haydée. And in the course of that evening his aggressiveness struck me more and more as that of a rejected suitor rather than a complacent lover. He went to great lengths to ferret out my weaknesses

162

and attack my foibles, thinking thereby to humiliate me in front of Haydée. His violent attack on my indolence provoked a spirited defense on my part.

"To do nothing," I said, "but to think while doing nothing, is exhausting. Far more tiring than working, I might add. Work is actually a form of laziness, the easy way out. People use work as a way of assuaging their bad consciences for not using their minds properly."

"If I read you right, you're the least lazy person on the face of the earth."

"I haven't taken a vacation in ten years."

"Counting thinking time as work, I assume . . . Adrien, what amuses me most about you is your constant need to justify yourself."

"No, contrary to what you think, my conscience is clear."

"You're a liar. You feel guilty because you don't have any money."

"Listen, Sam, that proves how little you know me. Have you ever heard of the Tarahumara Indians? Well, when they come down into the towns and villages, they go from house to house begging. They stop at the front door, knock, then turn sideways, their nose turned up in haughty disdain. Whether they are given alms or not, they always leave after a set period of time, without saying thank you . . . When I go begging, Sam, it's always sideways, with my nose in the air. Anyway, we're all slaves of other people. I find it less dishonorable to live free, gratis, and for nothing at a wealthy friend's house than to be on the government payroll. Talk about parasites . . . Most people today do dumb work, paper-pushing, nothing that contributes to the betterment of mankind. I'm not the real parasite: the bureaucrats and technicians are."

"I can almost hear you sighing for the good old days. As for me, I prefer the modern era."

"I'm just as modern as you are, Sam. More, actually. All you hear these days is that work is a means to an end. And what is that end? Why, leisure. We speak of a leisure civilization. The only problem is, by the time we get there, people will have lost all sense of what leisure means. Think of all the millions of people who work for forty years in order to win their moment of leisure, and by the time they retire are totally lost . . . and die. Frankly, I think I'm serving mankind better, and more honestly, by taking it easy rather than working myself to death. One has to have the courage to *not* work."

"More courage than going to the moon, or to Mars?"

"Apples and oranges, my dear Sam. You're confusing the issue. One does not exclude the other."

"For you, Adrien, going to the moon means to be rich. And you could be, you know. Your problem is—and that's what bothers me about you—you refuse to rise above your own mediocrity."

"It's true I have always been sorry not to have money. But mind you, don't rule out that possibility, Sam. I may surprise you yet. If I were rich, however, what you now refer to as my dandyism would be considered sloth, pure and simple. No heroism whatsoever. And I can't conceive of a dandy not being heroic."

During this conversation, Haydée, who was sprawled on the couch doing a crossword puzzle, seemed to be paying us little or no attention. At one point Sam asked her what she thought, and she replied that since whatever I said was always wrong, anyone who took me seriously ought to have his head examined. Saying which, she got up and refilled her glass, from a bottle on the table near Sam. Sam put his arm around her while she poured, then, growing bolder, slipped his hand beneath her dress and tried to caress her thigh. She broke loose; he tried to hold her; she wrenched free and fled toward the far end of the room. And then, unexpectedly, absurdly, tragedy ensued . . .

On a small pedestal was perched the Chinese vase that Sam had just bought from me. Haydée, flouting her pursuer, grabbed hold of the wooden pedestal, causing the vase to rock dangerously. Haydée did nothing to keep it from falling.

"Look out!" Sam called. "The vase!"

Too late. It fell and flew into a thousand pieces on the tile floor. Haydée, momentarily nonplussed, burst out laughing. But it was a nervous laugh, as though she was not quite sure what the consequences might be. In a second Sam was beside her, and he gave her a resounding slap. She screamed and ran out of the room.

"She's incredible, that bitch!" I said, not quite sure what to do or say.

Sam's despair was greater than his rage. He was down on his knees, trying to scrape up the pieces. I knelt down to help him, but he waved me away. In a toneless voice he said, "Your room's made up. On the second floor. You know the one."

I found Haydée in the bathroom, dabbing cold water on her reddened cheek.

"Haydée!"

She turned around and started to laugh.

"How can you laugh?" I said.

She kept on. I lost my temper.

"Haydée! That was a Sung vase. Do you realize that?"

"I didn't break it on purpose," she said, and suddenly she looked so sad, or her part was so well played, that I couldn't contain a smile.

"Look at you," she said. "You're laughing, too!"

"Haydée, all I can say is you're lucky Sam's an amateur. A professional dealer would have killed you on the spot. You're impossible. I should have known I couldn't let you out alone."

"That's what you get for leaving me with him for two days."

"What did he do to you?"

"Nothing."

"Did he try anything? What did you two do for forty-eight hours?"

"He didn't even try anything. We went sailing. And last night he took me to the casino. Very charming evening . . ."

"Is it *because* he didn't try anything that you're so upset?"

"If I told you I slept with him, would you believe me?"

"I'd believe anything, coming from you. I know by now that when you say yes, it probably means no, but there's a chance it also might mean yes."

I went over and kissed her on the neck. A long, loving kiss. She put up no resistance, and obviously enjoyed the embrace. I whispered in her ear, "You're a terrible little bitch, without an ounce of morality in your whole being."

She laughed. "All I can tell you is, I'd never espouse your morality."

"Neither would I. Anyway, tonight I feel like deviating from it."

I took her in my arms and held her tightly. She lifted her head, offering me her lips. I stopped thinking. Only the awkwardness of our position kept me from taking her there on the spot.

"Shall we go upstairs?"

"No," she said, "let's go home."

On the way home, the cool morning breeze added to my feeling of exaltation. My victory was my defeat. Haydée, in yielding, had won. What delighted me was not that I had reached my goal but that she had reached hers, or what I presumed that goal to be. She had valiantly overcome all the obstacles I had strewn in her path, which had only strengthened her resolution. I thought again of my pet theory. The events of the past three weeks were unfolding as though I had written the script, as though everything she had done had been done in terms of me, and of her desire to have me. Daniel, Sam, and now the broken vase were but so many stations along the path to her winning my precious person. The fortress of moralism with which I had till now protected myself was crumbling. Since my purpose in coming to Rodolphe's had been to enjoy myself, why not make my last week there as pleasant as possible, my relation with Haydée as pleasurable as I could make it? The prospect of a liaison so tightly circumscribed in time and space fulfilled my fondest desires for what absolute adventure ought to be: one week was the ideal length of time for an amorous adventure, in contrast to my usual one-night stands or those loves that had been erased by the waves in the shifting sands of my life . . .

As we were crossing the village of Gassin, I was about to pass a parked truck but was prevented from doing so by a car coming in the opposite direction. I stopped, and the two boys in the car recognized Haydée as they passed. The car braked to a halt a few yards down the road, and Haydée got out to go say hello to them. They were on their way to Italy, and I heard them telling her their address. She came back to fish a piece of paper out of her pocketbook, to take down their address. I heard them trying to persuade her to hop in the car right then and there and come with them. It didn't matter if she had no clothes; they'd lend her their shirts.

The truck behind which I was parked pulled away, and by now a car had pulled up behind me, blocked by me in front and by the car with the two boys to its left. I eased forward to let it by, with no other thought in mind but to be polite and to cut short Haydée's dallying with her two boyfriends. But I realized almost immediately that I was not going to stop, and that I was, for the first time, making a real decision . . .

This tale is the story of my tacks and turns. My daydreaming ceased all at once, giving way to the dream I had harbored during the early moments following my arrival at Rodolphe's. That vacation dream: now I had the possibility of living it! Calm, solitude: now I could have them for the taking, simply by asserting my freedom. I reveled in my victory, which I attributed no longer to chance but to my own doing. I felt myself slowly filling with the wonderful sensation of independence, of complete freedom; at long last I could do whatever I wanted.

But when I was back at the house, the emptiness and silence began to assert themselves, tighter and tighter, and I found it impossible to sleep.

After an hour of tossing and turning, I picked up the phone and called the airlines, to find out when the next available flight to London was.

V

CLAIRE'S KNEE

MONDAY, JUNE 29 — Lake Annecy, France. Jerome steers his motorboat toward the Vassé Canal. On Lovers' Bridge, Aurora, leaning on the railing, watches his approach. When he passes beneath the bridge, she turns and crosses to the other side, and calls out to him. Jerome, who turns the bow slightly as he comes in to dock, catches sight of her. He gets out of the boat and runs over to where she is standing.

"Aurora!"

"Jerome!"

"You see, miracles do happen! When I was driving through Paris the other day, I kept hoping you'd pop up at some street corner. But here I didn't even hope."

"I'm on vacation. I rented a room at some people's house in Talloires."

"Talloires! That makes us next-door neighbors. I have a house there where I used to spend my summers when I was a boy. I've put it up for sale, which is why I'm here. I expect to stay about three weeks. I can't really believe it's you! Do you know that I've been looking for you from one end of the earth to the other. Absolutely dropped out of sight, and no way to find your address. You've moved away from Paris?"

"No, but I moved from my old place. Are you still in Morocco?"

"No, Sweden. But what in the world are you doing on this bridge? You know it's called Lovers' Bridge?"

"My tea leaves had predicted that I would meet a gentleman in the near future. And it turned out to be you. If I hadn't called out to you, you wouldn't have recognized me. Have I changed all that much?"

"No, not at all. You're younger and prettier than ever. Anyway, if I didn't see you, it's because I don't look at pretty girls anymore. I'm going to get married. But I'll tell you all about it later. How about over lunch? I'll drive you back in the boat, if you're not afraid of drowning."

Madame W.'s house, where Aurora was boarding, was right on the lake, set back from the water by a well-kept lawn. The right-hand portion of the house was one story, which included an enormous living room and several bedrooms. The roof extended some distance beyond the walls, and this part of the house was surrounded by a porch on all sides. The left-hand side of the house was two stories high, and a wooden balcony, typical of the Alpine region, projected on the lakeside from the second-floor rooms. It was half hidden by the lush foliage of a cherry tree.

Madame W. knows Jerome and his family. In fact, she reminds him, they played together when they were children. The last time, he must have been eleven or so, and she fifteen. Jerome replies that in fact he remembers her brothers very well but not Madame W., confessing that at that age he hadn't yet developed an eye for the young ladies. Except, he adds, for a little eight-year-old blonde named Poupinette whom he had taken under his wing.

"In other words," Aurora remarks, "you haven't changed. You still chase after little girls."

Just then Laura, Madame W.'s sixteen-year-old daughter, comes in, her schoolbag under her arm. She is in her last year of high school. A lively child with an easy laugh and eyes that look directly into those of the person she's talking to, Laura fixes her gaze on Jerome. She tells him that she's familiar with his house, for she's become friends with the daughters of the people who've been renting it, and they've seen a lot of each other over the past few years.

"We used to play hide-and-seek in your house," she says, "and I must tell you we ate every pear on the pear tree. I love that house; I hope they're not going to tear it down."

Jerome reassures her; then, as they are all having tea, he relates how he and Aurora first met, six years before, when he was the cultural attaché in Bucharest. After that they lost track of each other, and, miracle of miracles, there she was standing on the bridge here in Annecy. Aurora remarks that if they lost track of each other, it was because Jerome stopped writing her. To which he responds by saying that he was intimidated to write to a writer, for it turns out Aurora is a novelist.

"So," says Jerome to Laura, who has been gazing at him during the entire exchange, drinking in his every word, "are you on vacation now?"

"Almost," she says. "We're out of school tomorrow."

"When I was in school, I somehow managed to skip the last few days."

"Not me. I don't want to. We have a teacher we detest. An old maid. Not only old, but hateful! The only time she's ever happy is when she's been so mean she makes the kids cry."

"Laura!" her mother scolded.

"But it's true," Laura insisted. "And you should see the gleam in her eyes when she does make the kids cry. She's positively in ecstasy. I tell you, she's hateful, and we're going to play a hateful trick on her tomorrow . . ."

"Really, she made *you* cry?"

"Not me personally. I never cry in front of other people."

"I must say that the spectacle of a girl crying renders me totally helpless. Especially if she's pretty."

"Am I to infer, then, that you only make the ugly ones cry?"

"Neither the pretty nor the ugly."

"I'm sure you do. Just a trifle, to see how much it takes. Aren't you ashamed to reveal your nasty side like that?"

TUESDAY, JUNE 3o — Jerome's house is situated in the town proper. It's a rambling old eighteenth-century house, devoid of ornamentation, its stuccoed exterior set off by green shutters. Behind the house stretches a terraced garden, beyond which is an untended field that in times past had been a vineyard.

Aurora, who has accompanied Jerome, is admiring the primitive paintings—the work of a Spanish soldier during the occupation of Savoie—that decorate the drawing room.

"There," says Jerome, "is Don Quixote on his wooden horse. He thinks he's going to fly away. They blindfolded him. The bellows makes him think the wind is blowing, and the torch gives him the impression he's nearing the sun."

"An allegory, my dear Jerome," Aurora says. "In fiction the heroes are always blindfolded. Otherwise they'd undertake nothing; the plot would grind to a halt. Actually, we all have blindfolds over our eyes, or at least, blinders."

"Except you, since you write."

"True. When I write, I'm obliged to keep my eyes open."

"And do you create the illusions? Do you handle the bellows?"

"Not I. The heroes and heroines dictate the action. Or their logic does."

"But you do, nonetheless, to some degree."

"I don't. All I do is observe. I never invent; I discover . . ."

They move on into the master bedroom, an enormous room dominated by a four-poster bed. When he's home, this is where Jerome spends most of his time. On a table, prominently displayed, is the picture of a young woman in her mid-twenties, Lucinda, the daughter of a diplomat. She and Jerome had met in Bucharest and had a stormy relationship while he was stationed there. Aurora is amazed that Jerome remained faithful to her, but he explains that they broke up, then met again in Stockholm, and that he now planned to marry her when he returned there the following month.

"Up till then I had been dead set against marriage," he says. "But since all our efforts to break up once and for all have failed, we've come to the conclusion we ought to stay together. If I'm marrying her, it's because I know I can live with her. And besides, the fact is that since I first met Lucinda, I've had affairs with lots of other women—as she has with lots of other men—and I've come to realize that I don't give a damn about any of the other women. I've reached the point where I can't even tell them apart anymore. Except for someone like you, of course, whom I love as a friend . . . But enough about me. What about you? How's your love life?"

But Aurora has nothing to say, or prefers to say nothing. The fact is, for a year she has been living alone. And enjoying it. And since she does enjoy it, she sees no reason to seek another way of life.

They go out into the garden. The highest terrace is traversed by a path flanked by rows of catalpa trees; the path leads to a circular platform overlooking the lower terraces. This platform is bounded by a stone parapet and a row of yews, between which one can see, down below, a number of tennis courts.

"Laura plays at the club," Aurora says. "You may see her

down there at five o'clock. I mention it because I'm reminded of a novel I once started, and finally gave up on, that revolves around a man in his thirties, maybe approaching forty, a rather sedate and proper gentleman, whose peace and tranquillity are upset once a day by two pubescent girls who play tennis at the house next door. One day they hit a ball into his yard. He picks up the ball and puts it in his pocket—why, he's not quite sure—and when the girls come knocking at his door, he pretends he hasn't seen it and goes looking for it with them. Then, when they finally leave, after apologizing for having put him to so much trouble, he slips down into another yard—that empty lot down there, for instance—and tosses the ball back onto the court. Now, the girls happen to know that that yard where the ball came from belongs to an elderly and rather feeble lady quite incapable of playing such games—or even of throwing the ball back—so they're greatly intrigued. The same events are repeated three or four times over the next few days, and this man, who till then was a model of sobriety and decorum, moves increasingly toward the edge of madness . . . But I got stuck. I didn't know how to finish the story. Now, thanks to you, I have a renewed desire to go back to it."

They head back toward the house. Aurora turns suddenly, as though to reveal a mystery. "I probably shouldn't tell you this, but since you're so thick-skinned as far as other women are concerned . . . are you aware that little Laura has fallen head over heels in love with you?"

"You're writing a novel again."

"No, she told me herself."

"If she did, that proves she's not serious. But if it gives you material for your story . . ."

"I'm sure you're not unaware of it yourself," Aurora goes on. "You must have seen the way she gawked at you."

"She looked at me very ingenuously."

"In this day and age there are no ingenues."

"Of course there are. She's still a child, and she's candid and direct, which is what makes her so attractive. If I had to concern myself with all the adolescent heartthrobs of the girls who cross my path, I'd never have time for anything else. Anyway, it's your job to observe, not mine."

"It's too dull to serve me in any way, too stupid."

"Why don't you simply admit that I don't inspire you."

"Actually, you don't. I was never tempted to use you as the basis for one of my characters."

"Too dull?"

"Yes, but I think insignificant people can be turned into interesting fictional characters. Still, I rarely take my inspiration from current people or situations."

"In general, I'm absent."

She laughs. "I'm afraid there's just no way you can ever inspire me. Even if you were to sleep with your teenage schoolgirl on the eve of your marriage, I don't think I could find it in me to turn it into a good story."

"And what if I *didn't* sleep with her?"

"The story would be better. It doesn't matter whether something actually happens. There's already a subject . . . In fact, there's always a subject. And there's the rub: for if we were to be seduced by every subject that comes to mind . . . The truth is, the subject does attract me, and the problem is, it attracts me too much. One thing I've always been incapable of doing is putting myself into my novels. And I have found myself in situations similar to the one I was suggesting to you."

"Interesting . . ."

"There have been times when I found men younger than me attractive, and my story resembles yours in that I never took it to its conclusion. I mean, I was never really in love with any of them. I could easily use that idea as a basis for a story, relating it to my own experience but then transposing it to other circumstances."

"Be my guest and transpose as much as you like. But don't count on me to carry this one to its conclusion."

"Are you afraid? What risk is there? She'll shy away at the last minute. She's a sweet little flirt. And I know her kind, from personal experience. No, the only risk you run is that she might turn out to be a drag."

WEDNESDAY, JULY 1 — Jerome is paying Aurora a visit. Her room is on the second floor, and opens out onto the balcony.

"It's a nice place. Quiet and peaceful," he says.

"Too beautiful to work in," she says.

He points to a sheet of paper in her typewriter.

"That's our story?"

"Before I can write about it, it has to happen."

"And since it's not going to happen . . ."

"Something always happens, even if it's your refusal to admit that it does."

"So that I'll always be your guinea pig."

The room is tiny. Jerome suggests that Aurora move in with him. He's rattling around in the house, and besides, she could observe him firsthand during his vacation, which might provide her with new insights for her novel. She thanks him, but she feels committed to Madame W., and she's enjoying the opportunity to live with a provincial family. In Paris she spends all of her time with other writers. Here she can live with other people on a normal, day-to-day basis. "Besides," she adds, putting her arms around Jerome's neck, "how do you expect me to run the risk of moving in with you, just the two of us in that house of yours? You know damn well I adore you."

They go downstairs; the house is empty and silent.

"You see," Aurora says, "I have the place almost to myself. The mother works in town, and the girls are always out running around somewhere."

They pause beside a photograph standing on the mantelpiece.

"Who's that?"

"Claire, the other daughter."

"Not much family resemblance."

"They aren't sisters. How does she strike you?"

"Oh, come on, Aurora, stop needling me."

They emerge out onto the lawn, at the water's edge, and, looking around for chairs, espy Laura, seated at the foot of a lawn chair.

"Hello there," she calls out, smiling and provocative.

"What are you doing here?"

"School's out. Finally."

Aurora suggests that she make them a fruit salad for lunch. No, she doesn't want any help, thank you; it's a secret recipe. Jerome remains behind with Laura, who studies him closely, her face wreathed in smiles. Jerome remains serious, and, with obvious skepticism, asks, "What puts you in such a good mood, the end of school?"

"Not really, since I have to stay here while all my friends are leaving. Luckily, next month I'm off to England, to live with a family in Cheltenham. Anyway, I'm usually happy. If anything, vacation makes me unhappy, unless it means going away, seeing new places, not staying at home like a stick in the mud. But, then, I have to wait here for Claire's arrival."

"Claire?"

"My sister. Well, not really my sister: my mother remarried, and Claire is my stepfather's daughter; my own father's dead. She'll be here in a few days. We're very close . . . Too bad my mother divorced."

"Divorced whom, Claire's father?"

"That's right. Mother had two husbands. And now she's all alone."

Aurora returns with the lunch.

"Laura's sad," says Jerome, "because school's over. I sympathize with her. What I found depressing was coming back to the scenes of my childhood. The first few times I did, I found it so oppressive I had to pack up and leave. Too many memories."

"Memories you don't want to add to?" Laura asks.

"Certainly not."

"And what about Sweden?" Laura says. "Do you like it?"

"Yes, I do. A lot. But it's not so much the country I find attractive; it's—"

"The climate," Aurora cuts in. "I know, the climate suits you to a tee; you've said it a thousand times before. So spare us from hearing it again."

THURSDAY, JULY 2 — Jerome has come to pick up Aurora. As they stroll along the shoreline of the lake, Jerome takes her to task for having prevented him, the day before, from mentioning his forthcoming marriage in front of Laura.

"What in the world are you talking about?" she says, with obvious insincerity. "I didn't prevent you from saying whatever you wanted to."

"You know damn well you did. When you cut me off with your snide remark about the 'climate' of Sweden."

"But it's true. You've always said cold climates agree with you, and that you can't stand heat."

"Come on," Jerome says, "that's enough."

"Anyway, why so compulsive about mentioning your marriage? Do you think they're all that interested?"

"Playing the guinea pig doesn't suit me at all. I don't know what you told that child Laura, but when I see her, I can't keep from running off at the mouth."

"So run off, my friend. Don't let me stop you."

FRIDAY, JULY 3 — Jerome, who is invited to have coffee at Madame W.'s, finally manages to make an honest man of himself and tell them all about his marriage plans.

"The reason I'm going to live in Sweden is, very simply, that I'm marrying a Swedish girl next month."

"Even I didn't know till the other day," Aurora notes, closely watching Laura's reaction.

"Her name's Lucinda, and she works for UNICEF. Right now she's on a UN mission in Africa."

"It must be hard for you to be separated," says Madame W. "Especially at a time like this."

"They're used to it," Aurora chimes in. "And besides, think how happy they'll be to see each other once they are back together."

"It's true," Jerome says. "We've known each other for six years, and we've often been separated."

"But you won't be from now on, I trust."

"No. In any case, much less . . ."

"Besides," Aurora says, "absence makes the heart grow fonder."

"That may be," says Madame W. "Maybe I'm too picky. I can't bear to be away from someone I care about, and yet here I am, after two marriages, all alone."

"But Daddy didn't leave you," Laura says with obvious pique. "You can't equate dying with leaving."

"It all ends up to the same, though, doesn't it?"

"But you can't blame yourself for that."

"I didn't say I was blaming myself." She turns to Jerome and Aurora and shakes her head. "I always end up arguing with her . . . All I'm saying is, given my need to love, and finding myself alone, I feel cheated. My failing, if it is a failing, is to still put too much faith in love, with a capital *L*. I think you," she says, turning back to Laura, "won't have the same problem. And you'll be happier for it. Don't you think so?"

"Me?"

"Yes, you. All the kids your age think love is an old-fashioned sentiment. Gone out of style."

"I never said that. And I don't care at all what other people my age think. If they're stupid, Mama, it's not my fault . . . Anyway, it's not true. In your day there wasn't any more love than there is today. More hypocrisy, maybe, but that's all. Sometimes I think you say whatever comes into your mind without really thinking it through."

"Laura! . . . You see how she treats me?"

"I don't like to talk to make myself heard. And damn it anyway: this isn't a conversation for me. I can't speak with any experience."

And with that she jumps up and runs toward the far end of the garden. Madame W. explains that Laura's ill temper is the result of her not being allowed to go on a trip with her school friends.

"Please don't mind her," she says. "I don't know what's got

into her today. I've never seen her explode like that in front of other people. I think she's upset that all her friends have gone off to Corsica together. I didn't think it was right to let her go so far away at sixteen. And besides, her sister is arriving in a few days. Not to mention that she'll be spending the month of August in England." She glances at her watch. "Goodness, ten past two. I'll be late getting back to the office. Aurora, will you be good enough to remind Laura about the errand she has to run for me at three?"

After Madame W. has left, Jerome lights into Aurora.

"Thanks a lot!"

"What did I do?" Aurora asks innocently. "Look, why don't you find her and cheer her up. You can use as your excuse the errand her mother wants her to run."

The garden extended north, bordering the lake, and led to a grove of walnut trees. Jerome finds Laura seated at the water's edge, tossing crumbs from a cracker she had taken from the table to a swan gliding offshore. When she hears Jerome coming, she turns her head; then, seeing who it is, turns quickly back toward the water. Jerome stops beside her.

"I came to remind you of the errand you have to run for your mother at three."

"Was it she who sent you?"

"No, Aurora . . . What a lovely spot. Is it your special spot?"

"Yes, I often come here when people upset me . . . Oh, I don't mean you. Or Mother, either. Actually, we adore each other, but somehow she always seems to twist what I say into something I don't mean."

"I'm sure she didn't mean to. Anyway, she didn't say anything bad about you behind your back."

"Didn't she go on about how cantankerous I am?"

"No. In fact, she said what a wonderful girl you were."

"I know. With other people, she's proud of me. But when I'm there, she always puts me in the wrong. It's part of her makeup: she's argumentative. I generally agree with her, first of all because she's my mother, and also because if I argue back, I know she'll win out in the end. But I do love her dearly."

"I know she loves you, too."

"I shouldn't have sounded off like that. I'm sure it made her furious with me. What did she say?"

"I don't know. That you were mad at her for not letting you go off to Corsica."

"But she knows very well that's nonsense. I'm the one who didn't want to go. The truth is, I like it here. Well, it is a little stifling sometimes, if you know what I mean. If I'm going to be depressed, I prefer to have it happen anywhere else than here. All my friends are away. I wonder if I shouldn't have gone to Corsica with them, now that I think of it."

"That's strange," Jerome says. "I've felt just the opposite these past few days. With all this beauty around me, nothing gets me down."

"I know. It *is* beautiful. But sometimes I feel it pressing in on me, as though it were trying to suffocate me."

"Then, why don't you go mountain climbing? Up there, nothing can press down on you."

"We used to, Claire and I, when we were little girls. We were always up in the mountains."

"So was I. I know all sorts of nooks and crannies. One of these days I'll take you up there, if you want to. Are you afraid of heights?"

"No, not at all. It's not the heights that bother me, or being down here in the valley; it's actually the beauty itself: too much of it for too long a time. I need to get away from it for a while."

"Just what I was saying an hour ago. When you love someone, it's good to be separated from time to time."

"I agree . . . I suppose we shouldn't leave Aurora back there all alone."

Laura gets up and starts to run. After a few steps she stops and turns. He joins her and takes the hand she has extended to him. For a while they walk hand in hand; then, suddenly, she slips out of his grasp and runs on ahead.

SATURDAY, JULY 4 — Jerome arrives at Madame W.'s in his boat. As he ties up, Laura comes down to meet him. She tells him that Aurora isn't there. Some friends came for her and drove her to Geneva for "five or six days."

"So," Jerome says, "you're all alone. What are you reading? If it's books you're interested in, I have a house full of them. Want to take a boat ride over to my place?"

In Jerome's living room Laura pauses before a photograph of Lucinda.

"She's very beautiful," she says. "But hard. I pictured you with a warmer woman."

"You're suggesting we're ill matched?"

"An initial impression."

"Actually, you're quite right. Lucinda isn't my type, physically. In fact, I don't have a type. Assuming a certain basic 'acceptability' on the physical side, I don't really care what a woman looks like or how she's built. What matters is her self, her character."

"Yes, but the self is revealed in the way a person looks."

"And what do you see?"

"That you two are different not only physically but morally as well."

"There you go again. You're right! When I was your age I had a picture in my mind of my ideal woman, and she was very different from Lucinda. Physically or morally, I have the distinct impression she's not really my type, as you've so astutely noted. But so what? My type, if ever I found her, would doubtless bore me to death. If I'm marrying Lucinda, it's simply because after six years I'm still not bored by her, nor she by me. So neither of us sees any reason why we shouldn't make it permanent. I suspect you're going to find that attitude horribly devoid of passion."

"It's true. I like to think that I'll love someone the first time I set eyes on him, not after six years. That doesn't sound like 'love' to me. That sounds like friendship."

"Are you sure they're all that different? When you think about it, love and friendship are the same thing."

"Not in my book."

"Really? I don't believe in love without friendship."

"Maybe. But with me, friendship comes later."

"Sooner or later, what does it matter? In any case, there is in the concept of friendship something very beautiful that I hope exists in love as well, and that is the notion of mutual freedom. A lack of possessiveness."

"I'm possessive, horribly possessive."

"You shouldn't be. It can poison your life."

"I know. Sometimes I think I was born to be unhappy. But I won't let it happen. I'm a positive spirit, I think only about the happy side of life. People are unhappy because they want to be. Whenever I'm down, I can bring myself out of it by realizing that tears are no help and by remembering how lucky I am to be here, and how much fun I'm going to have."

"What do you consider 'fun'?"

"Having a good time. Being alive. Today, for instance, I feel very happy. If tomorrow I wake up feeling blue, I immediately fasten on to something positive, and I'm happy for the rest of the day . . . But maybe if I'm in love, then maybe . . ."

"Maybe what?"

"When I'm in love, it preoccupies me so totally that I have a hard time fixing on something positive when I feel down. I forget how happy I am just to be alive."

"There's a contradiction there. All I know is, you shouldn't allow being in love to make you unhappy. It should be just the opposite. But I sense you're strong enough, and well balanced enough, to know that."

"You really think so?"

"I do."

"I'm going to confess something to you."

"Namely . . ."

"I don't enjoy being in love. I can't think; I can't enjoy life; I get nervous and upset."

They emerged into the garden. Jerome paused to admire the roses, then suggested he cut a bouquet for Laura. She refused.

"What would Mother say?"

"Offering a girl roses is fairly innocent."

"She'd find your offering me roses rather ridiculous, and she'd be right."

"All right, then, you give them to her."

"Give them to her yourself the next time you come."

"I will."

"Give me just this one."

"Only this one?"

"Only this one."

He cuts it and hands it to her.

"But not for your mother."

"No, of course not. This is for me, to keep in my room."

"Where will you say it came from if she asks?"

"From you."

"And won't she find that silly?"

"Not a single rose. A bouquet, yes, but not a single rose. At least I don't think she will. But—"

"But what?"

"But nothing."

SUNDAY, JULY 5 — Jerome, who has been invited to dinner at Madame W.'s, arrives with a large bouquet of roses. There is another guest, Jacques D., a man of about forty.

After dinner the conversation turns to the natural beauties of the area, and more precisely the specific points from which one gets the best views. Jacques maintains that the best spot is on the other side of the lake from Madame W.'s house, because it offers the best view of the towering Tournette ranges and the Lanfon peaks. Madame W. says that she would rather live where one has a view of these mountains rather than at their foot. She feels hemmed in by them. Laura disagrees: she thinks that living at the foot of a mountain gives you a feeling of protection, "as though you were in a cradle." But her favorite spot in all the region is halfway up the mountain known as the Aulp peak, which forms the base of the higher Tournette. She asks Jerome if he'd like her to show him the spot the next day. Jerome seems reluctant at the prospect of climbing more than three thousand feet through the woods—woods that as a boy he had climbed through a thousand times. Laura says that it won't take them more than three hours, and that if he feels like it, they can push on to the top of Tournette itself, and spend the night at the châlet there.

Madame W. chides her daughter for taking advantage of Jerome's good nature.

"That's not what's bothering you, Mother. Are you worried about Jerome and me spending the night at the châlet?" Laura says with mock ingenuousness. Then, without waiting for an answer, she turns to Jerome and says, "It's all set. You'll pick me up tomorrow morning." Then she gets up and kisses her mother, then Jacques, and finally Jerome good night.

"I'm not sure I should let her go with you," Madame W. says. "I hope you realize she's in love with you."

"I doubt that, madam. She's playing a game."

"A game you can get caught up in."

"She knows I'm getting married."

"I'm only joking. And the truth is, I'm pleased she's fallen for a level-headed man like you."

"Level-headed, I'm not so sure. I hope you're counting on your daughter's level-headedness more than on mine."

"When one is a month away from getting married, one is level-headed, isn't that so?"

"I suspect that is what Laura is counting on, too."

MONDAY, JULY 6 — At the Aulp peak, Jerome is admiring the soaring mountains that rise above, either wooded or massively rocky—Tournette, Lanfon, Roux—and the steep drop to the dark-blue waters of the lake below. The feeling of oppressiveness you get down below is almost as great up here, Jerome notes. Laura doesn't think so. They are seated on the side of the hill. Jerome's arm is around her shoulder, and she nestles comfortably against him.

"It feels good being here," she says. "I like the way you hold me. How do you feel?"

"Great, just great."

"Really?"

"Yes, really."

"Would you like it better if you were with your fiancée?"

"Well . . . if you put it that way, I guess in the final analysis I would."

"Why 'in the final analysis'? I would hope that your answer would be unequivocally yes."

"It is, since I'm leaving you for her. If I liked being with you better, I'd stay with you. But how should I know whether I'd prefer to be with you? What's the point of comparing? The fact is, I like it here, now, with *you*." He strokes her arm gently, then says, "You know, my girl, I find you rather daringly imprudent. In your place, I'm not sure I'd be so trusting."

"I'm not so trusting, but since I need to enrich my experience, I have to take chances. Calculated risks. You're taking a greater chance than I am," she adds, "since you're about to be married. I'm a free woman."

"I'm free, too. I respect Lucinda's freedom, and she respects mine. As far as I'm concerned, she can do whatever she likes, the hope—or rather the conviction—being that she won't do anything that would upset me. If everything one partner likes displeases the other, it would be crazy to want to live together."

"And would she be pleased knowing you were with me?"

"Sure she would, if she knew our friendship was purely platonic. Friends are still part of both our lives."

"Aurora, for instance."

"Right."

"I like her enormously."

"Did you two talk about me?"

"Of course we did."

"And what did she say?"

"That I should be careful when I'm with you."

She looks at him with her most seductive air. He tries to draw her close, but suddenly she jumps to her feet. "Let's go for a walk." Hand in hand, they follow the path that ascends toward the higher peaks. After a while both of them pause, a little out of breath. Jerome presses Laura to him. She lifts her head. They kiss. But again she tears free and dashes on ahead. He follows her up the trail, catches up to her, and his arms encircle her waist.

"Let me go!"

"All right. No more fun and games?"

"No. I want to be serious. I want a man to be in love with me, and I with him."

"You've got your whole life ahead of you."

"You sound like my mother. You know, I always had the feeling I'd get married very young. Some girls do marry at sixteen."

"Not very many. And I disapprove of those who do. I can't see any earthly reason why you'd want to marry now."

"You know that Mother's getting married again."

"To the man who came to dinner the other night?"

"Right. Jacques. And when they do, I'm going to find it hard living with them."

"But you still have years of study ahead of you. You can go live in Grenoble, or Lyon. Or even Paris . . ."

"I know I can . . . Listen, I want to tell you something, but you're standing too close. Step back a bit, all right? I think I had fallen a bit in love with you. No, no, it's true. And if someone like you came along and swept me off my feet, assuming I loved him, I'd go with him."

"And what would your mother say?"

"She'd be delighted."

"But, somebody my age?"

"Age doesn't matter to me. I never was in love with the boys my own age."

TUESDAY, JULY 7 — Seated next to Jerome on a bench in the garden, Laura goes on with her revelations.

"I don't like people my own age. I find them stupid. I may look like a little kid, but don't believe everything you see. I'm wise beyond my years. Ever since Mother divorced, she confided all her little secrets, all her problems, to me. I know a lot more than most girls my age. A *lot!* They're all still wet behind the ears. I can very easily see myself married . . . which doesn't mean I'll rush off and marry the first person I meet, of course."

"I just can't see girls marrying so young in this day and age. This isn't the time of Louis the Fourteenth, after all. Your mother lets you do whatever you want."

"Not so fast. She may seem to, but she's not as liberal as you think. And I think she's right to be strict, to fill my ears with sound advice. I may not agree with her, she may irritate me, but I often find she's right. She's right because—"

"Because?"

"Because I'm crazy. There are times when I feel like doing anything. I mean *anything!* But then I think of my mother and know how upset she would be, so I stop just in time. There are boys who will tell you I'm impossible. But I could just as easily be wild, and if I'm not, it's because of my mother. No other reason. If I had a father like Claire does, I think I'd be more tempted to yield to my crazy impulses."

"Is Claire crazier than you?"

"No, she's in love with a boy who's coming to spend his vacation here. You'll meet him. Those two are inseparable. My problem is, I've never really been in love with a boy, and that begins to worry me . . . That's not quite true: when I was young—I mean a real little kid—I almost fell in love with a boy twelve and a half. I can't say it ever came to very much, but I did love him. And, after him, nobody, really."

"In other words, your love life has been over for four years now."

"I want to love someone, but the only boys I get to see are my own age, and I have an instinctive fear of them."

"What kind of fear?"

"I don't know, some kind of instinct of self-preservation, I guess. And the handsomer the boy is, the more I'm afraid."

"You mean you're afraid you won't be able to resist him?"

"No, it's vaguer than that. The younger they are, the more they insist, and that bugs me. Say I find a boy nice, and whenever I'm with him I feel I love him, just walking hand in hand. But then after a while he begins to feel, 'Aha, she's in love with me,' and he begins to take on all kinds of airs. Self-importance. And then it's all over, like a balloon deflating. The younger they are, the less sure I feel with them, because they don't know how to handle things. I only feel comfortable with someone who might be old enough to be my father. I must have lacked paternal affection. Anyway, when I'm with an older man, it's as though I have found my father again. I want to share his work, give my opinion about what worries or concerns him, be with him always . . . I want to be a small, loving presence, and whenever I do, I feel wonderful."

She lies back, nestling her head on Jerome's shoulder.

WEDNESDAY, JULY 8 — Jerome moors his boat at Madame W.'s villa. He disembarks and heads toward the house. A girl taking a sunbath on the lawn gets up and comes over to him. He introduces himself.

"You must be Claire. I'm Jerome. Is Laura here?"

"She just went off somewhere. Vincent came to pick her up."

"Vincent. A friend of hers. He just came back from Sallanches."

"And is Aurora still in Geneva?"

"I think so. In any case, I haven't seen her."

"In other words, you're here alone. Where do you live, in Paris?"

"Yes."

"Lucky girl. Lovely day, isn't it."

"Very."

He tries to prolong the conversation, but her short replies make it difficult, and as he is still casting about, the sudden noise of a car entering the driveway cuts him short.

"Nice to meet you," he says, feeling three may be a crowd. As he reaches his boat and casts off, he turns back to see a young man of eighteen or twenty running across the lawn toward the girl, who stands waiting for him with open arms.

THURSDAY, JULY 9 — Jerome is in his room. A car honks in the street below. Insistently. It's Aurora, on her way back from Geneva. He goes down to meet her, and is introduced to the friend: a Romanian, as it turns out, who had driven her. He invites them for a drink and asks how her trip was. Lovely but uneventful, she relates. At least, nothing she can reveal without betraying the "highest diplomatic secrets," she says, casting an eye at her friend. But Jerome, no doubt, has a great deal to tell her.

"Yes and no," he says. "Nothing happened. Or so little it hardly bears relating. But since you thrive on non-events . . . You see," Jerome says, turning to the Romanian, "I too have my little diplomatic secrets."

"Professional secrets," Aurora says, correcting him. "You see, I'm using him as a guinea pig. I want to hear all about it, Jerome, no matter how insignificant . . ."

FRIDAY, JULY 10 — At the far edge of the lawn, where it meets the garden, Jerome gives Aurora a rundown of his "experience." She did serve a purpose, he says; namely, to provide added confirmation that he is above, or beyond, any amatory adventure.

"The only way a girl can interest or arouse me is if there's an element of curiosity involved. I did want to find out if the child wasn't stringing me along, in keeping with a well-planned scenario. Planned by you, I suspect. I kissed her the other day, to see what would happen, and I actually had to force myself. Even when I took her hand, not the way I'd hold a child's, or an old friend's in the course of a conversation"—he takes Aurora's—"but in a conscious gesture of sensuality, it bothered me. When we walked hand in hand, it seemed a burden, not out of guilt but simply because it seemed so pointless. The act of paying court to a woman other than Lucinda didn't make me feel guilty; it made me feel I was wasting my time. Lucinda is everything to me. There's no way to add to what is already complete."

"Then, why the experiment?"

"To please you. And to act as your humble and obedient servant."

"I'm very impressed," she says sarcastically.

"And to witness the experiment fail. One is never sure of anything until one tries it. If I were to keep away from women, not look at them, avoid them, my love for Lucinda would become a duty rather than a pleasure. I'm marrying her because I enjoy being with her more than with anyone else. My will doesn't figure in the equation. And if I had any doubts, they're gone."

"In any love equation, will has to figure, in however slight a way."

"I like it to be as slight as possible. And to discover, as I did the other day, how insignificant it is—believe me, it is a delightful feeling."

SUNDAY, JULY 12 — The cherries are ripe. Everyone has decided to spend the afternoon picking them: Jerome; Aurora, who is on the balcony, writing; Madame W., who is reading in a lounge chair; her daughters; Gilles, Claire's boyfriend; and Vincent, Laura's classmate. Like Laura, Claire is sixteen. What is most striking about her is her grace, the way she walks, her carriage, the willowy figure she makes as she passes. Laura's main quality is her vivacity; Claire is disturbing in her haughty nonchalance. The two main expressions her face reveals are an adoring look whenever she sees or hears Gilles and a look of indifference—almost defiance—toward the rest of the world. One has to give the young man his due: he is tall, handsome, well built, has a firm voice that doesn't hesitate to convey his thoughts, albeit with a trace of arrogance that, one senses, even Claire has trouble enduring. Once in a great while she takes exception, but their quarrels are patched up almost before they begin. Vincent is almost the opposite: rather small and coarse-featured. But he has bright eyes that sparkle with obvious wit and intelligence. He and Laura could play the main roles in *The Taming of the Shrew*, for they are constantly at each other. Vincent and she both pretend to be only good friends, but it is clear that he, in any case, is more smitten than he is willing to admit. As for Laura, who will ever know? If one were to believe what she says, he's the direct opposite of her ideal, physically, but their minds are clearly on the same level, and there is an obvious complicity between them. Laura seems suddenly to have lost all interest in Jerome, who is feeling a little lost among all these new faces and amid this shifting climate. He's wondering how he can slip away gracefully, but his eyes, on several occasions, pause on the legs of Claire, who is perched halfway up the ladder. Laura, as she passes, catches his wayward eye.

TUESDAY, JULY 14 — They're all off to the Bastille Day ball at the village square. Scarcely have they arrived when Aurora is swept away by an Italian who is going after her diligently. Jerome dances first with Laura, and Gilles with Claire, leaving Vincent to watch the activities, feeling a little left out. The next dance is a tango, and Laura leave Jerome to invite Vincent. Since Claire is leaving the dance floor, Jerome asks her to dance. She says she'd prefer to sit this one out, and remains glued to Gilles. Aurora and the Italian are whirling around the floor; Laura is clinging to Vincent in what seems to Jerome an exaggerated way. Passing close to where Jerome is standing,

Laura signals mockingly for him to invite a girl nearby. Jerome looks at her choice: a fat girl with glasses.

THURSDAY, JULY 16 — The tennis club. Gilles and Claire are waiting for a court. Jerome's attention is caught by the sight of Gilles' hand, which rests casually on Claire's knee as his eyes are riveted on the match being played on the court in front of them. Claire is snuggled up against him.

FRIDAY, JULY 17 — Aurora is paying Jerome a visit. From the terrace they can see the mixed doubles—Gilles and Claire versus Laura and Vincent—being played on the court below. Then they stroll back and sit down in the shade of the house.

"You know," Jerome says, "I much prefer your conversation to watching tennis. And, anyway, there was something I wanted to tell you. A little sermonizing, to tell the truth. You propel me into all kinds of experiments while you carefully refrain from trying any yourself. Is that fair?"

"Your experiments didn't lead very far . . ."

"I'm a tourist here. A bird of passage. My real life is elsewhere. Whereas for you this is serious, your life."

"I'm also a bird of passage."

"Not for long, I trust. You're too beautiful to waste your life flitting from one man to the other."

"My days of great beauty are done and gone."

"Find yourself a man you really like and stop complaining."

"And what if I made you a bet I'll find him before the year is out?"

"Who told you?"

"Tea leaves, my friend, tea leaves . . . And what is all this about finding myself a man? Where? Who? Do they just grow on trees?"

"They're everywhere. Say, what about that guy the other night, at the Bastille Day ball?"

"Oh, that."

"Confess: you didn't find him all that bad . . ."

"That's the whole problem. I like them all, which is why I don't settle on any. Why one rather than another? Since I can't have them all, I don't want any."

"Very abnormal attitude, my girl, and very immoral."

"Immoral, certainly not, since it keeps me chaste. I'm not going to throw myself at the first guy who comes along. What for? What would it lead to, except disaster?"

"I'm not talking about the first guy who comes along."

"And my attitude is that if there is a Prince Charming, he'll show up one day."

"Where, here?"

"Here as well as anywhere. I'm in no hurry. To hear you talk you'd think my days were numbered, before I become old and gray. I have a confession to make to you. Last year I wanted to check out my 'seduction factor,' so I made myself a pact to seduce no less than five young—*very* young—men in the course of a week."

"Five!"

"Actually, I only hooked three. But all handsome as hell."

"And did you enjoy it, aside from the glory of conquest?"

"Yes. I could have gone on indefinitely. But in the long run it's depressing, so I made up my mind to wait. I know how to wait—that's no problem—and there is a very enjoyable aspect to it, the sense of expectation."

"Assuming it doesn't go on too long."

"Don't worry."

"Your story is far more fascinating than mine."

"No, your involvement with the girls I find more interesting, since it's harder to pin down."

"In that case, it serves you right: my pubescent love is being washed away by the sands of time. Kaput! I have nothing new to tell you. Is she trying to use Vincent to make me jealous? I doubt it. Her experiment is finished, as is mine. Period. She's resumed her old ways, and I'm doing the same. You know . . ."

"What?"

"Nothing. What strikes me as amusing is that it's no longer you who is writing your novel: it's me. I have an idea, but my ideas frighten me . . ."

"No, tell me."

"You'll have to guess. It's only an idea, mind you not a proven fact. I took my role of guinea pig so seriously that I'm outdoing myself. Anyway, trying to put myself into the role of the fictional character, I wondered whether he might be able to feel something I couldn't. The fact is, I don't feel anything. This experiment has convinced me that I'll never chase another girl, be she young or old. But I'm speaking for myself, not your character. Do you follow me?"

"More or less. You're saying that you've come to a conclusion about yourself in this story, but not about the character I'm creating from you: for him, the experiment is still going on."

"No, it's over for him, too, at least in this experiment."

"So it's all over, for everybody."

"That's not what I said."

"What did I miss?"

"Try again. Actually, there's no reason why you should be able to read my mind, and I'm sure I haven't translated my thoughts very clearly. Laura almost figured it out, I suspect.

The problem is, when I talk about something, I give it more importance in the story than I mean to. Guess again, though I'm afraid you'll never get what I'm driving at. Let me give you a hint: it's over with *Laura*."

"You've already said that. So?"

"So, it's over with *Laura*."

"Oh, my God! You don't mean that Claire is also—"

"No, only an idea. And not that she's in love with me. But, I find myself—how shall I say—interested in her."

"A classic case. And Claire's in love with someone else."

"It's not only that. If I wasn't intrigued by her, what difference would it make? But let's say she disturbs me. No, she disturbs my character; and, to some slight degree, me. So slight I probably wouldn't even mention it if you hadn't made it clear you're especially interested in these 'slight degrees.'"

"Explain what you mean by 'disturb.' How does she disturb you? Her body?"

"In a way, yes. Physically, since that's the only aspect of the girl to which I can claim any knowledge. We've hardly exchanged a word since we first met. In fact, I think I'd have some problem talking to her, if it came down to it."

"So . . . the girl intimidates you!"

"True, I feel absolutely powerless in the presence of girls like her. Have you ever felt that way?"

"Sometimes. With very handsome men. I'm amused that you had the courage to admit your shyness to me."

"But I've never tried to hide it. Usually I don't have to take the first step. I've never run after a girl when I didn't feel she was disposed to having me chase her."

"And what about this one?"

"Listen, this is a very strange case. I'm not sure I can explain it, but there's no doubt she does arouse a very strong desire in me, one that's all the stronger in that it has no purpose, no goal. Pure desire, a desire for nothing. I don't want to do anything about it, but the mere fact of feeling this desire bothers me. I thought I was past feeling desire for any woman except Lucinda. And, to make matters more complicated, I don't want her. If she threw herself at me, I'd turn her down."

"Jealousy?"

"No. And yet even if I don't want her, I have the feeling I have some sovereign right to her, emanating from the strength of my desire. I'm convinced I deserve her more than anyone. Yesterday, for instance, I was watching those two lovebirds down at the tennis courts, and I said to myself, 'In every woman there is some vulnerable point. For some it's the neck; for others, the waist, or the hands.' And for Claire, in that position, in that light, it was the knee. Her knee was the magnetic pole of my desire, the precise point where, if I had been allowed to follow the dictates of my desire, I would have placed my hand. And just as I was thinking that, her boyfriend placed his hand there. In all innocence. Without malice aforethought. That hand, above all, was stupid, and that shocked me!"

"I see the problem, and for me the solution is simple: put your hand on her knee and exorcise your desire."

"Not so simple, my dear Aurora. Very difficult, in fact. A caress has to be accepted; it can't be forced. It would be easier to sleep with her."

MONDAY, JULY 20 — After having gone for a swim, Gilles, Claire, Aurora, and Vincent, together with some friends of theirs, are playing volleyball on the lawn. Jerome and Laura are sitting on the porch, watching them.

"When I think about it," Jerome says, "my ideal woman is delicate and very fragile. Looking back, I realize that all the girls I've loved have without exception been too healthy and hardy. Even Lucinda. Too athletic. Not that I don't like and appreciate her athletic side, but if I had to start from scratch and manufacture a girl to measure, I'd use Claire as my model."

"It's still not too late," Aurora says.

"But I've also told you that the physical aspect is secondary to me. If Claire did respond to my advances, I'd have to cease and desist. But I'd like that decision to be mine. Nothing is simple. Whenever I've desired a woman, she's always eluded me. All my so-called conquests are the result of unpremeditated liaisons. Desire followed possession, if you will."

Suddenly Claire gives a cry. The volleyball has hit her on the end of her index finger, and it looks as though the finger may be sprained. Gilles scolds her for not knowing how to play the game properly. Jerome goes over and asks her whether there is anything he can do. He brings her over to Aurora, who examines her finger and concludes, with a knowing wink, that all it needs is to be "massaged" a little. Then Aurora leaves, under the pretense of getting something to drink. Jerome apparently doesn't care to exploit the situation, and is content to engage Claire in idle chatter. Claire responds with a laugh or two, but is hardly more loquacious than before, although she does confess that volleyball is not her cup of tea, and that she plays only to please Gilles.

"You shouldn't do whatever boys ask you to do," Jerome observes.

"But I don't do 'whatever boys ask me to,'" she replies, mimicking him.

Aurora comes back bringing each of them a glass. She

starts to hand one to Jerome; then, as he reaches for it, draws back as though to throw him off balance. She catches his eye, and he follows her gaze: Claire's knee. He understands what she is up to: when thrown off balance he can, if he wants, make contact with Claire's knee. But he'll have none of it.

THURSDAY, JULY 23 — Gilles has borrowed Jerome's motorboat and taken Claire for a ride. He's opened up the throttle and is barreling through the waves, swooping in as close to shore as he can, without any regard for the rules of boating. Jerome is reading in the shade of the old cherry tree when a guard from the neighboring campground arrives to complain about Gilles' conduct. He's driving the bathers out of the water, despite the remonstrances of the camp personnel. Jerome apologizes and says he'll make sure it doesn't happen again.

While the guard is still there, Gilles comes ashore and, in response to the guard's complaints, tells him it's a free country and he'll do what he damn well pleases. One insult leads to another, and the two men almost come to blows. The guard finally leaves, and Jerome tells the two lovers that since they obviously have no sense of responsibility, he won't let them use his boat anymore. Gilles loses his temper and swears that he handled the boat in strict accordance with the rules of the lake. Laura arrives, intrigued by their dispute, and vehemently defends Gilles.

"You mean those damn campers are complaining again? Well, I hope you scared them out of their wits! Litterbugs, that's what they are. I won't tell you the number of times I've picked up their debris off the lawn. And they trespass whenever they damn well please, without so much as an 'excuse me' or 'do you mind.' They think they own the place. They're impossible, those people. I hope you scared them to death."

"Listen to her!" Jerome says. "I'll tell your mother how you contradict me!"

"See if I care! Anyway, she agrees with me. And what's more, my fine-feathered friend, remember that you're on our turf, and if you don't like it here, complain to my mother, not to me . . ."

FRIDAY, JULY 24 — In town, Jerome runs into Laura, who is on her way home after running some errands. Jerome asks if she'd like him to give her a ride home in his boat, which will give him a chance to stop by and say hello to Aurora. Why not? She says, and while they're walking to the dock, Jerome asks her whether she'd like to go mountain climbing with him again. She replies that she can't today, and tomorrow she's busy packing, since she's leaving for England on the twenty-sixth.

He says it seems a pity to leave each other on such terms. What terms? she wants to know. I don't know, he replies, but I have a feeling the friendship that started on the mountains the other day is stillborn. She says she doesn't know what he's talking about, especially since they've seen each other almost every day since, and what more does he want, for God's sake?

"That's just it," he says, "somehow I expected more."

"And I think it's fine as it is," she says. "And if there wasn't any 'more,' as you put it, it's your fault. You're the one who always kept his distance."

"I didn't want to force myself on you. You were always surrounded by your friends."

"You should have joined us. You're not such an old fogy."

Jerome confesses that the reason he didn't join them was that he found the young men a pretty sorry bunch. Vincent was all right maybe; but Gilles was a real loser.

"Gilles is my sister's boyfriend," she replies, clearly astonished by his attack, "and it's not my role to criticize who she goes with. And, besides, I think he's nice. They make a terrific couple."

"Come on, now," Jerome says, "you don't really mean that. She's far too good for him."

"You hate him because he doesn't kowtow to you."

"Are you crazy? I like people who have a little spunk. His problem is he's a complete phony. The worst. Claire ought to drop him like a hot potato. If she's blind to it, then why don't you open her eyes?"

"She loves the guy. What business is it of yours, anyway?"

"None, really. I simply thought I ought to speak my mind."

"That's true. You're jealous, for no reason. Then again . . ."

SUNDAY, JULY 26 — It's Laura's departure date for England, and her mother is driving her to Geneva. It's growing late, and they tell Laura to hurry up. She appears from somewhere beyond the garden, where she and Vincent—who's looking as though his world had just caved in—had been in heated conversation. With Vincent looking on, Laura embraces Jerome a trifle more tenderly than necessary. Finally they are off, and the others return to the porch. Any departure, even if it doesn't involve a lover or close friend or family, is always sad, Jerome thinks.

TUESDAY, JULY 28 — The day is cloudy and windy, but Jerome, who is leaving the following day, has some necessary business in town and takes the quickest route, by boat. As he is about to tie up at the town dock, he sees a couple walking in the public park, in close embrace. They're fairly far away, but Jerome is almost sure it's Gilles. He takes his binoculars: it's Gilles, all right. But the girl he's with is not Claire.

On his way home he passes Madame W.'s. Claire, who is there alone, tells him that Aurora's not there. Jerome asks her to remind Aurora that they are supposed to have dinner that evening, and that he'll pick her up at eight o'clock. She promises she'll give Aurora the message; then, with some hesitation, asks him if by any chance he's going to Annecy.

"I've just been there," he says. "Why?"

"Nothing. It doesn't really matter."

But her concerned air belies her words.

"I'd be happy to take you to town," he says, glancing skyward. "It looks as though it's clearing up."

Halfway there, the skies darken, and the wind begins to gust.

Jerome casts a wary eye at the thunderclouds and decides he'd better put in to shore as soon as possible. The first available landing is a private dock, and just as Jerome ties up, the heavens open, suddenly and violently. Claire dashes into the boathouse a few yards away while Jerome covers the boat, then runs to join her. They are seated precariously on some packing crates. Claire is wearing a light summer dress, over which she has a linen jacket. He asks her if she's cold. She shakes her head. She seems worried. He glances over at her, then scans the skies. It's clear the rain will go on for some time.

"Even if it clears," he says, "I won't have time to take you into town. You'll never make it to your rendezvous."

She replies, at greater length than normal, that she didn't have any "rendezvous," as he put it, but that she simply wanted to leave a letter at Gilles' place. Gilles, you see, had gone to see his mother in Grenoble, and she wanted him to find the letter that night when he got home.

"I have to confess that it pains me to see a girl like you wasting your time with a creep like Gilles," Jerome blurts out. "If only you were aware of how superior you are to him . . . You could have any man you want, young lady. Take advantage of it."

"Gilles is terrific!" she says. "So he doesn't play up to you the way Aurora and Mother do. Or Laura, for that matter. I think it's to his credit that he doesn't. It shows he has some character. Anyway, I couldn't care less what you think."

"You couldn't care less to know how your friend Gilles spent his afternoon?" he said. "I didn't want to tell you, but I think you'd better know. He didn't spend the day with his mother in Grenoble, but in Annecy, with a blonde, medium height—"

Before he finishes, Claire bursts into tears.

Jerome murmurs some words of consolation, but she only begins to sob all the louder. A minute of silence follows, punctuated only by her sobs, the pounding of the rain on the boathouse roof, and the occasional peals of thunder in the distance. Claire hunts for a handkerchief, but comes up with nothing. Jerome hands her his, which she takes, as the sobs slowly subside. One of her legs is folded under her, the other stretched out in front of her, the knee forming a kind of luminous landmark in the darkness. Jerome, completely absorbed by the girl's tears, gazes down at her. His glance moves upward from her knee along the line of her thigh to her belly, convulsed from her sobs, then back down again, slowly . . . Then, with a deliberate motion, he places his hand on her knee and begins to caress it with a circular motion of his palm.

Claire has no reaction. All she does, with some delay, is glance down at the caressing hand, probably determined to put a stop to it as soon as she has regained control of herself. But she remains passive, until the sobs have subsided, Jerome's hand meanwhile continuing its insistent rhythm. The rain ceases. Claire's eyes are almost dry now. Only a last solitary tear courses down her cheek. Jerome watches it, mesmerized. When it reaches the corner of her mouth, he removes his hand from her knee and gets to his feet.

"Let's head home," he says.

Seated in an easy chair, a cup of tea in front of her, Aurora listens to Jerome's confession. He confesses (was it the sudden storm, the impending departure?) that he was in a kind of trance, prey to an overwhelming need, of catastrophic proportions. Something stronger than his own will dictated the words he said without wanting to, forced him to do things he ordinarily wouldn't have done.

"She cried and cried; then she began searching her pockets for a handkerchief but couldn't find one. I handed her mine, and she dabbed her eyes with it before handing it back, but I told her to keep it. I'm sure that at that moment she must have hated me. If I had tried to touch her, or even to open my mouth, she would have cried, 'Leave me alone!' So I stayed there, embarrassed more than anything, watching her weep, pleased that my revelation had struck home but at the same time appalled at my behavior. I was ashamed to have made her cry, and I assumed she was ashamed to have broken down in front of a stranger, and that added to my embarrassment.

"What bothered me even more was the fact that I felt that she was not looking for comfort. If I had taken her hand, or tried to hug her, she would have resisted . . . Anyway, there she was, seated across from me, and there, too, at arm's length, was her knee, that smooth and shining, delicate, fragile knee. So near and yet so far. So near I could have reached out and touched it; so far because it was so unattainable. So easy, yet so impossible. It's as though you're on the edge of a cliff, and you know all it takes is one step and down you go, and even if you want to, you can't.

"It took courage, you know, a great deal of courage. I don't think I ever did anything more courageous—or more willful—in my life. I don't think I ever felt more that I was doing something that had to be done. For it did have to be done; right? Since I had promised you I would?

"So I put my hand on her knee; it was a rapid, assertive gesture that gave her no time to react. All she did was look at me—indifferently, I think; in any case, with hardly any hostility. But she said nothing. She didn't remove my hand; nor did she move her leg. Why, I couldn't say. I don't understand. Or maybe I do. You see, if I had tried to caress her hair or forehead, she would certainly have reacted with some classic, instinctive gesture of self-defense. But what I did took her by surprise. She probably assumed it was the initial tactic of an assault that was to follow. And when it didn't, she was reassured. What do you think of that explanation?"

"I think you've told it very well," Aurora says. "My only regret is that I don't have a paper and pencil handy so I could note it down verbatim. As for what she thought, what does it matter to you? I see you there in the semidarkness of the boathouse, a couple sculpted for all eternity. Who gives a damn about your thoughts?"

"You know," he goes on, "I don't exactly enjoy making girls cry. If I did it, it was because I wanted to teach her a lesson. Open her eyes. If I had had the feeling that I had shocked her, I would have removed my hand. But, not only did I not upset her;

I did her some good. What I took for a gesture expressing desire she took to be a gesture of solace. I can't describe the feeling of peace that came over me during that brief moment . . ."

Aurora found Jerome's story, and the accompanying interpretation, highly entertaining.

"A charming story," she says, "but devoid of both sound and fury. The only perversity it contains is what you claim to put into it."

"And I claim the results are highly moral on at least two counts. First, I exorcised my desire: the girl's body will no longer obsess me. It's as though I had possessed her. Second, I performed a good deed, in that I opened the poor girl's eyes to the truth about her boyfriend. She's rid of him forever, thanks to me."

"She'll probably end up with somebody worse."

"No, I don't think so. Now that her eyes are open to the dangers that kind of boy presents."

"What I find most amusing is the fact that the crux of the matter is that you can't bear for any woman to escape your clutches."

"The living proof that some do is sitting right there: you, my dear."

"I don't count, since I'm not playing."

"Maybe that's what bothers me about you. Different rules for different people. I'm your willing guinea pig, nothing more, but in my eyes you're a real friend, someone I care about. And in case you've forgotten, everything I've done I've done out of friendship for you."

"Laura was for me? Claire was for me? I hope you're not going to throw in Lucinda, too?"

"Listen, you probably won't believe me, but if you hadn't been here, nothing would have happened, even if I had met both these girls in one way or another. And since you're leaving, nothing further *can* happen. Thanks to you, though, I've reached the exquisite peak of subtle experience, and I don't want any further developments."

"Where does all this leave Lucinda?"

"Lucinda? Why, in the future I shall be a horse with blinders. All the rest, the other girls, have been swept away as if by magic. You are a magician, Aurora!"

"Did you ever doubt it for a moment?"

"Not really. Otherwise I wouldn't have put myself into your hands the way I did."

WEDNESDAY, JULY 29 — Nine in the morning. Jerome, in his boat, moors for one last visit to Madame W.'s. The sky, swept clean by the wind, is a sparkling blue, and the lake shimmers in the morning light. Aurora, who has seen him land, comes down from her balcony to say good-bye. He asks her to say good-bye to Claire for him. She asks him whether he'd like her to wake Claire up, and he says not to bother.

They embrace, and Jerome tells her how badly he feels about going off to get married and leaving her to her solitude. She smiles mysteriously and says, "Solitude? Who says I'll be alone?"

"What does that mean? You have a lover?"

"A fiancé."

"You never breathed a word. I tell you everything, and you keep everything to yourself."

"You never asked. And besides, you know him. I introduced you to him the other day."

"The guy who drove you back from Geneva? Not bad!"

He climbs into his boat and casts off. As he disappears down the lake, he can still see Aurora's silhouette waving to him in the distance. As Aurora turns back toward the house, she sees Gilles parking his car. He asks Aurora if Claire is there, but before she can reply, Claire comes down the stairs. Aurora goes upstairs to her room, preferring not to witness what she suspects will be a stormy session between them. From her balcony perch, however, half hidden by the branches of the cherry tree, she can't help watching the two lovers pace to and fro across the lawn below, in heated discussion. Snatches of their conversation drift up to her. Gilles' explanations seem little by little to get the better of Claire's accusations. True, he didn't go to Grenoble as he had said . . . His car had broken down . . . On his way to take the ferry he had run into Muriel, who was in a terrible state of mind . . . some terrible problem with the boy she was in love with . . . He was only trying to help . . .

They walk over and sit down on the bench near the lakeside. They embrace, their kiss long and sensous. The boy's left arm is around Claire's shoulder, and his right hand is caressing her knee.

VI

LOVE IN THE AFTERNOON

Prologue

It is eight o'clock in the morning. I get ready to leave. I slip on my raincoat. I go back into the bedroom to pick up a book from the bed table. From the next room a child's cry is heard: "Mama!"

I pause at the bathroom door and knock lightly.

"Helen."

"Come in," my wife says.

The door opens to discover her naked, from the back, stepping out of her bath. She grabs the bath towel and drapes it around her as she turns to face me.

"On your way already?" she says, turning her cheek for a kiss.

"Sorry," I say, "but I have a tough day ahead of me. Ariane's crying. I don't have the time to pick her up."

"Don't worry, I'll take care of her."

I put my arm around her waist and pull her to me, letting my lips wander over her still-moist shoulder.

"Hey . . . you're going to get all wet!" she says.

"It's okay. I'm wearing my raincoat."

We live in a suburb west of Paris, a half hour from the Saint-Lazare station. The train platform is jammed at this time of day, and the train itself is even more crowded. So crowded, in fact, that I can barely get my book out of my pocket.

On the train, I much prefer reading books to newspapers,

not only because newspapers are cumbersome but also because I can't immerse myself enough in the papers. Books lead me farther afield, and at present I'm very much taken with books on exploration. Today's book is entitled *Voyage autour du Monde*, by Bougainville. Half an hour in the morning, half an hour at night: that's about the proper dosage, as far as I'm concerned, for my reading time on the commuter special.

In the evening I also read, but something else. I enjoy reading several books at once, each having its own time and place, but all having the power to transport me out of the time and place in which I live. I couldn't read if I were alone in a cell, with bare walls around me. I need someone there, a physical presence.

When I was a student, I could never stay in my room after dinner, unless I had to study. Now, Helen and I rarely go out. She's an English teacher at the Saint-Cloud Lycée, and she spends most of her evenings preparing for her courses and correcting papers. For me to be a thousand leagues away from her in my thoughts only makes her physical presence all the more reassuring . . . Why, among all the possible beauties, was I turned on to her beauty? I still haven't found a satisfactory answer.

Seated across from me on the train is a young woman busily correcting papers. She is married, I know, having looked at the third finger of her left hand. She doesn't look like a teacher, but neither does Helen. Every now and then she lifts her head and gazes vacantly into the distance. She has beautiful eyes . . .

Now, when I see a woman, I cannot judge her without thinking in categories of the "chosen" and the "reprobates." Not only do I no longer have the unfailing taste I used to have, but the criteria which once seemed absolute to me have eroded to the extent that I'm incapable of ferreting out, at first glance, that certain something that any woman had to have if I were to find her irresistibly attractive.

Since my marriage, I find all women attractive. No matter what they're doing, no matter what their movements or occupations, I bestow upon them that mystery I used to be at pains to strip them of. I'm curious about their lives, even if they reveal nothing that I don't already know. What would have happened if I had met this woman three years ago? Would she have caught my eye? Would I have fallen for her, wanted to have a child by her?

I walk in the throng of people exiting from the station, which breaks up into smaller streams that take this street or that.

I love a big city. Suburbs and provincial towns depress me terribly. And despite the mob and the noise, I never tire of plunging into the moving throng as I would into the sea, reveling in its depths and in swimming back up to the surface, a solitary swimmer, letting myself be carried by the currents but ready to strike out on my own as soon as the wave breaks and disintegrates. Like the sea, crowds are tonic to me, and encourage my dreams. Almost every thought I have comes to me in the street, even those that relate to my work.

My modest office is nearby the station. My friend Gerard and I have gone into business for ourselves, and our office consists of three rooms: my office, Gerard's, and a third for our secretaries.

By the time Fabienne, one of the secretaries, arrives, I'm at my typewriter composing a letter. She apologizes for being late, but I tell her not to worry, it is I who am early. She asks if I would like her to take my place, but I tell her that I'm still trying to compose the letter properly, and that if I make any typing errors, I'll be happy for her to make a clean copy. Meanwhile, would she be an angel and fetch me a certain document in the files.

Even as I type, I watch her as she looks through the files for the paper I need. No question: the girl is pretty, elegant, and well built. Not that her obvious physical attributes detract from her professional qualities. For Gerard and I cherish the latter, which is not to say that we disdain the former. We both feel that one's working environment is important, and we see no reason not to make it as pleasant as possible. Having as our working companions two pretty girls is, we find, both enjoyable and stimulating, although I hasten to add that "hands off" is our credo. This said, I don't mean to imply that gallantry is dead. On the contrary. The very fact that Fabienne is off limits for me, as I am to her (she's about to be married), allows us to engage in those little games of flirtation that we would both find difficult to play if our co-workers were middle-aged or stiff-jointed old biddies. Still, our office conversations are strictly business. We avoid small talk assiduously. I never confide in her anything about my private life, and she is as circumspect about hers. Anything I may have picked up about her life outside the office has come from the barrage of phone calls she makes, day in and day out, to her fiancé, some scraps of which I can't help overhearing.

This morning there appears to be a minor drama. Her boyfriend calls a few minutes after she has arrived. She answers him somewhat testily, saying that it's hardly the proper hour to start calling; yes, she's fine; no, he shouldn't worry, she was simply a little upset this morning, but right now she's very busy and he's monopolizing the phone. She hangs up with a broad smile in my direction, which is a signal for me to turn back to my typing, which I had halted so as not to make it hard for her to talk on the phone.

Martine, also a real beauty, arrives at that point, wearing a new coat that Fabienne finds stunning, really stunning. Gerard enters as if borne by the wind and puts an end to the idle chatter. Martine, a steno pad at the ready, follows him into his office.

At one o'clock both girls take a break from their work and go down for a bite. Gerard, who lives only a few blocks away, goes home for lunch. I hang on until two, to avoid the lunchtime crowds. Anyway, I generally don't eat a big lunch, but go down between two and three for a salad in the local pub. I generally avoid business lunches, unless I can't get out of one, and try to make all my appointments late in the afternoon.

I'm seated at a café terrace on the Place Saint-Augustin, having a salad, when a former classmate of mine strolls by, someone I run into now and then. He works in the area—some sort of press attaché, if memory serves. He sees me and comes over to say hello. I invite him to join me.

"I ran into Gerard the other day," he says. "I gather you're really doing well."

"Yes, almost too well. We're probably going to have to expand. Which means bureaucracy will inevitably rear its ugly head. Now I can still work when and how I want; for instance, waiting to have my lunch until everyone else is back in his office."

"Don't worry, I'm a nine-to-fiver," he says. "My office has all sorts of rules and regulations, but that doesn't mean I have to follow them. You think you're the only one who can dictate his hours, but there are thousands like you. Just look around."

I glance up and down the street. "Looks to me as though the street is filled with women and the over-sixty-five crowd."

"What about all those guys with briefcases?"

"That one's a salesman."

"And that other guy is clearly a lawyer . . ."

"Or a teacher . . . or maybe a spy. Anyway, I find the crowd reassuring. I like to see the streets full at any hour of the day or night. That's one of Paris's great charms. If you doubt me, check out some provincial town at three or four in the afternoon. Nothing more sinister in the world, I guarantee. Suburbs, the same thing."

"It sounds as through you suffer what I call 'afternoon syndrome.' I've got a bad case myself. Even in Paris, I only feel safe after I reached the cape of four P.M. That's probably a direct result of our stupid habit of luncheons."

"That's why I don't have luncheons," I say. "I keep my anxiety in check by running errands in the afternoon."

I walk through the aisles of a big department store. Women, women everywhere, mostly very elegant. I pause at a counter displaying shirts, look them over, but don't buy any.

I emerge from the store and stroll up the boulevard Haussmann. I pause in front of the window of a men's clothing shop, then decide to go in.

I try on a dark-blue shirt, which the salesman tells me fits me perfectly. I look at myself in the mirror, obviously not very convinced.

"How about the green one over there?" he says. "Do you like it?"

"No, not at all."

"This one goes very well with your complexion."

"True, but it's not exactly what I was looking for."

"What don't you like about it?"

"Nothing. I just don't like it enough to buy it. I know blue's my color, but I need a change . . ."

"Then take the green!"

"It's not right for me . . . I'll think about it . . ."

I go into another store and ask to try on a turtleneck sweater. An absolutely stunning girl, whom I assume to be the salesgirl but who on closer inspection has to be the owner, says that all she has in my size is white, and a beige she doesn't like herself, so she can't recommend either. She looks me straight in the eye, then adds, "Why don't you drop by next week sometime."

Just as I'm about to leave, she reaches behind her and pulls out a sweater, which she hands to me.

"See, it's really not very handsome, and I don't think it's your style."

Then, seeing my eyes wander over several of the shelves, she says, "The sweaters over there are not your size, and that shelf you're looking at is shirts."

Without consulting me, she spreads out a whole rainbow of the shirts on the counter.

"Now here are some colors that I think you might like," she says. "Especially this one."

She deftly slips a shirt from its cellophane envelope, removes the pins, and holds it up against my chest. "It's perfect for you. It brings out the color of your eyes. Why don't you try it on and see for yourself."

"But I don't want a knit shirt."

"So what? Why don't you try it on anyway? If you don't like it, you don't have to buy it."

"But . . . I warn you, I'm not *going* to buy it."

"Try it on anyway, just to satisfy my curiosity, if not yours."

I finally yield, and go into the dressing room. The truth is, it looks terrific on me. I have a feeling that it was made for me and tailored to my exact measurements. I check the price and see that even that doesn't give me an out: it's quite reasonable. I pull the curtain aside and look at the saleslady questioningly, trying to think of some defect I can dream up.

"The collar doesn't fit just right," I venture timidly.

She bursts out laughing. "You must have forgotten to take out the last pin!"

She comes over, takes out the pin, pulls the shirt down a little in back, and gently caresses the material.

"It's a terrific buy," she says. "Pure cashmere. Soft, light, and you don't have to iron it."

"I'll take it," I say.

The clock on the Saint-Lazare station is striking six. From the neighboring streets and the nearby subway exits crowds of people hurry toward the station, climb the stairways, and spill out onto the station platforms.

Six-thirty. I'm still in my office, in conference with a business associate. Fabienne knocks and opens the door slightly. She has her coat on.

"You don't need me anymore?"

"No, thank you. See you tomorrow."

As soon as I open the front door, Ariane, who has heard me arrive, calls out to me. I go into her room, where her mother is just tucking her in for the night. Helen notices the package I'm carrying.

"Let me guess," she says. "It's a sweater."

"Close," I say. "It's a knit shirt. I'm afraid I let myself be talked into it. Let me try it on and see what you think."

I go into the bedroom and my eyes light on a shopping bag from the same store I had gone into earlier that afternoon. While I'm trying on the shirt, I call out to Helen, "Hey, I didn't know you'd gone into town. What time were you in the store? We could have run into each other. Strange, we never seem to."

Helen loves the shirt, feeling its soft texture with her hands, then rubbing her cheek against it, while my lips gently caress her hair. Then she says, "I just got home a little while ago myself, and I'm afraid dinner is going to be late."

We both go into the kitchen, and I help her peel the potatoes.

"You make me feel better," I say. "I was afraid that I'd been had."

"I never thought you were so easily influenced."

"Yes, but the saleslady was very clever. She made me feel that she didn't give a damn whether I bought the thing or not. Actually, the minute I laid eyes on it, I knew it was for me. That almost never happens with me."

I'm in my office. Fabienne opens the door.

"I have a lunch date. Do you mind if I leave at twelve-thirty?"

I tell her that's fine with me, and she adds, "By the way, I didn't think I've told you yet, but I'm going to get married, probably this summer."

I congratulate her and ask her if she intends to quit her job after her marriage.

"No, I'd like to stay on, if that's all right with you. My fiancé works for his father and I could go work for him, but I'd prefer not to. He also doesn't think it's a good idea. Actually, I won't have to work once I'm married. He'd be happy to have me stay home, but I find that prospect dull. I prefer to work, even if my earnings are only enough to pay for a maid."

We've invited friends of Helen's to dinner, Mr. and Mrs. M., both of whom are teachers in Nanterre. The conversation turns to the question of couples who work together.

"Actually," says Mr. M., "the fact that my wife and I both teach in the same school doesn't really bring us closer together. Agnes is a math teacher, and I teach literature. Opposite ends of the spectrum. Total lack of communication. In a way, I suspect your work and Helen's are more compatible than ours."

Helen and I both burst out laughing.

"Helen hasn't the foggiest notion of what I do."

"And Frederic doesn't even know the title of my thesis."

"That may be," I say, "but your profession is directly responsible for my studying English again, and half the books I read these days are in English."

Gerard and I are in my office discussing a business matter with someone who is both a friend and a business associate. We've finished our agenda, and I ask them if they would like a cup of tea. Fabienne comes in with the cups.

We are on the subject of boring business receptions.

"What irritates me most about these receptions," says Gerard, "is all these guys who feel they have to drag their wife to it. It's as though they didn't get enough of cultivating their marital boredom at home, and they have to parade it out in the big world. What's more, a lot of these women have professions of their own. My wife's a doctor, and Frederic's is a teacher, so they both have their own professional obligations, without our having to impose ours on them."

Martine comes in with the teapot. Gerard asks her if she would like to go with him to the reception he had been referring to. She doesn't seem to take his invitation very seriously.

"I see," he says, "you have to check with your fiancé first . . . Ah, you've broken up with him! Do you have another one yet? . . . These girls are always a problem. They're always 'about to be married'! And, well, when you have a fiancé, there's no way you're going out with another man . . . Now, take my wife and me: we almost never go out together. The fact that I love her, and that I'm virtually faithful to her, doesn't mean that I can't appreciate the company of a pretty girl. And I can't picture myself accepting some boring invitation to one of these receptions unless there was some hope that I might meet some pretty girl there. That's the least one can ask of these dumb evenings."

I'm walking in the street, through crowds of women. I sit down at a café terrace and watch the women passing by.

If there is one thing I am no longer capable of, it's doing the whole seduction number with a girl. I can't imagine what I would find to say to her, or even if I would be able to dream up a reason for talking to her in the first place. I don't want *anything* from her, and if it comes down to that, I wouldn't even want to proposition her.

Yet I feel that marriage is hemming me in, as though I'm living in a cloister, and there are times I feel like running away. The prospect of peace and happiness stretching far into the future ultimately depresses me. I find myself looking back on the not-too-distant past, when I was assailed by the doubts and torments of uncertainty, the awful feeling of not being sure. I dream of a life filled with loves that are just beginning—and loves that will last forever. In other words, I dream of the impossible . . .

When I see lovers in close embrace, I think less of myself or of what I was than of them and what they will become. That's why I like big cities so much: people come into your life and then disappear, and you never see them grow old. What makes the Parisian streets so fascinating to me is the constant, fleeting presence of these women you see going by at every hour of the day or night, and whom you are almost certain you will never see again. It's the simple fact that they are there, indifferent, conscious of their charm, satisfied to check it out and see whether it works on me, as I am constantly doing with them, as though there were some sort of tacit agreement between us, often without so much as a smile or even a glance. I deeply react to their seductive powers without actually being seduced. I add that none of this in any way affects my relations with Helen. Quite the contrary . . .

I tell myself that these women passing by necessarily prolong my wife's loveliness. They enrich her through their own beauty and in return receive some parcel of hers. Her beauty is the guarantee of the world's beauty; and vice versa: when I embrace Helen, I embrace all women.

That's one side of the coin. The other is that I feel life passing me by while other lives are unfolding parallel to mine, and I feel frustrated to be a stranger among them, frustrated to not have encountered each of these women, if only for a moment, stopping her in her rush toward God knows what work, or what pleasure.

And I dream: I dream that I possess them all. For several months now I have had the same recurring daydream, which grows clearer and clearer as time goes on. A childish dream, probably inspired by something I read when I was ten years old: I imagine that I am the proud possessor of a little machine that you hang around your neck and that emits a magnetic fluid capable of annihilating other people's will.

Still watching the women walking past the café terrace where I sit, I put my machine to work.

The *first woman* is sauntering by. I accost her a trifle ceremoniously.

I: Excuse me, ma'am. Do you mind if I ask whether you're in a great hurry?

She: Frankly, I'm not.

I: Do you have an hour to spare?

She: If you want the truth, yes.

I: Would you enjoy spending it with me?

She: I'm not quite sure.

I: Let's give it a whirl. That way you will know for sure.

She: That's true, I will. Excellent idea.

The *second woman* seems as though she's not sure of her way. I smile at her; she smiles back.

I: Ma'am, I'd like to kiss you.

She: Me, too! (She throws her arms around my neck.)

I: And what if your husband were to see you?

She: He's not here, is he? Shall we go up to my place?

The *third woman* is walking her dog. I approach her by a circuitous route and slip my arm around her waist. She lifts her head and gazes at me ecstatically.

I: With you, I see I don't even have to waste a word.

She: Your eyes say it all!

I hail a taxi.

The *fourth* is standing in a classic pose on the sidewalk, apparently waiting to pick up a client.

I: Excuse me, miss, are you a professional?

She: Twenty is the going rate.

I: Sorry, I charge fifty.

She: You look as though you're worth every penny.

And she takes out her checkbook and writes me a check.

The *fifth* woman is walking with a boyfriend. I ignore him and go up to her.

I: Hello there!

He: What the hell do you want?

I: I wasn't talking to you.

He (taken aback): Oh, I see. (He steps aside.)

I (to the girl): How about joining me?

She: You see I'm with him.

I: Send him packing.

She: What will he say?

I: Let me take care of that. (To the boyfriend): You don't mind my taking your girl, do you?

He: If you want an honest answer, no.

I: Really, which do you prefer? That I take her . . . or that I beat the hell out of you? (And I flex my muscles, and grit my teeth.)

He (hurrying off): Okay, okay, if you put it that way.

The *sixth* is running across the street. I grab her arm. She spins around, furious.

I: How about having a drink with me?

She: No.

I: Why not?

She: I'm on my way to see somebody.

I: I . . . uh . . .

She: Stop stuttering! Anyway, you're rude, crude, and un-attractive. I have a boyfriend, and he loves me as much as I love him. So buzz off!

Wondering what has happened, I look down at my little machine. No, it seems to be functioning perfectly . . .

Part One

Such was my frame of mind when Chloe came to see me. I can't honestly say whether or not I was happy to see her again. She reminded me of a time in my life that I considered dead and gone. I had known her when I was engaged to a girl named Milena, in a relationship that was complex and stormy, and with whom I broke up just before I met Helen. At the time, Chloe had been living in just as stormy a relationship with a friend of mine named Bruno, who today is married and whom I have virtually lost touch with. I knew that Bruno was wildly in love with Chloe, and she cheated on him left and right, to the point where one day he tried to commit suicide. He was saved, and thereafter I did my best to detach him from Chloe. She was well aware of my efforts, and I had every reason to believe she was not overly fond of me, although on the surface our relationship was very cordial.

I had always had trouble trying to situate Chloe—intellectually, morally, and socially. Although she had little education, she was highly intuitive, and many of her observations and judgments were surprisingly astute. In many respects vulgar, she also had good taste in many areas. She had no set of standards that I was ever able to detect, and I have seen her in many situations in which she was extraordinarily kind and generous and in many others in which she was unrelentingly nasty. Bruno had spent money on her as though there were no tomorrow, and by the time they broke up, he was virtually destitute. In all fairness, however, I can't really blame her for that, for gold-digging was not among her vices. She enjoyed twisting men around her finger, and whenever she did extract money from a man, I noted that she never gave anything in return. When I knew her, she was a salesgirl in a boutique on the rue de Sèvres. But it wasn't long before she lost that job, and thereafter she seemed to hang around in nightclubs, apparently sponging off first one person and then another for lodging. The next thing I knew, she was a fashion model, and doing quite well, but that, too, aborted before long. I saw her several times after that, always with a different man to whom she was "about to be married," and the next thing I knew she had run off to California with a young American painter, which was the last I had heard of her.

One day, as I come back to my office about four, as usual, Fabienne informs me that someone is waiting for me, a young woman who wants to discuss something personally with me, all of which arouses my interest. I open the door and at first do not recognize Chloe, who is sitting with the light behind her. She sees that I don't, and is upset. I do my best to smooth things over, but she obviously feels slighted, saying something to the effect that why should she have expected me to remember her after so many years. Besides, she was only passing by, and when I receive a phone call announcing that my next appointment is here, she gets up to leave.

I tell her not to be foolish. Of course I have a few minutes for her, that I'm curious about how she managed to find me. She says she happened to run into an old friend of Bruno's and he gave her my address. Since she was only a block or so away, she thought it only normal that she stop by to say hello, and is only sorry to have picked such a busy moment. Her apology is so sincere and so sweet that I'm sorry I didn't greet her more warmly. To try to repair things, I ask her what she's up to. It turns out she's a barmaid at a nightclub in Saint-Germain-des-Prés while waiting for something better to come along.

The only time she's ever free, she tells me, is in the afternoon. As I escort her out of my office, Fabienne having announced the arrival of my next appointment, I say, in an effort to be polite, "Afternoon is sometimes good for me, too. Give me a call someday, and let's have a drink together." I don't really believe she'll take me at my word.

. . .

Lo and behold, the following week she does call when I'm out of the office and asks me to call her back at such and such a number. I don't, but when she calls again, I take it. She would like to see me as soon as possible. Can she come by right now? I tell her it's out of the question, and make an appointment with her for two the next day.

She arrives ahead of time, while I'm still finishing up a letter, and wastes no time getting to the point. She's looking for a job. Couldn't I take her on as a secretary?

"Not here," I tell her. "Those we have don't seem to have any intention of leaving. Besides, we need qualified people."

"But I am qualified," she exclaims, heading for the typewriter as if to prove it on the spot. "I spent a year in the States working as a secretary."

"Can you handle accounting?"

"No, but I can learn."

She begins to laugh, amused by my obvious effort to put her off. Don't worry, she says, she's not in a hurry.

"Anyway," she adds, "I'm a big girl. I can take care of myself. I'm not going to put the bite on you."

She gets up to leave, saying that no matter what, she likes me, has always liked me, even though we didn't always see eye to eye. If I didn't remember, too bad for me; she did. I reply by saying that my feelings toward her were, as she knew, colored by what she had done to Bruno. And she doubtless also knew that I had done everything in my power to convince Bruno she didn't deserve him.

"And you were right," she says. "I was all wrong for him." Then, "Don't stand there trying to look so tough. You couldn't be a bastard if you tried."

Her flattery, cleverly enveloped in irony, succeeds in disarming me so completely that instead of cutting our conversation short I ask her whether she'd like to have a drink downstairs with me, for old time's sake.

We go to a little bistro nearby, where she fills me in on the details of her life since she's returned to Paris. She's living with a man named Serge, who's a business associate of the man who owns the Agamemnon, the nightclub where she works. He's only a friend. She doesn't love him, she's with him for want of someone better, and intends to pack up and leave at the first opportunity. The nightclub, too. She asks me all about my life, about my wife and how we live, and I tell her, among other things, that my wife is pregnant. Our second, I add. Oh, no, I hasten to reassure her, I didn't marry Milena. I lead a very quiet life, a far cry from the old days when I was a night owl. She's all for it; she only wishes she had the same kind of quiet life herself. She finds her present life a drag. The work is exhausting, the nightclub seedy. The only thing is, of course, she earns a lot more money there than she could as a salesgirl or receptionist, but nonetheless she intends to leave as soon as she can. And never look back.

One swallow does not a summer make: we need to buy a new bed for Ariane, and I meet Helen and Ariane in a department store to pick it out. By now Helen is showing. Ariane's old bed will be for the new baby. As we're leaving the store, we run into Chloe. Seeing or sensing my embarrassment, she introduces herself as an old friend of mine and Bruno's. She congratulates us both on our marriage, makes a huge fuss over Ariane, and leaves with a big smile.

"Is she Bruno's old flame?" Helen asks. "You always described her as a bitch. She seems very nice."

Six o'clock. I'm still at the office. Chloe calls to tell me she's a block or two away and can she drop by for a minute. When she arrives a few minutes later, she's carrying presents for both the new baby and Ariane, a sweet little apron for the latter. I tell her she shouldn't have gone to the trouble. She replies that she loved doing it; she adores children, and also giving presents, so the combination was irresistible.

"By the way, congratulations on your choice of a wife. She seems terrific! Just don't ever let me catch you playing around!"

I tell her I'm the most faithful man in town, and don't intend to change. She's delighted to hear it, but in a teasing tone she can't help adding that for a husband as much in love as I claim to be I have one of the worst cases of roving eye she's ever seen. Anything in skirts, so it seems. She knows she's touched a vulnerable nerve.

"You're right," I say. "When I was with Milena, I never looked at another girl. I was a slave to that woman. But now, with Helen, who is as sure of me as I am of her, I see no reason not to enjoy the prettier sights in town. As they say, it's only looking, and that can't hurt you. Besides, I don't feel I have to justify what I think or do, or whom I look at, to Helen, and she feels the same way."

But Chloe will have none of it.

"If you want my two cents," she says, "I see it as your way of preparing some pleasant backup situation. Oh, maybe not right now, but whenever the day arrives when your darling little wife becomes boring or dumpy or simply no longer turns you on."

I take the bait and, as I tidy up my desk prior to leaving the office, explain to her exactly how I see things. Locking the doors—first mine, then that of the outside office—I tell her that freedom is the value I prize most highly. I could have gone to work in a big company for lots more money, but I decided not to. We're struggling, and I can't deny it's hard. For Helen as well as me. She's teaching full-time and trying to write her thesis, which she plans to work on during her maternity leave. As we walk downstairs, Chloe chuckles and says, "I'll bet your new baby comes into the world wearing horn-rimmed glasses."

When I arrive home, I show Helen the presents, and, much to my surprise, she's delighted by them. She even goes so far as to suggest inviting Chloe to dinner. I say that we couldn't if we wanted to, since she works in the evening, and anyway, I'm not sure I want to. I see no reason to go out of our way to be nice to her. I want to reassure Helen, in case she has any doubts, about my former relations with Chloe, and I adopt a tone of condescension and even pity when I refer to Bruno's "ex-mistress."

I hear nothing from Chloe for the next several days. I figure that, having satisfied her curiosity about what had become of me, she has moved on to other, more interesting concerns. I feel slightly relieved, and also slightly resentful.

But then, much to my surprise, I arrive at the office one morning to find her perched in the waiting room, a suitcase at her feet. She looks as though she hasn't slept all night. She tells me that she has walked out on Serge. He doesn't even know; he was still asleep.

"I couldn't fall asleep last night," she says. "I kept tossing and turning, and all I could think was, 'What am I doing in this guy's bed?' I feel he's a complete stranger. So I snuck out of bed, packed my things, and here I am. Do you think I'm crazy?"

"If you were going to leave," I respond, "the sooner the better, I always say."

She doesn't know where she's going to stay, and wants to know if I can put her up, at least temporarily. I tell her we don't have the room.

"But where will you put the baby?"

"In with its sister. Or, if we hire a nurse, we'll have to clean out the place we now use as a storeroom."

"I can repaint it, without any help," she suggests. "Or maybe I can bring in a few friends to help me. And when the baby comes, I'd love to take care of it. I love babies. And you won't have to pay me. I'll do it in exchange for room and board. Think how much money you'll save."

She laughs as she sees my face grow more and more concerned, and says she was only fooling: someone has put her on to a room in Montmartre.

"And as for working, I can wait awhile," she says, pulling a roll of bills from her pocketbook, explaining she hasn't yet had time to get to the bank.

She asks me if I could take a few minutes out of my busy day to go with her to look at the room. Since it's a sublet, she'd prefer to have a witness to whatever transactions take place. I tell her I'll be happy to go right now, if she can only give me a few minutes to rearrange my calendar a bit. I dictate a couple of letters, give instructions to Fabienne, and, as we leave, introduce Chloe to Gerard.

On our way downstairs, Chloe launches into a tirade against bureaucrats, a tirade that goes on until we've found a taxi several minutes later. "An artificial and useless race," she says of them. "Without exception."

"Whenever I go into an office," she says, "I have a feeling of entering some never-never land. People rushing about. For nothing. If every office in the world were closed down, we'd never notice the loss. Pencil-pushing, and paper-shuffling— that's all offices ever produce."

"And when you serve your customers in a nightclub," I respond, "does that strike you as especially creative?"

"I'm giving them pleasure."

We arrive at the address. The room is small and very dark. The landlady, at first taking us for a couple, says she doesn't think the room would be suitable. "There's only a single bed," she protests, which provokes gales of laughter from Chloe.

Sensing that Chloe is keeping up a good front but really fighting off depression, I invited her to lunch at a restaurant not far away. During lunch she confides in me further, confessing that she's been very down, in fact during the past few weeks has even thought of killing herself.

"I'd like to," she says, "but I'm too much of a coward. If all we had to do was lift our little finger to return to the great void, half the people in the world would do it. Maybe everybody. What is there to live for? If people aren't satisfied or happy with their lives, it would be more logical to end them. But we don't. And why? Out of fear or cowardice . . . While I was with Serge, it would have been relatively easy. All I would have had to do was open the gas jet. I was tempted to, more than once, and that was one of the reasons I wanted to get out of there . . . I don't expect anything out of life. Love? I no longer believe in it, assuming I ever did. The only bond between Serge and me was pity. Mutual pity. He was a little crazy, and so am I." She nods at two middle-aged ladies at a nearby table. "Is that what I have to look forward to?" she says. "To end up like those two biddies over there? No, thanks."

"But you won't be like them."

"I'll be worse. I'll be a bum."

"Unlike you," I say, "I find it comforting to observe other people's lives. There are, of course, lives that are happy and others that are sad, but none to my mind is ugly or degrading. The only thing that would make me contemplate suicide is if all lives were identical. It's their variety that makes it so stimulating."

"All people are ugly, and they lead ugly lives. The only exceptions to the rule, in my book, are children. Too bad if later on they become ugly, too. They'll always have had their childhood to look back on. The only thread that binds me to life is the hope of one day having a child. But I'd want it all for myself. I wouldn't even let the father see it."

She also says that she's made up her mind never to live with a man again. If she has a lover, they'll have separate apartments. The days of giving a man permanent access to her bed are gone.

"But I must be boring you out of your mind with all this drivel! Please forgive me. I can't tell you how wonderful it is, though, for me to have someone to talk to like this. Even if you don't agree with a word I say, it's such a help just to be able to talk."

I find myself moved by her confessions. I take her hands tenderly in mine, and kiss her lightly on the side of the forehead. She nestles catlike against my shoulder.

"It's a two-way street," I say. "Listening to your very real worries helps deliver me from my imaginary ones. I know it doesn't make any sense, but one day I'll explain it to you."

Before she leaves, she asks me if I can help her in the next day or two to pick up the belongings she didn't have time to pack when she left Serge's. I have a moment's hesitation, but finally say I'd be happy to.

In order to avoid any unpleasantness, Chloe waits until Serge has left town on a business trip. "Just to make sure my information is accurate," she says, "would you mind calling the club and asking for him." Since she still senses that I'm not wildly happy at the prospect of breaking into Serge's room, she adds, "It's my room as much as his. And I still have the key."

Despite my reluctance, I have to confess that the idea intrigues me, and I can already picture myself as a detective novel's hero on a touch assignment. The plot thickens when we discover, as we arrive there, that the room is secured with a padlock. Chloe loses her temper and begins to pound and kick the door, so loudly that I'm afraid everyone in the building will be up in arms. Fear of scandal propels me to new heights of ingenuity. With my trusty boy-scout knife I attack the hinge screws, and in less time than it takes to tell, the door is open. Chloe moves about, picking up everything that is hers, leaving nothing behind, including several photos of her on the wall, which I help to remove.

In the taxi Chloe throws her arms around my neck and kisses me, laughing.

"I'd give my right arm to see Serge's face when he gets back," she says. "I love you," she says, hugging me again. "You really saved my life."

. . .

When I am finally alone, my euphoria melts like the April snow. I am suddenly reminded of Chloe's past, and am terribly afraid she might take advantage of my obliging nature, even if she doesn't want to hurt anyone. I make up my mind to see her less frequently, for now that she is free of Serge, why should I think she won't show up every afternoon in my office? Yet, to my surprise, the exact opposite happens. I don't hear from her for a week, and my initial fear of having her on my back slowly gives way to the somewhat disagreeable sensation of having been used by her like an old rag: thrown away after use.

And then one day she appears in my office, unannounced. I conceal my pleasure in seeing her by speaking in a tone two or three degrees rougher than usual. She apologizes for having dropped out of sight, but she had heard of a decent job and had been tracking it down; besides, she didn't want to trouble me further with the long litany of her misfortunes. Now she could reappear with her head held high: she has landed a job as a waitress in a restaurant. She'd started the day before. It is a lot better than the club. The only problem is, she no longer has the whole afternoon free, only from four to seven. When I don't seem to be overwhelmed by the status of the new job, she explains to me that it's a high-class place, where she'll rake in fat tips and meet much more interesting people than she ever did at the Agamemnon. "People with good positions," she adds, "who may be able to help me. Not all those penniless creeps who used to hang out at the club."

The fact that our respective jobs make it more complicated to see each other now makes our meetings all the more precious.

Chloe is never quite sure when she'll be free, since the clients at her restaurant are often businessmen who linger. And, for my part, I can't change my normal timetable, for people have grown used to my making appointments late in the afternoon.

My conversations with Chloe no longer seem like the burden I once feared they might be; on the contrary, they come as invigorating breaks in my business day. With Chloe I feel oddly at ease. I confide in her as I have never confided in anyone, even my most secret thoughts. Thus, instead of repressing my fantasies, as I used to do, I have learned to bring them out into the light of day and to free myself from them.

I have never been as open with anyone, least of all with the women in my life, with whom I always thought I had to put up a good front, to wear the mask I thought they wanted to see. Helen's seriousness and intellectual prowess have led me gradually to keep our conversations on a superficial level. She likes my wit, and a kind of mutual modesty has grown between us, a tacit understanding to refrain from discussing anything we feel really deeply about. Probably it's better that way. This role I play, if indeed it is a role, is in any case more pleasant and less stiff than the one I played when I was going with Milena. I suspect that an element of mystery is indispensable between two people who live together.

Out of respect for Helen, I carefully refrain from saying anything in front of Chloe that might be construed as disparaging to her, and in fact go out of my way to paint her as a woman endowed with every grace and virtue under the sun. This constant praise has finally got under Chloe's skin.

"I can't believe you sometimes," she finally bursts out. "You seem to feel you always have to prove that you love your wife. For God's sake, if you don't love her, or if you love her less than you did at first, that doesn't mean the world's coming to an end. It's only normal. Just as normal as it is not to be chained down to one person your whole life. Nobody really believes in the concept of marriage anymore."

"I don't love my wife because she's my wife but because she's the way she is. I'd love her even if we weren't married."

"No, you love her—*if* you love her—because you think you have to. Speaking for myself, I wouldn't stand for anybody loving me the way you love Helen. But then, I'm the exception that proves the rule. Since you're a bourgeois, follow your own staid, middle-class rules: hang on to your wife, but find yourself a mistress. Think of it as a safety valve: it'll be good for you, assuming you do it in moderation. Not a bad idea, don't you agree?"

Our meetings became more and more frequent, but now, circumstances have forced us not to get together for more than a week. I am completely snowed with work, and the following week looks to be just as bad. What is worse, I am going to have to spend all day Wednesday out of the office, to see some government official, and that is the only day she has free all week, because the restaurant is closed.

"If you're not free in the afternoon, why don't we spend the evening together," she suggests. "You can tell your wife you have to attend one of those cocktail parties you were talking about."

I reply that I would be ashamed to lie to my wife that way; and, what is more, it would have a serious effect on the purity of our relationship. Chloe laughs with obvious scorn, but then, doubtless fearing that if she argues further she'd only strengthen me in my resolve, she takes a whole other tack.

"Actually," she says, "I only wanted to ask you a favor. Some guy I know has offered to introduce me to an important businessman who owns a string of clothing stores, and I might be able to find a job there through him. The only problem is, I strongly suspect that this guy has his own reasons for introducing me. So if you show up with me, he'll see that it's not as easy as he might think. Besides, I'd really like to get your reaction to him. I can't believe you'll like him."

"Who is he?"

"I met him at the restaurant."

"You never talked to me about him."

"Why should I have? He's not that interesting. I meet new people every day. This guy is on the handsome side, and he knows it. He claims to have seduced every pretty girl in town, and he swears I'm next on his list."

"Are you?"

"Not on your life! But I'll make him sweat a bit before he finds out. Are you jealous?"

"Me? Why should I be jealous? But I don't have a very strong feeling you really mean what you say about him. You sound like a fifteen-year-old."

"Well, I'm not. When any man comes after me, even if he doesn't stand a chance, I can't say it leaves me cold. One more reason why you ought to come with me on Wednesday. I can't wait to see what you think of Gian Carlo, and to see how he reacts when we show up together . . ."

Evening. I'm reading while Helen is working on her thesis. She has boxes of notes, and she carefully studies her file cards, jotting down what she needs, now and again lifting her head to stare into space, lost in thought. Her gaze never once is turned in my direction.

"Okay, that's enough for one day," she says finally. "One has to know when to stop. In my condition, I think it's a good

245

idea to finish up my work in the afternoon and go to bed early. If you don't mind, I think I'll go to bed and read."

"Not at all," I say. "By the way, next Wednesday I have a cocktail party I really ought to attend. Do you want to come with me?"

"Are you crazy? But please go if you feel you should. I'll take advantage of it to go to bed even earlier than I had planned. I need all the sleep I can get."

The following Wednesday, Gerard and I leave the government offices at six o'clock and grab a taxi back to the office. The secretaries have left. There is a message for me: "Chloe called. She says to tell you she's sorry but she won't be able to come this evening." I have trouble concealing my disappointment in front of Gerard. I go into my office, close the door, and dial Chloe's landlady.

"No, I'm sorry, she's not here," she tells me. "In fact, she hasn't slept here for the past three days—that, I can tell you."

When I arrive home, Helen is already in bed. I explain to her that the more I thought about it, the less I thought of going to that cocktail party.

"Why didn't you call me?" she says. "I didn't prepare anything for dinner."

"I didn't want to keep you up, since I knew you wanted to go to bed early. Go to sleep. I'll fend for myself. Don't worry . . ."

Having finished dinner, since it's still too early to go to bed, I go into the living room, planning to read for a while. But I have trouble concentrating. Nor do I feel sleepy, as the hours tick by. Finally I fall asleep in my chair, and Helen finds me there the next morning.

"What happened to you?"

I stammer that I couldn't put down the book I was reading and that I must have fallen asleep.

All the next day—in the train, the office—I find myself nervous and distraught. I feel as though I'm liable to lash out against anyone, under any pretense. What irritates me most is that Chloe doesn't seem to care about my self-imposed role as platonic confidant. She treats me exactly as she would have a lover and thereby forces me to react jealously.

A few days later I receive a postcard from Italy, which says, "Sorrento. March 10. I've gone away for a short vacation. See you soon. Chloe."

Part Two

Our child was born on March 17. It was a boy. We could tell almost from the first day that he wasn't going to be an easy child, and Ariane, who was, began to react to her brother's arrival by becoming difficult herself. Helen was at the end of her rope. I suggested that she prolong her maternity leave, which was due to end when school reopened after the Easter vacation, but she said she really wanted to get back. So I told her that although it might strain our budget slightly, I was going to hire a mother's helper.

I allowed Helen, of course, to choose the girl, and expected an ugly duckling to arrive. But to my surprise the English girl she hired was lovely and willowy. At any other time in my life I might have feared her presence would prove upsetting to me, but this was prevented by the dual factors of Helen's presence and Chloe's absence. Chloe's effect on me was such that when I thought of her, her memory made any thought of another girl impossible. In the course of the previous months Chloe had succeeded in demystifying all women for me, both physically and morally, and I couldn't work up any curiosity about the soul or psyche of our English visitor, or even any interest in her lovely body, which she did not hesitate to parade for all eyes to see, rushing naked from the bathroom to the baby's room every time the child began to whimper.

Finally, a few days after Easter, Chloe reappears. I try to enumerate coldly and unemotionally my list of complaints, but I cannot pull it off as I had planned.

"I don't understand why you're so upset," she says. "I did call you. Would you have preferred that I spell it out, that I told you I was going with Gian Carlo? I thought you would have guessed, after what I told you."

She's very pleased with herself. Too often had she let herself be taken advantage of by this kind of fellow. Someday, she had sworn, she would get her revenge. Well, she had got it, in spades. She succeeded in making him fall madly in love with her; then she took off with an English student she'd met, a real Adonis, but really too young, and then she dropped him after a few days.

"So there's my tale. Vacation time is over. But before I left I quit my job and that awful room I was living in. For the moment, I'm sponging off some friends I met in Italy, who drove me back to Paris. I still have a little money left, so I have time to look around."

Slightly tanned and obviously relaxed, having replaced her eternal blue jeans with a rather elegant outfit, Chloe has never looked more beautiful, and I cannot help comparing her to Helen, to my wife's disadvantage. And I am ashamed at the thought, realizing that the poor dear is barely out of the maternity ward. Still, I feel more comfortable and natural with Chloe, if that is possible, than I did before she left for Italy.

At home, on the contrary, I find myself artificial. The birth of the boy, the arrival of the mother's helper, my wife's creased brow, as though she were bearing the weight of the world, make me feel all too strongly that I am indeed a father. I play my role, and watch myself playing it. To amuse the children, and also to cheer up Helen, I suspect, I resort to all kinds of silly games and antics, making a complete fool of myself.

With Chloe, too, I am both spectator and narrator, for she hounds me with questions about my new son and how it feels to be a father. This is the happiness aspect of it all: the pleasure of living my life on the one hand and relating it on the other. Not that I am unaware of the duplicity involved, but I confess that it does not bother me in the least. And yet there are times—when I catch a glimpse in the mirror of us, Chloe and me, as a couple— I am shocked, as I know Helen would be shocked if she were to happen upon us unexpectedly. And I wonder how Helen would react if she were to see us shopping together, with me—whom she never consulted about her wardrobe—giving advice to Chloe about this or that skirt or dress.

. . .

Then Chloe begins to sink into a deep depression. Her money is running out. She can't find any work. One day when walking together in the center of town, she begins to bitch about the noise, the crowded streets, and then says that she's wasting her time, and wasting mine, too. I suggest we sit down and have a drink. She refuses. She wants to go home, hails a taxi, and dashes out into the street. I run after her, grab her by the arm, and hold her, and as the cars whiz past us, she breaks into tears and follows me meekly back to the sidewalk and thence to a garden bench.

There, on the bench, she throws herself into my arms. Her eyes are still moist.

"You see," she says, "you're the only reason I have for going on. Without you, I would already have killed myself a hundred times."

"Don't say that!"

"But it's true. Why isn't everybody like you? They're all a bunch of lousy bastards!"

"I'm nice with you because our relationship is platonic. But don't take me for a softy: in business I'm tough as nails."

She looks up, bursts out laughing, and then takes my head in her hands and covers my face with kisses. She pulls back, puts her arms around my neck, and offers me her lips. I kiss her, in a long and sensuous embrace. Then, running my fingers gently through her hair, "Listen, Chloe . . ."

But no sooner have I opened my mouth than she takes my hand and says, "Let's go for a walk, okay? No more talk."

. . .

I overhear Fabienne talking with some client on the phone. I'm only half listening, but something she says makes me prick up my ears. Some boutique is looking for a salesgirl.

"I'm sorry for listening to your conversation," I say, "but don't you think Chloe might be good for that job?"

She was hired the next day. The store is near the Madeleine, a scant five minutes' walk from my office. In addition to the owner, two salesgirls work at the boutique. Chloe comes in at twelve and stays till eight. The other girl, who opens up, leaves at about six. Neither of them takes a break for lunch, simply sneaking out for a few minutes to the bakery next door for a pastry or a cup of coffee.

But the logistics of our meetings become considerably more complicated. The only day we can conceivably spend any time together is Monday, when the store is closed. Still, since Chloe is pressuring me to stop by and see her, I go over one day at about two o'clock. The other salesgirl takes advantage of the early-afternoon lull to go out for a coffee, leaving us alone. Chloe is happy as a clam: she has the owner wrapped around her finger, the work is pleasant, and, what is more, she's found a room in the same building where the store is. She'll be moving in shortly.

A customer comes in, interrupting our conversation. For fear of embarrassing Chloe, I signal that I'll see her later, but she signals back for me to stay. The customer is asking Chloe a question she really can't answer, but she tells the lady she knows someone who can, so please wait for a minute while she fetches her. She dashes out of the store toward the bakery, and I take refuge in a tiny office filled with fashion magazines, one of which I pick up and leaf through while the customer is on the far side of the store looking at dresses. Assuming I work here, she asks me if she can try one on. "Of course, madam," I say unctuously, gesturing broadly toward the dressing rooms, hoping that Chloe will return in time to see me performing my new functions.

Sunday. I'm taking photos of Helen and Adrian, whom she's holding on her lap.

"That's good! Hold it! Excellent of both of you. Now I want one of you alone."

"But you already have hundreds!"

"But I want some better ones. I don't know whether I'm becoming a better photographer or whether your beauty is increasing constantly, but when I look at some of those wedding pictures of ours, I can't figure out how I ever came to marry you."

"That's exactly how I feel about you!"

I smile; she smiles. Click!

Monday. The store's not open, but Chloe has decided to come in anyway to rearrange some of the shelves and racks. I'm surprised by her interest in her new job, which strikes me as not quite in character.

"You see," she tells me, "the reason for all this zeal is that the boss is leaving shortly for Saint-Jean-de-Luz, where she has another shop. I really want her to be impressed with me, so she'll give me as much responsibility as possible while she's away. You'll see: before long I'll be the manager here."

She opens a box of dresses that has just arrived.

"Isn't this stunning? I think I'll try it on."

She slips off her dress, under which she is wearing a black body stocking, and puts on the new one.

"Not bad, eh? How do you like it?"

"In all fairness," I say, "I've never gone overboard for any dress in my whole life. I've never thought a dress was pretty or ugly in its own right. I must say that this one is stunning on *you*. But it's not the dress I admire; it's the person wearing it. You're beautiful!"

Without saying a word, she takes off the dress and tosses it over her shoulder. She slinks forward and assumes a classic ballet pose, then extends her arms toward me, with her left leg slightly raised. I take a step or two forward and glide between her arms until my body and hers are touching from head to toe. I place my hands on her hips and run them tenderly over their contours, as though to verify their perfection.

"Yes," I say, "you are beautiful."

She lifts her head lovingly to mine. I bend over and move my lips within an inch of hers, still not certain I will actually kiss her. The seconds tick away; I can feel that the spell is broken. Her expression hardens; her smile freezes. I try to say something.

"Listen, Chloe—"

"No, I'm not going to listen," she says, going over and slipping back into her dress. "I know what you're going to say: you're going to ramble on about your wife."

"Wrong," I say. "I'm not thinking of my wife now, but about the friendship we're on the verge of ruining."

She laughs wickedly.

"I don't believe in love," she says. "There's not any friendship between us, neither on your part nor on mine . . ." Then after a brief silence, "Don't you understand that I love you, that I've come to realize over the past few months that I've fallen for you?"

I shrug my shoulders. "I hope not. If I thought that were true, I'd go out that door and not look back. What you want is to have me to yourself. You want me to leave my wife."

"Not necessarily. I'm happy the way things are. It's enough for me to know that I love you and that I've told you so. I have a very fertile imagination, you know. I can even imagine making love with you when I'm with another man."

"You're out of your mind!"

"No. What is crazy, though, is to pretend you love someone when you really don't. I can't love someone just because we live together. So many guys . . . you allow them into your bed and they immediately think they have a pass for life. It's not true, not even if he were the father of my child . . . Did I tell you I desperately want a child?"

"Yes, you did."

"Well, you'll be happy to learn I've found the father."

"Ah?"

"Yes, you!"

She comes over to me and looks at me fixedly.

"Don't laugh; I'm very serious. I have the very firm intention of having a child by you; and, as you know, I always get what I want. I thought it over very carefully. I find no one else I want to father that child. You fulfill all the conditions: you're already married; you're handsome, tall, and not too dumb. And you have blue eyes. I want my child to have blue eyes. I trust you agree that my logic is impeccable. Any questions?"

"And what do you think my wife will say?"

"She doesn't need to know. In fact, even you will never know for sure whether you're the father."

"So what's the point, as far as I'm concerned?

"None, maybe. But I'm more interested in my own concerns than in yours. You think I'm joking? I'm not. My logic is, as I said, irrefutable. You're the one who isn't logical."

At the house, we've invited several friends, including Mr. and Mrs. M., to dinner. Before going in to sit down, we spend a few minutes in the children's room. The mother's helper has just finished giving the baby his bottle, and they all bill and coo over him. Everyone tries to figure out whom he looks like, or which trait comes from the father and which from the mother. In her new dress Helen looks especially pretty. She's in high spirits, and obviously enjoying herself. The general good humor only makes me pensive. My wife finally detects that I'm distracted, and for a moment her face clouds over.

The following Monday, Chloe has already moved into her new lodgings, which are on the top floor of the building. The tiny apartment consists of what used to be three maids' rooms, but the partitions have been knocked down so that the place now consists of a main room, kitchen, and bath. It's really quite pleasant and spacious. With considerable ingenuity, using a few shelves and stools and boxes, most of them taken from the boutique storeroom, Chloe has fashioned herself a most original place to live. As she prepares coffee, she says how happy she is to have a place of her own at last.

"No one will ever come up here," she says. "If ever I sleep with someone, I'll go to a hotel or to his place. Even during the day I'll invite no one, be it boy or girl. Except you. I'm tired of the same old nightlife. From now on, you can come and see me here. It's so much more pleasant."

She carries the cups over, and I sit down on the edge of the bed. She sits down on the floor at my feet and snuggles against my legs.

"Isn't it nice, being here together?"

When I've finished my coffee, she takes the cup, places it on the rug, and kneels between my legs, facing me, her arms around my neck. She places her head on my chest. I put my arms around her, lift the tail of her blouse, and slip my hand inside, letting it wander idly over her skin. It is a peaceful time of day, and somehow distressing.

From the open window the sounds of the pigeons drift in, and, from farther down, kitchen sounds, maids conversing back and forth through open windows.

"You know, Chloe," I say, without letting her go, "right now I'm very much in love with my wife." I make a point of stressing the "right now."

"Yes, I know. If you are, then don't feel you have to come up here," she says, pulling away from me and jumping to her feet.

"Let me finish," I say, raising my voice. "I mean that right now, although I love her and desire her physically more than ever, I'm also completely under your spell. Maybe we ought to sleep together. I have to tell you my resistance is crumbling. But it's not just the sleeping together that bothers me. It's that given the way I feel about you, it becomes more than that. And I don't think it's possible to love two women at the same time, do you?"

"That depends on your definition of 'love.' If you're talking about passion, then the answer is no. But passion never lasts. If you feel like sleeping with two women, or several, and you have a tender feeling for them all, what's wrong with that? People do it all the time. Actually, to my mind polygamy would be far more natural for all of us."

"It's barbaric. Women are slaves."

"Not necessarily, if women practice it, too. If you followed your natural inclinations, you'd sleep with as many girls as you like, and you'd let your wife do the same with men. I know I'm right, and one day I'll persuade you I am. I know that sooner or later you'll cheat on your wife. Maybe not with me. But whoever it is will have benefited from my spadework."

"If I lived in a society where polygamy was practiced," I say, "I'd be polygamous, and I'd probably have no problem. But in the society we live in, I can't base my life on a lie. I already keep too many things from my wife as it is."

All of which Chloe finds very funny.

"And what makes you think she doesn't keep anything from you? If you want to know, I saw her one day with another man."

"Where?"

"Near the Saint-Lazare station. About a month ago, before I started working."

"So?"

"So nothing. Don't look so upset. They were simply walking together and talking. She didn't see me, but I recognized her."

"What's so extraordinary about that? She often comes into Paris. It was probably another teacher. What did he look like?"

"Nothing to write home about. On the ugly side, actually. He must have been a teacher. I'm not suggesting anything beyond the fact that they were walking together. But the thought crossed my mind that when we walk together in Paris and you're so afraid you might run into her, wouldn't it be funny if we ran into *her* with another man!"

I laugh and tell her that I suspect, in fact, one of her fellow teachers, a Mr. M., is rather smitten with Helen. But, I add, I doubt there's any physical attraction there. That's why I don't think about such questions, and why I never will.

"Here's what I suggest for the next time we meet," I tell her as I'm about to leave. "It is pleasant here—too pleasant. I'll work it out so I'm free all next Monday afternoon. We'll go have lunch together somewhere, maybe in the Bois or along the quais, wherever you like. We'll have all the time in the world to talk everything out. Okay?"

The following Monday at one-thirty I climb the stairs to Chloe's place. I knock several times and get no response, but I can hear the water running. Finally she hears me.

"Oh, there you are! The door's locked. Come in this way."

I can hear the lock on the bathroom door being slipped back. I go in, to see her arm disappearing beneath the shower curtain. As I head for the bedroom, she says, "Would you mind passing me the towel?"

She reaches out again and grabs it.

"And would you also mind putting the bath mat down?"

While I'm complying, she opens the curtain and emerges, swathed in the towel. Holding on to it with one hand, she slips a still-wet arm around me and gives me a kiss.

"Don't worry," she says, "it's only water. It doesn't stain. And since you're here, how about drying me."

Not quite sure how best to proceed, I pat the towel gingerly as it remains about her.

"Come on," she says, "you can do better than that!"

I remove the towel and carefully dry her from head to toe. When I'm finished, she takes the towel and wraps it around her waist so that it covers her legs. Then, holding on to my lapel with one hand, she takes the towel and tosses it over her shoulder, almost losing her balance. She flattens herself against me. I put my arm around her waist and cover her neck with kisses.

"Your coat is prickly," she says, pulling away from me and gesturing for me to remove it. Which I do.

Completely reassured as to the course of subsequent events, she leaves me, walks into the bedroom, and heads toward the bed while I begin to undress. I unbutton my shirt collar and start to remove the shirt. Just as I start to pull it over my head, I pause for a moment and take a step toward the bedroom door and glance at the bed: Chloe, leaning on one elbow, is smoothing out the wrinkles in the bed and fluffing up the pillows. She glances over her shoulder in my direction, sees me with my shirt half over my head, and laughs. I step sideways, out of her line of vision, and find myself in front of the bathroom mirror. A comic sight, indeed, my shirt looking like some strange monk's hood. I smile at myself, but my smile turns into an angry grin, and with a shake of my head I bring the shirt back down to where it should be.

In the next room, Chloe is no longer fussing, and there is an oppressive silence that lasts for several seconds. Then I open the faucet full blast. Covered by the sound of the running water, I head for the bathroom door, open it, and leave, having grabbed my suitcoat.

I fear that despite my precautions, Chloe may have heard my precipitous departure and might call after me. I dash down the stairs as fast as my legs can carry me and emerge out into the street, completely out of breath. I'm in such a state that I keep on running down the street, bumping into several people in my flight.

Back at the office, Fabienne is on the phone. When she hears me enter, she turns around, and I have the distinct feeling, from the look of surprise on her face, that my unexpected return has put a crimp in her plans.

I walk quickly into my office and stand for several seconds next to the window, to catch my breath. Then I go over and shut the door, which in my haste I had left ajar. I pick up the phone and dial my home number. Helen answers.

"What's the matter?"

"Nothing. I simply wanted to see if you were there. A meeting I was supposed to attend this afternoon was postponed, so I thought I might come home early. I just wanted to let you know."

"But you could have simply come home. Why did you bother calling?"

"Because . . . because I was here beside the phone. I'll see you shortly."

When I walk in, Helen studies me carefully, a trifle concerned.

"I was worried. You sounded so strange on the phone. Are you all right?"

"Fine. My day got all fouled up at the office. So, I decided, why not take advantage of it and come home rather than linger there. But I didn't want to bother you."

"You never bother me," she says. "I'm working. But I always work better when you're around. Today, though, for some reason, I felt lazy. I had . . . uh . . . an errand to run, that's all. And I'll put it off."

"Where, in Paris?"

"No, here. But it's of no importance."

"Go ahead and run it. I don't want you to change your plans for me."

"No, unless you'd prefer me to go."

"Don't be silly! You're the reason I came home. I didn't have anything special to tell you; I just wanted to see you. To see you in the afternoon. We never get to see each other in the afternoon, except on Sunday."

She sits down on the couch. I sit down beside her and put my arm around her shoulders, which are bare. She's wearing a light, sleeveless summer dress.

"To tell the truth, there's something about afternoons I don't like. Sometimes I feel upset, full of angst, afraid to be alone. Have you ever felt that way?"

"It's strange you mention it, because now that our English nanny takes the children out to the park in the afternoon, on those days when I'm not teaching I feel odd, and somehow lost. I suppose I have to get used to it. It's also odd to have you here at this time of day."

I start to get up, and she grabs my arm.

"No, stay. I'm happy, so happy I can't tell you," she says, but her laugh sticks in her throat. "The only thing is, I must look silly."

I hug her tightly, and for a moment we remain locked in close embrace without talking. I'm the one who breaks the silence.

"Helen?"

"Yes."

"I'd like to tell you something."

"Ah!"

"Why 'ah'?"

"I thought you told me you didn't have anything special to tell me."

"I just thought of it this minute. And anyway, it's completely silly, and I probably shouldn't even say it. But here it is:

here I am sitting beside you, and you intimidate me. You intimidate me because you're beautiful. You've never been more beautiful, in fact. But you also intimidate me because—and this is even more incomprehensible—I love you. It doesn't make any sense, does it?"

"No, on the contrary, I understand it very well."

"I tell you because I'm always afraid you'll mistake my shyness for coldness."

"But I'm the one who's cold. Much more than you. You're perfect. I could never love a man who always wanted to pry into my innermost thoughts, even if his intentions were the best."

"Yes, but I sometimes feel bad that I don't talk to you more than I do, that I don't reveal what I'm thinking and feeling; whereas there are times when I spend hours talking with people I don't give a damn about, people with whom I'll never have any but the most superficial relations. Superficial, or fleeting."

She doesn't answer me. She's lowered her head.

"Helen?"

I bend down and look into her face, which she's trying to hide.

"Are you crying?"

"No," she says, turning up to look at me, her eyes still moist, "can't you see!"

And, burying her head in my shoulder, she starts to laugh nervously, but before long it turns into uncontrollable sobs.

I caress her bare shoulders, cover her neck with kisses, and slowly the sobs subside. I unhook the back of her dress and slip my hand inside, gently caressing her back. I whisper in her ear, "Are we all alone?"

"Till five o'clock. But let's go into the bedroom."